A Man Divided

A Man Divided

ROBERT KALICH

BETIMES BOOKS

First published in the English language in Dublin, Ireland, in 2021
by Betimes Books

www.betimesbooks.com

ISBN 978-1-9161565-6-2

A Man Divided is a work of fiction.
Names, characters, places, and incidents are either the product of the author's
imagination or are used fictitiously.

Cover design by JT Lindroos

To Brunde

TABLE OF CONTENTS

PROLOGUE

DUCK

At five in the morning, I met Duck. He was wearing his uniform: long coat, shiny blue suit, white shirt, red tie, an American flag in his lapel. He refused to wear a mask or cover his manufactured blonde hair. He appeared not that different from so many other New Yorkers who reside near 1818, where state-of-the-art towers are mushrooming over a territory recently dubbed "Billionaire Row." Why would the President of the United States take the time to meet up with the likes of me? I offered Duck a deal his ego could not refuse.

In Manhattan the very best time to schedule a meeting has always been before the lights turn on. Even now, with the virus dominating the premises, Duck had slipped away from his security detail. We met at Columbus Circle. Walked adjacent to Central Park over to 1818. In the lobby was the night porter, Geraldo Camacho, mopping the marble floor. Camacho didn't look up from his mop and pail. He did wave to me. Duck and I quickly entered a private boxcar that led directly to my penthouse. I unlocked three bolts with privately designed keys. Stepped into my luxury retreat. Duck followed me inside.

"Would you like a drink, Mr. President? I have purple label, vodka, pineapple juice. I can prepare coffee. Perhaps you just want New York water."

"Cut the crap, Singer."

His lack of pretense caught me off guard. I did expect him to be more presidential.

I poured Duck a glass of pineapple juice.

Duck peered at an antique rocking chair I had since my father passed. "I had one of them," he said, plopping down into it. Rocking himself. "Always loved my chair. It's gone now, like most of who I am is gone. I just don't know me anymore. That's the reason I accepted your invitation, Singer. We did have some good times in the old days. I'm sure the time I spend here with you will be real." He paused. Took a swallow of juice. "My life isn't close to real any longer." He jumped up and started walking around the study. He went from one room to another inspecting my bookshelves. Just about floor-to-ceiling wherever you looked. Even the kitchen. He started pulling one book off the shelf, one after another. "Never saw so many books in my entire life. Did you read all of them? Which one is your favorite?"

How do you answer a question that oblique? My library is my sanctuary. My books, amigos. Eleanor gripes all the time that there is no space for her life. Only mine. But Duck wasn't only griping about space – "I haven't read a novel since I was in college. In fact, even then I hated reading," he said.

It was as if Duck was an old friend who desperately needed to talk to someone. If not a buddy, a business associate who had gone belly-up. Perhaps that is Duck's strength. Not his glibness. His charm. The way he can disarm just about anyone.

"Donald ... Is it okay if I call you Donald?"

"I told you, cut the crap, Singer. I'm the same guy I was the day we first met. When was it?" He didn't wait for me to respond. "I remember it was through Haskell Gold. Gold was the best pro-football handicapper I ever knew." Duck smiled. "I used to get his picks." He paused. "Is Gold still around? That crazy bastard was also a pretty sharp card counter. You know I had him banned from playing Twenty-One at my casino." He smiled. "What a prick he was. You know, my dad wasn't afraid to do a real estate deal with anyone. Not even Isaac Becker or his mobster cronies. But with Haskell Gold, he refused to deal."

"Haskell Gold's dead." That was my one response. I didn't want to contradict him. Actually, Fred Trump was the one responsible for Gold, Becker, and me meeting Duck. Duck was 22 at the time. Sitting in on a deal that Haskell Gold was trying to put together with his father. Isaac Becker was going to participate in the financing. I was there for no particular reason outside of the fact that I loved being around Becker. In those days I idolized the guy. Duck was there to learn the family business.

There were many subjects I wanted to explore. His psychotic conception of freedom. His refusal to wear a mask to protect other people. The contempt he shows by not wearing one. His power-plays against governors who have refused to reject Dr. Fauci's pleas to engage in public health policy. You could call what I was doing research for this book I'm writing but I was also personally curious. I also wanted to discuss Russia and Putin.

Duck took two swallows of juice. His Adam's apple bobbed. In a voice that sounded conspiratorial, he murmured, "There's something about you, Singer. I'm going to tell you something I wouldn't even tell my late dad. You know how the media's always saying I stuff girly magazines into my desk drawers. That's not true. What I have there are six extra pairs of briefs. Every time I talk to Putin I shit in my pants. Maybe you can tell me what you think I need to do to get reelected. That's a whole lot more crucial to me."

His Prussian blue eyes revealed an intensity that wasn't there before. "Tell you the truth, Singer, your homeless project is not the only reason I'm here. What I'd like you to do for me is reach out to your buddy, Walter Li. What I'd like you to do is talk to him about working more directly with me. Tell him I can pave the way to new Bobets for Global Health and several of his other companies from China to Russia. Right here in the States. One hand feeds the other, Singer. Hell, if anyone knows that it's you. Your partners were Gold and Becker. Those two worked with gangsters to get what they wanted." He grinned, "You know what it takes to get to where you want to go. I my case, it's to get re-elected." He took several swallows of pineapple juice. "What do you say, Singer. Will you hook me up with Walter Li?"

Duck stared at me as if it were a matter of staying or leaving. It was obvious to me that money for financing his re-election was rumbling in his stomach. I knew I was going to connect him with Walter Li but I wanted to stall before giving him a definitive response. My main reason was a perverse one. I knew Duck would get up and leave once he had achieved his goal. I was on my own sort of ego trip. Duck being in my apartment. As much of an asshole as I say he is, for me it still was special to have him there. As moronic as my justification sounds, it was the way I felt at that moment. I just wasn't ready for Duck to walk out the door.

I asked about Dr. Fauci.

"Our relationship is similar to the one Billy Martin had with Steinbrenner. They couldn't get along but they did."

"What about Deborah Birx?"

"She's quite a lady. The truth is I like her."

A few minutes later.

"… The very most I'll put up is 1 percent of the seed money." He stuck out his hand. I wouldn't agree. Duck must have felt he was losing ground. Especially when he again brought up Walter Li. And I again deflected to small talk. Duck sensed it immediately. He was as sharp, if not sharper, than me.

"I remember the day we were at the Kentucky Derby, Singer. Must have been almost forty years ago. Gold and Becker were also with us. Both of them were calling you "Broadway Bob." Telling me that you were the number one college basketball handicapper in the country. Becker went on and on about how much dough you made him that season. Believe me, Singer. I was impressed."

"At that time in your life, you were thin, handsome, ready to take over." I tried to flatter Duck as much as possible and still not sound like a flunky.

"That day at the Derby you know what really impressed me? You won all five races you bet on. That's something I never forgot. I also remember you telling me that day that you paid your way through grad school by betting on the trotters."

"Incredible," I said. "Your memory, I mean."

"It never lets me down," Duck said beaming.

I went over what I had in my mind concerning my homeless project. I had stayed up half the night preparing. I realized that there would be roadblocks. I felt I could always throw in more of my own money. Wipe out obligations that Duck never met. Debts that he spit on when he made his relentless moves to the top. When I spelled out some of those IOUs, Duck turned fire-engine red. "I did those bastards more favors than there are ants on an anthill," he shouted. For a long while Duck continued his tantrum, then he calmed down. Changed the subject. "Whatever happened to that first wife of yours?" He grinned at me. "I still remember the way she'd cross her legs." He smiled. "She was a real beauty. You had your share. I had mine. What's your new wife like?" he queried.

"Eleanor and I have been together over twenty years." He responded with, "You are certainly a different person now than the one I knew back then."

I tried to question him on Putin.

"I told you, Singer, those kinds of questions are strictly off limits. What I want to talk about is my re-election. That's the only thing that concerns me right now."

I deflected to an experience that we had shared in the past. He interrupted in a matter of seconds. "You know Walter Li and I did do some important things together. I can get to him without your help. But it will be a whole lot easier if you join my team. What do you say, Singer? The homeless project. My re-election. Are we a team?"

I started making small talk on Walter Li. Duck bought in. "Li's quite a negotiator. The kind of guy that might have started with less than nothing, but his success with Global Health... It's no accident." He stopped. "Tell me more about your wife, Singer. Sounds to me as if you got lucky."

"Eleanor's a brilliant woman. She has her MBA from Yale."

"I never had much success with that type of woman."

"Eleanor's not like that. Her great-grandfather was a Texas Ranger. He died at the Alamo. Her mother is one sixteenth Native American. We have a son. Reid's 19. He's a lot brighter than me. Maintained a 4.0 grade point average for his entire freshman year at Georgia Tech."

"Wow! Your son puts me to shame. I was fortunate to maintain a C average in college. If it weren't for my father ..."

We spoke of my dad. His parents both came to America from Poland. My maternal grandfather died before I was born, owned a chain of banks in New York. But when the depression came in '29, he jumped out of a window. Duck didn't flinch. He raised an eyebrow when I mentioned that at one time, I was seriously involved with a woman from Akure, Nigeria. "Imagine if you married her and had children," he quipped. I asked about the First Lady. His response was a grimace. Then a softer side was revealed, "Last night was a bad night for me. My wife was in a dark mood at dinner. I had to walk around on tiptoes, sanitize my conversation. What I got in return for my efforts was linear, careful, rational responses. The tension affected me. I didn't get much sleep. I couldn't tweet or do much of anything other than feel sorry for myself." He choked up. "When you can't talk to your own wife, what's the answer?"

"Now let's get back to Walter Li, Singer. I'd be asking you to do more but I can see you're one of those gung-ho New York liberals, but we're not. Walter is a legit Republican. He's a major contributor to the Republican Party. Are you going to put in a good word for me or not?"

Duck was like one of my bookmakers from Brooklyn. A show-me-the-money sort of guy.

༄

It was now 5:51 a.m. The sun was coming up. "Let's go outside onto my rooftop. It's the perfect time."

Duck slowly strode to the front of my landscaped escape. He stared north at Harlem. Gazed at Yankee Stadium. In the late evening you can see a halo over the Park when the Yankees are playing. He turned his head to the left. Peered at the Hudson River. Squinted at Jersey, then looked east, glimpsing all of upper Fifth Avenue. He leaned forward over the rails, admiring Central Park.

He turned to me. "There's no city in the entire world that compares to this one. Let me tell you, Singer, no one is ever going to convince me not to reopen this town. New York, like this country, needs to be reopened."

I debated with Duck as best I could. My arguments not to reopen pretty much run of the mill Dr. Fauci. Duck said things like, "We can't keep our country closed down. It's unsustainable." He threw out numbers. Frightening numbers. "Do you realize how many millions of Americans are unemployed? And it's only getting worse."

I brought up the 6 percent of Covid-19 cases that are fatal. That if we reopened, the percentage might stay the same but the increase in deaths will be exponential.

"Americans will have to accept that reopening will kill people. We do not have a choice."

"People will die!" I exclaimed.

"Look, Singer. I've given this a lot of thought. The candy-ass in me might even agree with you. But I'm POTUS. I don't think we can survive like this. We must have our economy running again. After my getting re-elected, it has to be my number one priority. I told you, Singer, talking about this stuff is off limits. Let's just stay away from it. I'll get enough static as soon as I get back to my office.

"Do you have any idea how many emails and texts I have to return when I get back? And they're all looking to me for answers. What am I supposed to tell my task force? FEMA! The Guard! Pharmacies! Hospitals! Doctors! Nurses! Meat workers! Oil and Gas! Shipping! Wall Street! The Blacks!" He paused. "What am I supposed to tell the Blacks when the police keep killing them? I'm the one they blame." He pursed his lips. "Screw all of them. I'm nobody's fall guy. I'm doing the best I can. No other president in the past one hundred years had to deal with the kind of cards I have to play. People mention the Spanish flu we had in 1917. Did you know that Woodrow Wilson lied about it? And this pandemic is a lot worse. We have a trillion more people. Of course, I'm losing it. It's only going to get worse. Yet I got to do something. I get blamed for everything." He stopped. Slumped down deep into the Chesterfield. "You got to hear me, Singer. I came here because I need your help with Walter Li. Not because you want to name a homeless shelter after me. Though the truth is, that's appealing to me."

It was approaching 8:35 a.m., the time Duck advised me he had to take off. "You think things have been easy for me. You think I haven't thought of quitting. But I won't quit. I'll tell you this, Singer. Those impeachment hearings. Sometimes I do wish that they had found something out. But I'm not a quitter. The country needs me. I might know a whole lot more about real estate than I do about Covid-19, but I got great people working for me. Great people." He stood up, "You know, Singer, talking to you this morning has been like talking to my old man. I can't explain it any better than that."

Duck stretched. "I feel pretty good now," he said, grinning at me. He patted down his blonde hair. Tightened the knot on his red tie. "I'm ready to start my day," he said cheerfully. We ended up making the deal he wanted. "I'm going to allow you to use my name. But remember, Singer. I'm not putting up one dollar." He smiled as he stepped into the elevator. "THE DONALD J. TRUMP SHELTER FOR NYC INDIGENT POPULATION. Has a nice ring to it. Doesn't it?"

PART ONE

DAYS OF COVID

March 8th, 2020. Just another calendar date. It isn't. I'm packing my things. Joining my wife. Destination Justice Lane. Eleanor stays in North Salem, New York, most of the time. I reluctantly come up from New York City on weekends. It's an ultra-fancy suburb, you know. The house is surrounded by woods, wildlife, spring breezes, and has a swimming pool and a golf course, it's miniature, don't get excited; it has winding roads, a corral, an Audubon trail, a guest house that's huge. That's a good thing as my identical twin will be joining us in a few days, and a day or two after that Reid. He's a freshman at Georgia Tech right now but the school has ordered all of its students to go home.

"Ba, I think if I continue focusing, I'll finish this semester with a 4.0."

Reid's not a liberal arts major as I would have preferred. Hell, what I would've really wanted was him to be another Willie Mays or Mickey Mantle. Reid's major is mechanical engineering. Yes, my son is a nerd, but taking physics and advanced calculus and having a passion for robotics is not something his mother or I have a problem with. This summer, Reid and two of his classmates were to go to Australia, enjoy the beaches, but now with Covid-19 lurking in the air, that's off.

"I'm planning on signing up for some summer school classes, Ba."

That's my son. Not a day goes by that I'm not proud of him. The problem is Eleanor is freaking out because of the virus. She's not the only one panicking. Most of my friends have already deserted the City. For me, it's not the virus that's my primary reason for leaving.

"Robert, I don't want to be here without you. I want to hold onto every moment we have. Every minute counts. You're 83 years old. Please, Robert. I'm worried…"

So, I'm writing a novel. But how do I begin? I guess by introducing myself. My name is Robert Singer. I've never felt better. More capable of living life than ever before, and I feel profoundly grateful. I'm most thankful for having Eleanor and Reid at my side. Let me confess right now: I've known my share of women. I've experienced all kinds of pre-Me-Too relationships and those you might describe as friendly kitsch. I even attended fundraisers with our quacking duck President and those sickos, Epstein & Weinstein. Not much to say about them other than "good riddance."

My own first love, Victoria Lurie, was definitely based on my erections. It lasted for seventeen years. The first twelve were a "good deal." I had an on-and-off-again affair with Victoria through her first three marriages. Then we were caught by husband number three at the Plaza Hotel. Less than three months later, "You must marry me," Victoria hissed, and being a cantor's son must have rubbed off on me. Hell! It wasn't that at all. It was what my old friend and partner, Isaac Becker, always said, "A pussy hair can pull a battleship." I married Victoria Lurie. You could say I had a screw loose or that I was built that way. I've since chopped off those branches.

At 62 I met Eleanor, my soulmate. That's not me speaking. That's Eleanor's mother. Mrs. Caintrell smiled at us the day we told her that Eleanor was pregnant. "You two are soulmates," she said. We've been together over twenty-one years now, and Ely and I, we have something imperfectly perfect. Now, let's jump forward without any more convolutions and talk about people who are dying to others who are stepping up while I hush up and stop dwelling on how I lived my life.

Every day I listen to half the country saying that Duck doesn't care about people dying and the other half saying, "Everything he's promised, he's done." Of course, I'm disturbed by Black people being killed on the streets. Of course, I'm concerned with everything that is happening that I had fought against in the Sixties. But talking about it, well, maybe I'm not such a good talker, but I can pound a little on the typewriter keys, and I realize the only way for me to say something is to get on my ass and write about it. That my restlessness wouldn't disappear or, for that matter, my frustration with Duck and all the other ducks by just going to Barnes and Noble and picking up a book to read. I've done enough reading to last a dozen lifetimes; besides, I have a personal library at my New York residence, at last count nine thousand eight hundred and eighty-eight books. That's right, I read. That's why I'm convinced that reading and blathering will not alleviate the feeling that is eating me up any less than by going to Marea or Per Se for another gourmet dinner or chatting with my freakin' billionaire friends who never read a book since the day they left college or have a single thought on anything outside of making more dollars.

I didn't always hang out with unidimensional people. I started as a fresh-faced caseworker for the NYC Department of Welfare. I hate to admit it, for too many years I stayed at that dead-end civil service job that offered only a pension and health benefits. The truth is, I did enjoy helping people in the beginning. But it's impossible to continue extending TLC when you have a wife beating down on you 24/7, telling you what a loser you are. Soon you see yourself as a loser. Don't get me wrong. I'm not blaming Victoria. It was me, mostly me. I was the one who fucked up. I was the one gambling. In those days, I was up to my elbows in deep shit.

After Victoria got rid of me, at the age of 33, I met Julie Burr at the Welfare office, and for a while, things looked up. We became involved. Soon I forgot the divorce I was going through with Victoria, the debts I had, the prospects I didn't. The way I was living, a gravely ill mom and a dad who prayed from dawn to dusk.

Now I'm going to leap to Wuhan, China. Not the pandemic but to my own evolution. I found a way to make handicapping college basketball profitable. I went from a dismal loser to legendary, or, as they say today, Iconic. I soon became known as "The Handicapper." For thirty-one years, I won. Then I invested a chunk of my considerable wealth in a trusted friend's startup pharmaceutical company in Wuhan. I acquired 38 percent of GLOBAL HEALTH stock at the initial offering price. Well, you know what can happen when you have seed money and can invest. The rich get richer, as always.

All right, enough said on that. This might sound corny, but for me, who lived a lifetime in the lower depths, the past twenty-one years have been a godsend. At 62 I was burnt out. There wasn't much to look forward to other than handicapping games, gardening on my penthouse terrace, and an occasional fling. Then I met my future wife.

"Hello, my name is Eleanor Caintrell ... I have an MBA from Yale."

I thought, "A Yaleee!" Nothing's perfect. Eleanor had wounds. Deep inside of her. She had a diminished sense of self. An unnatural predilection for feeling engulfed. Starved of love since coming out of the womb can do that to you. I wanted to protect Eleanor from the moment we first connected. It was just as obvious to me that I needed Eleanor to rescue me, and between these two negatives came the greatest positive of my life. Together we uplifted ourselves and raised Reid, who is just about everything we would want him to be.

So that is where this mixed bag of a book is beginning. Hodgepodge and reality from an ancient author who can only imagine this new normal with as dystopian an existence as he lived his cold life till the age of 62, when pipe dream and reality collided, or, as my identical twin, Richard, the legit writer in our family, said in one of his novels: "My twin did everything wrong. He scoffed and scorned the traditional life; never washed mother's dishes when young; never studied in school; never went into the army, getting off on a feigned psychological exam (conversion hysteria the neurologist called it); never sang one note at our bar mitzvah; gambled for a living; never did an honest day's work; bounced lucky in his old age. Married well and today and for the past twenty years has all that money can buy, as well as love, family, and a son to love and who loves him."

Back to how I met my wife ... I walked up the stairs that led to Eleanor's railroad flat. Outside the door were copies of *Wall Street Journal*, *Crain's* and *Fortune* magazines. I rang the doorbell. "Come in," a tremulous voice peeped. I stepped inside, advanced through a long, dark corridor that led to a modest living room. Eleanor was sitting on a shredded grey sofa with three cats on her lap. I peered at her. Took a deep breath. Smiled. She didn't. The catatonic stare I received lasted for at least ten minutes. "Do you want me to leave? What's wrong? Do you want to have dinner?" I must have uttered those queries for the better part of what seemed like an hour. Eleanor's response – a stare. Silence! It was only much later in the evening, when we finally did go out to have some Greek food. When we returned to Eleanor's flat, she whispered in a tremulous voice that I believed transmitted the deepest parts of her being, "I've never been happy one day in my entire life." Those ten words changed my life. This penetrated me like a police officer's bullet. Ely's sadness was something I could feel. I knew I wanted to help. I did not realize that my ability to assist would be so puny. Yet this novel is not exclusively about our relationship and it's not only about the coronavirus or four hundred and one years of inequality. It's about how confusing and absurd life is. How impossible it is to be a human being; to have so much and yet know so little.

When I returned home that night, I kept hearing, "I've never been happy one day in my entire life."

Am taking a detour. Duck just passed the Defense Production Law and General Motors has promised to obey. Duck is talking to Michigan's governor. She didn't kiss ass, it seems, and Duck is peeved. He's acting like a spoiled brat. It's beyond me how we have this joker in charge. What went wrong? Just about everything! I'm not a political animal. Know less about politics than my son did when he was ten. But I'll tell you this much: I am leaning toward voting for Dr. Anthony Fauci if he runs for President in '24. I probably won't be around in '24. Not with the things Dr. Fauci is saying about the virus.

As we go through this global calamity, I keep thinking, NYC needs heroes and valor and common sense and leadership. People to step up. We also need personal protective equipment and brains and humanity. Then I think NYC is not that different from the rest of our country. Right now, we have a whole lot less of what is needed. From politicians caring to ventilators to doctors. Then, I think, we have a hell of a lot too. Independent thinkers. People who don't play follow the leader. I can imagine new companies sprouting out of the ground. Talented young people soaring into view. I mean, we can come back, get off the floor, move forward. Do the exceptional.

My son just walked into the room. He reads what I'm writing. "Ba, don't be naïve. We'll never come back as long as we're racist." Reid leaves the room. I return to my thoughts on Covid-19 and the number of people who we will probably lose. The sorrow it is going to cause. Then I think, in spite of Duck and all the ducks, Yes, we still need duck hunters, if you catch my drift, and then I think what about Africa and the Sudan and India and China and, well, you get my point. All of us are in this together. That's why we must open our eyes, shake the hands of healthcare workers, essential warriors, home attendants, doctors. Doctors that are now getting down and dirty in the trenches. Life and death physicians. They're real Audie Murphys out there, heroes doing whatever it takes to keep us alive!

My biggest fear is once this is over most of us will forget the other. Only a sliver will remember that one of us over another isn't superior. It's inferior. I want federation in my foxhole. Don't you?

Of course, I can talk like a bigshot. I have my family with me. Enough in the bank. Diamonds buried on my rooftop. I made those serious dollars wagering on college basketball. And each year after the first five years of gambling I would buy a pear- or round- or square-shaped diamond, at Tiffany's or from Isaac Becker, who had his own burial grounds. Isaac was one of my investors. I'd squirrel these carrots where I'd better not say. I also have Franklins buried under maples, oak trees, ledge boulders and I'd definitely better stop right here as it sounds like I'm cracking up. I'm not! If my son wanted to live the life I lived I'd break his skull. I mean that. I actually only started living without looking over my shoulder since Eleanor. But that's not the story. At least it's no more of this story than all the rest of what I'm writing. This I will tell you. My life has not always been domesticated, nor did I always have the kind of peace of mind and contentment that I do today.

At this moment, I'm at my desk. I have a checkbook. I'm aiming these checks like arrows at the neediest targets. Why wait to acknowledge people in my will. I have so much more than my family needs, and so many of us are in need. Just about every one of us needs a Santa. So many paycheckless friends, out of work strangers, homeless people; so many of us are making out benefit claims. So many human beings who need immediate assistance, and as I discovered over my 83 years, there are very few One-Percenters with a big heart.

I just received a phone call from Omkar BeHarry. He's a young man from Ghana who works the front desk at 1818. That's my NYC building address.

"How you doing, Mr. Singer?"

We spoke for a few minutes about his wife, their infant daughter, Emily. We spoke about some of the other employees at 1818 I'm on a first name basis with. I scribbled some notes, extracted what I could of what these men and women needed. "Checks will be in the mail," I told BeHarry. "You got my word on that."

Eleanor met me at 1818. From there, we drove to North Salem. Five days later, Reid joined us and two days after that, my twin brother. You might want to think of my twin as a Saul Bellows character. It took him five days to pack. He had never left the City for more than a week before he came up here. Dick is staying in the guest house, which is luxury for him. My identical's entire adult life has been spent in a tiny studio apartment, without a bed; he sleeps on a rattan mattress. It's a sliver of cotton. He's never lived with a woman, nor did he ever once think of having a child. If he was asked to babysit Reid for more than ten minutes, Dick would freak out. "I've got more important things to do," he would yell at Eleanor and me, and head for the door. Dick has always lived his life without anything other than his beloved books from floor to ceiling, an Underwood typewriter that has evolved into an Apple laptop, and red, green and blue pencils for underlining in those damn books that he never stops reading or adding to. Out of it has come, I must admit, some damn impressive novels. Yet, as a man, he's the American Dream in reverse. Living 50 percent of a life. The 50 percent he doesn't live, and there's no other way of putting it, is as isolated as a winter blizzard. Now all of us are together on these North Salem acres, which have trees and meadows and groundhogs and bobcats and foxes and brown bears and deer and most of everything. Eleanor has stocked the house with plenty of food and supplies, enough for six months of virus. As I told my wife just yesterday, "The things you purchased are a whole lot more important that my Kiton jackets and Tom Ford trench coat and your Gucci handbags and designer dresses and whatever else we have jammed into our fourteen closets."

Dick loves the guest house. He insisted that he needs to be left alone. To my twin, most everything is noise, other than Franz Kafka, Albert Camus, David Bobson and some other avant-garde superstars. To my brother, these are the only kind of people who have anything important to say. Oh, yes, do not let me leave out Samuel Beckett. He's another genius my brother genuflects to. Dick is as idiosyncratic as anyone you will ever encounter, but, and there's always a but, he can write. Maybe not with Kafka or Camus or Beckett, but with just about all of his contemporaries. In the past forty years, Dick has never received one commonplace review. He has compiled a body of work that deserves a Pulitzer. He's been nominated for two. Has won his share of prestigious blue ribbons and if you know anything about identicals: What Dick does, I do not have to do, and what I do, he doesn't need to do. Heads and tails. It's as arbitrary as that.

"I need to be left alone," Dick told Eleanor when he stepped on our grounds. "I'll make my own dinners. I'll visit you less than you want. I'll stay here for whatever time this pandemic needs to be resolved. Don't let my brother bother me. I'll call you if I need anything. You don't have to worry about me. I repeat: Don't call or visit. And keep Reid away. He will only want to talk about his engineering classes, and I don't give a rat's ass about math or computer science or robotics. Then again, I am interested in physics. Tell Reid he should call me."

Dick is definitely as weird as I am describing. I will tell you this for a fact. Whatever amount of time he stays with us he will rarely change his clothes or his linen or take more than one shower a week. No, the showering part isn't actually true. Since his novels have been recognized, he's been taking more and more showers. That is my twin brother in two pages. Oh, he did tell Eleanor, "Thank you for what you're doing for me. You're probably saving my life."

It's not that Dick is an elitist or a psycho. It's just that he doesn't have the patience for most of the people who are inhabiting this earth. He's always attempting to write something that has never been written before. He strives to do what other writers wouldn't dare to write or just can't write, or perhaps because of the economics involved, wouldn't get five cents to write. But as my twin would say, "Words are the enemy of writers. Words are boring. Any book that needs more than one hundred and eighty pages to say something is masturbatory."

I didn't have to twist Eleanor's arm. She just started cooking and cleaning and continuing to pay five housekeepers and all the landscapers, gardeners and other help that isn't here. I'm keeping my mouth shut. It's something that I always wished for. A housewife. As for Reid, he's also chipping in. Not all the time. Most of the time he's down in his basement, which is his staked-out territory. He has his life there. The space is about the size of Georgia Tech's football field. Reid is continuing his studies on the internet. As you know, my son is a mechanical engineering major. The only engineer I'm familiar with is the one from *Miss Saigon*. Oh, I have one friend, Harvey Litt, who went to Music and Art high school. He was president of his senior class. Damn good tennis player and real good looking. Harvey loved to paint, too, but his father forced him into engineering. He went to Columbia and after that took an advanced degree at Princeton. He did some important work for the government before being whittled into a married man with a son who ended up in Australia. Harvey's son did get himself a superior education. He went to Wharton, got himself an MBA. Used his father's money to pay his tuition. A considerable amount of money, that is, when you add it all up. I know that for a fact as my own Reid started his privileged life at the 92nd Street Y, from there to the Cathedral School and then to Choate and now at Georgia Tech. His education won't be over for a long, long while, but let's get back to Harvey Litt's son. He's now making moves on epicurean women on Australian beaches, not communicating with his mom and dad, refusing to return to the States. Half of me is feeling that the boy is a loser, the other half of me is feeling that he's closer to blue skies than his father ever was. What I'm saying is that there's more ways than one to live this life. I'm not judging anybody. Especially not any of my Black friends that left the States because they just couldn't take American racism anymore. Another story for another day. Right now the story is Covid-19. People are dying, none of us is living normal and I'm not sure I'm comfortable writing about the virus yet. Let me say a few words on my son.

I am more than elated that Reid is home from Georgia Tech and sheltering at home with us. It's my pleasure to put up with his correcting us on everything we do wrong, though at the same time, it's draining.

Here is a letter I kept for over six years. It says more than I ever could:

Dear Ba,

I know it seems like I really don't care. Ma probably thinks I'm just writing this because she told me to. I would hope that you of all people can tell the difference.

What you have given me is unique. Thank you for showing me that there is more than money and power and grades and exams and school. I am just beginning to realize how fortunate I am, that I am responsible to help those less fortunate. Again, as I get older, I realize how rare this knowledge is. I always thought those truths were just part of me. I was sure you thought so too. But now I know they were born out of the perspective you gave me. A perspective that is almost always a lacking in the money class I was born into. I sincerely hope you never feel you haven't made your mark on me. Father's Day is for appreciation, and I hope this letter at least shows that. However, I wish I could thank you more for all you have done, but I know this pursuit is pointless. So, I'll just close by saying I love you, Ba.

To this day, whenever I read this letter, it does something inside of me. You know what I mean.

The truth is, when I peer at my son, I still see the kid in him that I cling to, even more so than I held onto college basketball during my handicapping years. That was a past life that was existentially a challenge, an adventure, so very dangerous. There was a time I had three contracts out on my head. Now that part of my life is no more than a bad memory. A life the majority of you would say is not a life worth living. Maybe it wasn't. Maybe it was. I lived it and for me it was worth it. I would do it again. As for my son, as I said before, I'd break his skull if he wanted to follow in my footsteps. No question. I'd break his head.

I do think I've adjusted to living life as I do. I mean, domesticated! Tranquil! Civilized! Damn, I'm more than grateful that I landed on my feet. Isaac Becker always said, "You live by the sword you'll die by the sword." I didn't. I have friends who certainly did. One of my best friends recently has been transferred from Sing Sing to Fishkill. He went to prison when Reid was four and he won't come home till Reid is twenty-one.

There's no March Madness this year. It's always been the greatest time of the year to me. Ask Five Star Camps – Howie Garfinkel. Ask Cal Ramsey. Ask Rodney Parker. You can't! None of them is here any longer. What's real rough about not having March Madness is that the senior basketball players will never get a chance to compete in the NCAA tourney. What a terrible way to leave school. It's as if they lost the girl that they loved. That's made me recall Sheila Bauer. The redheaded schoolgirl I was dating in 1956, '57 and '58. She told me this at her front door after our last date, "You're always going to put books and writing out front. Serious people can't be happy. I want to be happy."

I don't miss the NBA. I'm burned out on dunks and three pointers. I loved the game a whole lot more when Bobby Davies and Bobby Wanzer were the backcourt for the Rochester Royals. Call me old school or whatever you wish, but I've seen virtually every player in the history of the NBA. I even penned a Basketball Rating Handbook on every player in the game. Hell, I even scouted with Fuzzy Levane and Dick McGuire when they worked for the Knickerbockers, and I can tell you this right now. Give me Magic as my point guard, Oscar Robertson everywhere, Wilt in the middle and Elgin and Larry in the corners and you can pick your next twenty-five. With this here pandemic, sports have disappeared.

To keep myself occupied, I have books to read, a typewriter to pound, Duck and Cuomo to listen to, Dr. Fauci and Deborah Birx to keep me informed, TV movies to watch at night and boy do I love movies. I have been watching on the average two a day. Last night, *Sleepless in Seattle* and that ending at the Empire State Building when Meg Ryan meets Tom Hanks and the eight-year-old boy. It still makes me cry. And after that I watched *Frankie and Johnny* with Pacino and Pfeiffer. Michelle Pfeiffer certainly was a beauty. I also watched *Baker Boys* last night. Pfeiffer was even more beautiful in that one. My Eleanor is a gem too. She has the kind of character in her face that the artist Georgia O'Keefe had. I am lucky. Not because my wife is beautiful outside. But because she's even more beautiful inside. Enough for one day. I'll close by saying, if I'm grieving, I don't know it yet.

Going to make this short and sweet. Before you begin wondering what it is I did or do, I'm going to spell it out. Some patience, please.

Yesterday in back of the guest house, I stepped on a basketball court, circle-to-circle. A miniature golf course, as well. I had hardly noticed either one before. I am definitely one of the deplorable privileged. The first thirty-five years of my life I was your everyday working stiff. Living on nothing, hustling, borrowing, struggling. Living paycheck to paycheck; my powerlessness and despair became more intense each year. I started reaching. My reach led to obsessively gambling, streaming is a more accurate term, on baseball and basketball. Even on the one major American sport I never fell in love with. Football! So here it is, December 1969, it is the fifth year of Victoria and my blissless marriage. I am in front of the TV, praying, "Please God, let me win this one. Just this one. That's all

I'm asking." I lost. Kicked in the Sony. Two seconds later, Victoria is in the room. "Get out," she screams. "Get out." I was 33 years old. Within a month my first wife moved out of the City to some hamlet provided for by someone called "Her Protector."

Our last night together went something like this:

We were living in a pre-war building off Central Park that Victoria had accessed through lies to her lawyer and in court. It was not that I'm Mr. Morality but I couldn't go along with her lies to collect alimony. I did! If I tell you a pussy hair cannot pull a battleship, I'd be lying. That December night, Victoria had returned to the City from Bermuda where she had been with "Her Protector." She was wearing red, red lipstick, silver fingernail polish, mascara, rouge, nylons, two-inch heels, she had a bronze tan. I knew who her lover was. He was a successful TV producer who looked like Robert Taylor. He lived on Fifth Avenue in the same building that Isaac Becker resided in. He was only one of Victoria's lapdogs. For some reason, maybe it was the game I had just lost, maybe it was that I was losing games all that week, maybe it was that I had nothing to fight back with but that night I really hit rock bottom. And let me tell you, bottoming out can drive one mad. Mad enough to tell yourself: "I'll show her." For one week, I lived in a dump called the Nassau Hotel. When I ran out of money I moved in with my parents. My mom and dad provided a life raft, Kosher food, paid the rent. I think I said this before, if not, I couldn't afford a postage stamp at that time in my life. I was tarred to Civil Service employment. Let's push back to 1961. The year I graduated from Columbia with a Master's in Journalism. That year I quit the Welfare Department, landed a job with the *New York Daily Mirror*.

Editorial assistant sounds like something. It paid $48.00 a week. When I was guilt-tripped into my marriage by Victoria Lurie, I returned to the high roller social work position. Everything is relative. I was again working for the City. My salary paid the vigorish, the high interest on my debts. I was forty thousand behind. That might not sound like Mount Everest. Believe me, it was. My annual income at the time was approximately $17,500. I was now 33 and moving into "the twins' room," as my mother liked to call it. I had my books packed in cardboard cartons. I had other things too, like a toothbrush and a ballpoint pen. For the next twenty-three months, I lived in the twins' room. It wasn't that bad. I tried like any other college graduate to find honest, meaningful, serious work. I failed to succeed. Yes, it is all on me. I'm not that different from my twin brother. I, too, am a sort of a misfit, don't drive, don't do high tech, not that high tech was around in those days, but I didn't have whatever it takes to land one decent job. I kept exploring. The only thing I was superior at besides scribbling (my stories were unequivocally rejected) was sports. I knew baseball and basketball. Had been published by A.S. Barnes. My rating handbooks on basketball and baseball were filled with my compilations, original formulas. I had rated every player in the history of both sports. And even then, with that knowledge under my lean belt, a large part of me still believed you could win at sports gambling. I knew you couldn't. I felt you could. Did you ever have that kind of feeling about something? Well, I did about betting on baseball and baskets. I knew you couldn't beat Las Vegas or your neighborhood bookmaker. I had painfully proved that to myself, as Victoria has hissed, "You gambler! You loser! Get out... Get out... Get out..." Knowing I could not buck my head against Vegas lines (correct numbers, power ratings, odds, point spreads) I was neutralized – any wiseass interpolations on my part meant zilch, absolutely nothing, less than nothing. Yet I kept researching. What the hell, I was up shit's creek either way. To repeat: Las Vegas lines were always correct and the 11-10 *vigorish* is the dispossess notice that puts every gambler in the poorhouse. Sports books, neighborhood bookmakers, tracks, casinos were as secure as a priest is in St. Patrick's on Christmas Eve.

Still, I was as confident as a Baptist is that there's a heaven, that I knew everything there was to know concerning hardball and roundball. What I didn't know was that I was wrong! What I didn't realize was that there were four thousand games, give or take, played in college basketball on a Division One level, that Las Vegas was not equipped to intellectually, technically, digitally have the correct numbers placed on all of those games. I researched, I studied, I stayed up all through the night. On weekends, day and night. I would come home from work and chart, power rate, apply trends, theories, go over scores, teams, rosters, coaches, courts, just about everything I could think of that could influence a score. What I discovered was that one hundred and fifty games a season, give or take, 150 games out of approximately 4,000 Las Vegas point spreads in Division One college basketball were wrong. Even a loser like me understood that the only games to wager on were those one hundred and fifty. So, I continued doing homework. Planned how to take advantage. Not that different than today's hedge fund hotshots or that surly SOB on TV. I watched *Billions* the other night. I liked it. Then I watched a second episode and then a third and realized that it's nothing more than a quacking duck that finds ways to skim off the bottom of the deck. Believe me, I don't have any reason to B.S. you like Duck does. I am not saying this because I want your vote, but *Billions* is just a bunch of actors with a sharp TV writer and sophisticated jargon. The show sounds right, but it isn't. Granted, it's entertaining and clever and looks great but the real deal is a whole lot more brutal and gory and a whole lot less entertaining. For two years I saved pennies, put together a $250.00 bankroll. Still owed banks, cards and people forty dimes. Hunted for a mistake in the Las Vegas line. Found one in late December 1971. I was going on thirty-five. Made my first bet. Twenty-five dollars. Three years later I was on my way to being an aberration. To be euphemistic: "THE HANDICAPPER."

I'm aware this insert is out of context, but it's relevant. It's something Duck said, I was like a kid asking for a Gordie Howe autograph. "You were 'The Handicapper' and Isaac Becker was jockeying with CBS to buy the Yankees. You two were the kind of men I wanted to be. The way you two showed up everywhere with beautiful women. Becker was with that gorgeous Israeli woman and, of course, you were with your first wife, or had you left her by then, you might have been with that Dominican actress, Gabriella Blanco. I'm not sure. Anyway, I just wanted you to know I always looked up to you. You were the man back in the day..."

I started collecting dollars. Stashed away one-third of my winnings. Invested a second third. The last third went for partying with women that didn't make me smile or laugh or feel good inside. They were women that did not nourish me, and, to be fair, I might not have been Weinstein or Epstein or Isaac Becker or Duck, but I didn't nourish them either. I took in limited partners, men that were for the most part grim, heartless, ruthless. Inside I became hardened, dehumanized, disconnected. I stopped embracing people. Stopped liking who I was. Then, twenty-nine years and eight months later I met Eleanor. Now let me add one more fact. Real money is not the first ten million. Real money is ... as I started to tell you earlier ... that in 1994 I invested in Walter Li. His startup, Global Health. The company is in Wuhan, China. The price I paid for GH stock was eighty-two cents a share. I purchased 38 percent of Walter Li's company, if you calculate it dollar for dollar. By the year 2000, Global Health was selling on Nasdaq at sixty-three dollars a share. Now let me tell you, Walter Li and I, we go all the way back to kindergarten, playing stickball on Riverside Drive. Just two Westside boys growing up together. What did we have in common that kept us connected? Both of us hero-worshipped Mickey Mantle. Both of us loved basketball and were interested in theoretical economics. But none of that was it.

"What I want, Walter, is to write a great novel."

"What I want, Robert, is to own my own Fortune 500 company."

At NYU, I was as much a free spirit as I was a philosophy major. At Columbia I received a Master's in journalism. Walter admired Hume, Descartes, Plato, Spinoza. I had a yen for Sartre, de Beauvoir, Camus, the German existentialists too. They were part of my pile. I was not that different from my identical. The difference, he was focused, and

I was a tangled web, a mixed bag, a hodgepodge, a Harry Haller torn between legit theatre, finance, elegant economics, sports, philosophy and literature, a life of the mind floating here and there, like today's virus. In less fanciful words, I was an eclectic who took on much too much. Including too many women. Walter Li, on the other hand, had more economy, a more focused brain. He was not sidetracked by words, poetry or a blank page. Walter Li and I remained friends but eventually we did go our separate ways. It didn't happen all at once. Actually, we're still friends. We talk once in a while.

"Have you kept in touch with Julie Burr? How is she?"

"Julie never returns a phone call. I've tried calling her for years. I guess when you get the kind of alimony settlement she got, even a friendship like we had means very little."

Walter Li went on to berate me in many of the same ways my twin brother does. "It was you, Robert, who screwed up. Not Julie."

Walter brought up Victoria. "Don't you have any good memories of Victoria?"

"What I remember, Walter, is Victoria having a champagne glass, holding a dry martini, her elbow on an end table. Sipping her drink as I walked into the apartment at two or three in the morning. I was out just about every night in those days. 'There you are,' she'd scream. And two minutes later she'd be checking my body for scratch marks, examining my underwear. Sometimes she'd fling her drink at me, start hissing, 'You gambler, you loser!' She'd exhaust me with her relentless tirades."

The one way I had to shut Victoria up was with my primordial desire. Both of us shared that lust. By the end, we were both living on fumes. Both of us were defeated, incapable of lifting a newspaper or carrying a dish to the sink. Both of us were clinging to one another as an old couple cleaves on to life at the end. Victoria would finish off our evenings by taking her icy fingers, grip my bowed penis, take me in her mouth, whisper, and this is the thing I remember as if it took place this morning, "Robert, It's mine. All mine," she'd victoriously, pathetically, pathologically hiss.

PURE CARBON – let me explain. I have thirty-six shadow boxes on my rooftop terrace. Each one purchased from Hayneedle. I use them as planters. The boxes are 28x28. They're made out of teak. All of this means little. What means something is that three of these boxes not only contain fertilized soil, and life, they're also hiding something dead. Colorless, crystalline minerals consisting of pure carbon that have the greatest clearness of any substance. Unflawed, transparent stones, diamonds, that have been cut into gems of great brilliance. These three waterproofed state-of-the-art shadow boxes have vaults in them. The three boxes are not facing the park. They're at the back end of the terrace where, at dusk, the sun disappears.

At seven in the morning I brushed my teeth, gargled with peroxide, returned to Eleanor in our king-sized bed. My wife wrapped one arm over my belly. We remained like that for a minute or two, then, Ely whispered, "I love you, Robert." No other words were spoken. I was able to squeeze both her hands as we were crisscrossed on the bed and I thought, knew, that there was nothing in my lifetime that has been any better.

One hour later, both of us left our bedroom. Eleanor to prepare Reid's breakfast. I to begin writing. First, I had to navigate the stairs. I held on to the banister. I made my way to the kitchen, opened the fridge, poured out a glass of orange juice, swallowed a swig, then another, then hurried to my Smith-Corona. As I did, I peered out of a window. And saw men wearing masks, landscapers that I'd hired, six Hispanic men pushing wheelbarrows, rakes, pulling out roots and debris, mowing grass, pouring gravel. They're not essential workers, just people earning a living. I think or understand or whatever fellow-feeling it is I have inside me, that these men could be me. I go to my desk. I start writing checks to help.

As I'm scribbling, I receive a phone call from Walter Li. Walter keeps bringing up, "We're infants when it comes to how we use our communication networks. China has spent billions and billions on surveillance. They have pings covering every road. What do we have? And that's only one way we're behind. Another thing that gets to me is why we're so passive. Why isn't our government flooding Russia as they do us? We should be telling Russian people how corrupt Putin is. Not one word out of our President on any of Putin's atrocities."

I started rambling on how there wasn't going to be a baseball season. "Robert, remember our economics professor at NYU?"

"Sure do. Mr. Bowtie. Julius Bachman."

"What did Professor Bachman always tell us?

"He'd start all of his lectures with "Children! Don't fill your head up with gobbledygook. Think big picture."

Ventilators, masks, shield, gowns, protective equipment, essential workers, separation, mitigation. It's a whole new language. Duck has spoken to Dr. Fauci and A-Rod about Covid-19. Before I start I will stop. That's enough on Duck's mindless meanderings. Just about every one of us eight million six hundred thousand New Yorkers has a pet peeve when it comes to Duck. Why isn't that true in all the States, with at least a minority of the Republicans? I ask myself that all the time.

Eleanor's own terrors are manifesting again. She's been acting strange. Leaking out of fear. This Covid-19 virus is bringing out the worst in her, along with the best. Eleanor began the day with, "Stay out of my room. I'll talk to you later." My wife has quarantined herself from Reid and me. The past two days have been rough ones. Sore throat, trouble breathing, gasping for breath in the middle of the night. At this moment, Eleanor is at the top of the staircase shouting down to me, who is in our white-tiled gleaming kitchen slicing an apple to drop in my raisin bran. "I'm glad your brother isn't coming over here today. He always makes me feel so ugly."

"It's not Dick. It's your parents who made you feel ugly. They're the ones who did a job on you."

Actually, my wife looks great. And I don't mean for her age. Eleanor is 55 and looks 34. She's in great condition. As for being fashionable, I've never been with a woman with more hair salon appointments. I know I'm sounding inane, but it's a whole lot better than panicking or hallucinating or falling apart over the virus, and I've done a good deal of that, too, as of late. Since Eleanor has quarantined herself in separate quarters, I haven't been able to sleep. I'm so dependent on holding my wife's hand, snuggling up against her, that when she's not around, I spend half the night staring at the ceiling. The other half I find myself living one kind of Kafkaesque nightmare after another. Last night I heard Eleanor gasping and screaming. "Don't come in here. Stay in your room. I'm okay." And then I had a weird dream. I was with Duck in the White House. There was a pool of blood ... Right now I'm having Raisin Bran with apples and prunes. Eleanor is at the top of the staircase. "I feel much better, Robert. I don't have a temperature. I'm going to take a walk in the woods."

Back to Eleanor's comment. "Your brother makes me feel ugly." My retort was the same one I've consistently told my wife for the past twenty-one years. None of us escapes childhood trauma. Eleanor had a mother who didn't know the difference between a hug and a smack. And a father who didn't use a wrench but he did use a buckle or a tree branch. Both of my wife's parents have improved since then. Both of them are even loving at times. But those clueless years are still at my wife's diminished core.

I've been up since four in the morning thinking, writing in my head. It's a whole lot better than what I put on paper.

Now that I've moved to my desk, the words are not flowing as easily. I'm sputtering them out as if I was a thinker and that's the very last thing I want to do. My twin brother does that. He uses his brain to conceive, understand, think things through. Dick creates books that are more than themes and plots and character arcs, strong or weak stories, but he gets little pleasure by doing so. My stomach tells me what to write. Perhaps that's the reason I love writing. I am sitting here now with my Smith-Corona in the early morning and I feel a rush. By catharting, I am purging out demons. If not demons, the evils over my lifetime. Especially that of being 83 years old and on the way out. I would want to be at the beginning of my life. Thinking of my future but all I have is a past. Yesterday I spoke to Milo Powers. He went to NYU with me in 1955 and '56. Then his father could not pay the tuition any longer and Milo had to leave. We've remained close friends over our lifetime. Milo has always been one of the most talented people I know. When we went to Jilly Rizzo's cocktail lounge, he played the drums, when we went to the Rego Park Jewish Center, he stood in the middle of the dance floor singing "God Bless America." That was the night I met Arlene Fox. We danced the foxtrot and before we knew it we were tongue-kissing as if there was no tomorrow. There wasn't. I never saw Arlene Fox again. That night Milo also sang "Foggy Day in London Town." Milo had a great voice. Eventually he entered show biz. That's when he became a singer/songwriter and a womanizer, but my friend is not a cultural cliché. Before too long he gave up writing noisy songs for money and started doing more serious art and, like most artists, ended up with a whole lot less.

Back to Covid-19. Today the Defense Product Act is on everyone's mind. GM has consented to manufacture ventilators, it's about time. The Javits Center is opening with at

least 1,000 hospital beds. I learned that earlier this morning listening to Andrew Cuomo. The governor has been
making inspiring speeches on TV. He speaks daily for an
hour or more, sometimes including his 92-year-old mother,
Matilda. So what! God Bless! The governor also speaks
about his daughters. Never heard him utter a word on a
wife or girlfriend. I like Cuomo. I think he's presidential.

I really don't care much about politics, not like Milo
Powers. Milo just called me, "Robert you still know people.
What would it take to hire someone to take that moth-
erfucker president out?!" Politics and blogging are Milo
Powers' thing. His blog site has over six thousand followers. Every day he vomits out his frustrations against Duck.
Duck's politics of division are always Milo's main gripe. I did
know the kind of animals Milo was referring to. They have
either passed or are no longer capable of getting physical.
There was a time I did do some business with Duck. One
of my friends who passed and his father-in-law were in real
estate. They dealt with Duck. I provided them seed money
for one deal that included two million dollars for the purchase of cement. Another time I was involved with Duck
was when we met for the very first time. I was at Eden Roc
or it might have been Les Club. It was during my Broadway
Bob years, a few years after I left *The Daily Mirror*. Victoria
had divorced her third husband by then, maybe it was her
fourth. I was seeing her without exclusivity, yet it was still
torrid and serious. Victoria was more than a ten, had a body
that was, well, it was … Duck noticed us on the dance floor.
He boldly walked over when I trotted off to go to the restroom. He came on with Victoria like the dealmaker he is.
That's all Victoria told me other than that Duck never got
anywhere. "Robert, he's just a kid and he's definitely not my

type." I'm sitting here trying to get this right. Now I'm not sure if that happened before or during our marital years.

The coronavirus has spread on a global level. Over 184 countries and counting. Some say nations. What's the difference between country and nation? I asked around. No one had a satisfactory answer. Not one nation has a monopoly on Covid-19. If we learned anything, it's that we're all as powerless as a welfare recipient. Still, we will survive, most of us, and the world will move on and probably remember this time in history as a footnote.

Six months later I check these pages: Who would've believed that forty-five million Americans would be out of work. Hundreds of thousands of Americans would be dead. In New York, 6 percent of all nursing home residents would be gone. Who knew?

I told Reid just last night that 10 years from now there'll be another Aaron Judge, another Mike Trout, another Mookie Betts, another Justin Verlander. That he's not missing that much in losing most of the baseball season. That tomorrow's players will have comparable statistics and skills and that whomever you choose to root for or against will be hustling and playing the game as honestly or dishonestly as Jeter did, or A-Rod. That there isn't any hope for our natures to change. Maybe a few new laws will come into our rearview mirrors, but people will be people, they will slide into second, steal a base, do all the wonderful and terrible things we've done before. Scratch the surface and that's what you get: endless, palpable, predictable – reprehensible separateness, polarization, hate, rage, libido, ego, and whatever other gook there is that comes to the surface. And yet there are still movies on TV like the one I saw last night. It was pretty good until the end. That's when it fell apart. The protagonist in the film ends it with, "I still believe in a just and loving God. War ending. People once again befriending one another. Political rhetoric – bullshit!"

Our new reality is disorienting. Lately, I feel out of whack. Even my dreams are. They're more like revelations or disclosures. Last night I dreamt I was at Birdland, the jazz club. First, I was listening to Al Hibbler doing his rendition of "Unchained Melody." Then I was listening to Charlie Parker, then Count Basie and then I was at Yankee Stadium watching Vic Raschi and Hank Bauer and Gil McDougald and Gene Woodling and Cliff Mapes. All these years I've loved baseball. Still believe the game represents the best of what America has to offer. It's the best of what's in us, and yes, the worst too, but things have improved somewhat since Jackie. We still have a million miles to go. I tell my son, "What's more perfect than a hot summer day, a diamond, a green outfield, a player hitting the ball on the nose, a pitcher making a pitch," my memories of the Thumper and Stan the Man and Joe D. and Willie and Henry and a million other field of dreams Mozarts and Beethovens.

Reid has his mother's blue eyes. He still smirks at me as if he were 10, his temper tantrums he directs at his mother. I bring this up because my mind keeps jumping from baseball to jazz and then to Reid and mechanical engineering. My son can be glued to his laptop and also he can be complex. Last night he was screaming at his mother that Duck must go. "Ma, in 2017, 83 percent of taxpayer money was given to the top 1 percent." He even knew the amount. Two trillion dollars.

How I ended up on my feet, don't ask. Maybe the last book I wrote tells my story, but this one I'm writing now, it also tells my story. It definitely has more depth, less filter.

Eleanor hates when I repeat myself. She's even more uncomfortable when I mention my wealth. "Eleanor, what do you want me to say – I stayed at the Welfare Department. That I'm collecting a Social Security check. A civil service pension." This book won't only be about Eleanor and me holding hands or how beautiful my wife is and how much I love her, or how lucky I am. It will be about an octogenarian and Covid-19. How he's scared shitless to leave his suburban retreat. How he's losing his grip. How he's terrified of becoming inadmissible evidence, how it's taking him over as the water in our pool does when you move from its shallows to its depth. "Robert, stop feeling so much self-pity," Eleanor exclaims. I do and I don't. I'm strong and I'm weak. Who wants to give up living, not any of us who are sane. At least no one I've ever known who has a family they love and more money hidden underground than they could ever get to spend. I'm grateful. I'm doing the best I can. Yesterday I was able to hug my son. Kiss him on top of his head. It was the first time since he's been home. The fifteen days of super vigilance are over. Reid and I and his shoulder-length sandy locks I am now able to touch. No more 6 feet of separation. About time! I've waited two weeks and one day just to kiss the top of my son's shaggy head, give him a hug, talk to him up close. And what do I get in return? Three minutes-worth of sarcasm, caustic blasts, accusations, putdowns, but I realize that's my son's way of telling me, as I once told my father, "You're not 19. You're not cool. Your life is one big irrelevancy. It's my time now!" And Reid is absolutely correct. None of us octogenarians should be that consequential. And that goes for politicians as well.

Eleanor will be preparing lunch soon. Reid is in his room. He probably went back to sleep. You know how teenagers are. They stay up chatting on their laptops till three in the morning. Reid loves it down in his quarters. He has everything he needs: an autographed uniform of Aaron Judge, another of Carmelo Anthony, and another of Roger Staubach, and another of Malcom X and another of Martin and another of Einstein and another of some guy name Ronaldo. I'm not keen on soccer. Reid has had some clashes with his mother since he's been here. I could never believe that a mother and son could regress like they do but they can. All it takes is one poke and old wounds come to the surface. All the hard work over a lifetime is obliterated, the damage inside us explodes, all our sanitizers and washing of hands for twenty seconds and protective equipment and civilized behavior and handcuffs are removed and whatever else there is, and the garbage is as ready to kill as when we walked the earth a billion years ago. In my way of thinking, that human virus inside us will last a whole lot longer than Covid-19. We can only address it with band-aids. "America is great. Everything is great. We will get bigger and greater and…" Now Duck is going on TV to perform his great and greater act. This is a weary hour. The more we try, the more shit there is. People are dying. Black kids are being murdered. We will go on. Most of us, that is!

This morning I told Dick to get out! Take a walk! "We have acres and acres of woods, a heated pool, a basketball court, you can get some exercise, some sun, some recreation. You can observe birds, anthills, chipmunks, deer, foxes and their kits, you can get to enjoy something alive rather than tap a laptop or read a book."

Dick wouldn't budge from our guest house. He was reading some heavyweight thinker. Underlining with his blue and red pencils, jotting down footnotes, the exact way he did when he was at CCNY in 1955. I remember him in those days reading some publication from Duquesne University that delved with depth, and I mean real depth, into existential psychology and psychiatry. My identical's copies of that bulletin had underlining on every page and footnotes in the margins as he poured through the essays as if it were the only thing in life worth getting to know. That press went out of business as most literary endeavors have nowadays, yet in its day, this modest periodical had giant thinkers like Harry Stack Sullivan, Merleau-Ponty, Karl Jaspers, Soren Kierkegaard, Hannah Arendt, even the anti-Semite, Martin Heidegger.

Two hours after my twin finished the work he was doing, he called. "Should I walk in the sun or sit on a bench outside the house? Which do you think is better for me?" Dick is like Reid was when my kid was 5. Actually, my twin isn't even 5 years old when it comes to common sense. Of course, he doesn't think so. Ask my brother and he would tell you that with any luck he'd be running a Hollywood studio. Mind you, he's never been to Hollywood. It's true that from his tiny studio in Manhattan he's made minor deals on some of our stories and treatments. That's it. Minor deals. What's kept my brother going for his entire life is his serious writing, but what's kept him entranced is the possibility of a Hollywood breakthrough. It still is what keeps him ticking.

Dick never wanted a family. The only thing he ever took as crucial was his quest to write a book that belonged on the shelf. Of course, he has come a whole lot closer to writing a breakthrough novel than I have. But I have a lot more fun trying. That's a fact. If a more thorough answer is required, here's one that both of us have learned is as close to an answer as we can shake hands on. As identicals, I'm a body writer that uses my belly as consciousness. I take off and let things explode from inside. The result is some of the work is richer, more lyrical, more fluid than Dick's. But the downside is that I'm careless. I do not pay attention to detail. Don't strive for perfection. I say fuck it. It's good enough. Dick, on the other hand, is terrified of using his body. He's all mind. His novels are scrupulous, attentive to detail, less and less expansive. At this time in his life there's little passion, mostly precision, and with less abandonment and carefreeness, he's more like a scientist or a mathematician, not only in syntax and grammar but in form and expressing his ideas. The result is Dick might not be commercial, but he's achieved something that's the difference between being a basketball player who puts his head down and charges to the one who sees the whole court, makes the right pass. Eleanor likes to say, "Combining Dick and me as people or as writers would make for one hell of a novelist and person." Dick is a fine writer. Perhaps a great one. Yet he is known only by people as rarified as Brian Evenson, John O'Brien, Brian McHale, Warren Motte, Trevor Dodge, or Svetlana Pironko, his publisher in Europe, and maybe five thousand other men and women who focus their attention on contemporary literature with an emphasis on experimental and avant-garde fiction. People who can appreciate the difference between saying something that's pioneering and not just a story that compels you to turn the page. He certainly doesn't write for the market I write for. My first novel made several best-seller lists. Was a Book of the Month Club selection. I think I said some of this before and just saying it now gives me a queasy feeling. Why? I admire Dick a whole lot more for never compromising than I do myself, who sold out years ago and never regained whatever it was that I started out with in the realm of getting the best out of oneself.

Anyway, my twin brother is quarantined alone, just one hundred yards down the road from our main barn-yard. In fact, I suggested to him that he give his new novel the title *I Was Alone Too Long*. Also, Dick has never lived with a woman. Forget about marrying one, he's never lived one day with one. He has chicken, his fruit salad and his Bulgarian salad for dinner and his cornflakes in the morning, and whatever else he loves to eat, which isn't much, and he has his computer, his red and blue pencils, a few choice books that he brought with him to read, his iPhone, his favorite novel, *The Fall* by Camus, Beckett's *Waiting for Godot* and his own manuscript, which he is working on. Dick just texted me: "Are you sure I should leave the guest house? Are you sure I won't get lost if I walk in those fuckin' woods? Are you sure?"

That's my twin brother: his pants are stained, his shirt streaked with blots, his fingernails filthy, admittedly he has improved a little, he now takes showers daily. Yes, my identical is odd, he's also pretty damn perfect. He is the only person that I've ever known who when he walks in his neighborhood is on a first name basis with so many of the homeless that I feel embarrassed on how much more hands-on and real his connection is than my checkbook donations. He is the only person I know who told all his dates, "I can only give you a subway token to get home with and the last thing in the world I would want is marriage or children." He is the closest person I know to Prince Myshkin, yet he's not an idealized character. When I scream at him that he's lived half-a-life, that writing his novels isn't worth the price he's paid, he'll give me a sheepish look and in his eyes I can see that he agrees. In his entire lifetime my twin has only loved two women. Two average women with beautiful faces. He held onto their rejections for his entire life. There was a third. A college girl he was in love with. I remember her. For four years he sat in the CCNY dance lounge and ogled her. Never said a word to her.

Dick just phoned: "I read your first fifty pages. You have never written more beautifully. The problem is today everyone writes well, possesses craft. The only thing important is what you have to say. Are you shattering the glass? That's something you're never going to do, so here is what I'm suggesting. If you're going to talk about the people in your life tell the damn truth. You know them. Tell the world if they are morally oblivious. Don't pull your punches. Characterize them for who they really are.

From outside my window you can see the woods. Actually, from every window in the house. There aren't many birds to spot. Some hawks, some blue jays, sometimes a robin red-breast rests on the grass, sometimes a bald eagle wings by, but the woods are the woods. Still, not one green leaf as of today. Nothing but brown bark, dry trees waiting for the late spring. Maybe some of the oak and maple buds will soon be appearing. Perhaps next week or the week after, but right now, brown bark, bare trees.

Eleanor just walked into my study. I'm beginning to find some rhythm in what I'm writing and my wife jolts me with, "In Ecuador, people are dead in the streets. They can't be buried. They're just piling up." Then Ely tells me that her friend's 42-year-old husband is in the hospital. That he can't be visited. He's on a ventilator and it looks like …

You can't get away from it. We're not going to museums, the planetarium, the theatre, movie houses. We're not sailing or hailing yellow taxis or Ubers. We're not cursing out traffic, we're not going to see baseball, watch the NCAA tourney or the NBA. We're not eating out or walking in Central Park or breathing in New York City's delicious polluted air. We've stripped our lives down to the bare essentials here on Justice Lane. I'm not complaining. We have a state-of-the-art house. It's perfect. Aesthetically flawless. Functionally it provides us with whatever is needed. There's even an oil painting of Lincoln by a celebrated 19th-century artist over our fireplace. It makes me feel strange in some way, as if Abe is with us. It also makes me sad, as I know for a fact that my son doesn't give a damn about the oil or about Lincoln, nor is Reid stirred by the Gettysburg Address. Lately, all I hear from my son is, "Another African American was murdered today. This country sucks!"

"History follows a pattern of events that recur in different eras." The proverb has been traced back to Rufus' *Historiae*. It was later used in *Scenes of Clerical Life* by English novelist George Eliot (1819-80).

On September 15, 1976, I was at the Booth Theatre in NYC for the premiere of the choreopoem by playwright Ntozake Shange, *For Colored Girls Who Have Considered Suicide/When the Rainbow Is Enuf.* It was Shange's first work and most acclaimed theatre piece. The characters were: Lady in Brown, Purple, Yellow, Green, White, Black and Orange. Orange was played by Shange. Sitting next to me and my girlfriend at the time, Julie Burr, in the first row of the Booth Theatre was Doris Petty. Doris was wearing a Howard t-shirt under a leather vest. I commented to her that I had several friends who had attended Howard. We sort of connected and when the show ended, I invited Doris to have a bite with Julie and me. "Or if you prefer a drink. I warn you, I'm not a drinker and neither is Julie."

"Coffee will do," Doris responded.

Doris Petty was not exactly a double for Dorothy Dandridge. She looked more like Ruby Dee. Over coffee she told us, "I'm working on a documentary on Stokely Carmichael and when I finish it I'm going to do one on Black men in America incarcerated unjustly." It was obvious to me that Doris Petty was a serious individual, and when I told her that I had written *American Racism*, "I know who you are. I read your book when I was at Howard."

American Racism, by Robert Singer, published 1969.

"The author calls for new attitudes, new energies, new self-assessment on the part of the Black man in order to reach the educational and economic goals he needs to meet the White man as an equal. He demands a spiritual revolution to spark such attainment.

"'Assert yourself,' he urges the Black man. 'Use the talents within yourself. Be right. Be prideful. Be ambitious. Be quantity and quality. Become a soldier for your rights, your human rights, your equal rights. Demand your freedom and become! That's the word – Become!

"'Don't you think it's time to make tomorrow look different and feel different from today? Don't you think it's time to change yourself, to revitalize your ego, to redefine your emotions? The aptitude is there, the ability is obvious. You, Black man, must harness your energies so that you will no longer be tempted by cruel misdirection and destructive misuse. Without your help, your challenge and your change, tomorrow will look and feel like today.

"'What is really meant by Black Power? It is a world, a dream, an unknown island. That the Black man will move to and soon inhabit. It is a movement, a cause, a reason for life. Black Power is pride, dignity and manhood. It is the means and the end, the sum total of assertion. It is respect and leadership. It is recognition and mutual concern. It is dialogue and monologue, with you and me and with every other responsible citizen. It is: seek worth and self-esteem. You, Mr. White, must see me for what I am. A man with individual identity.

"'It is good and it is fair.'"

"Nigger lover," Victoria snapped at me as she looked over my shoulder when I was writing these words. She continued doing so for the remainder of our marriage. Why did I stay with her? To this day I am haunted, become nauseous, when I ask myself that question. The only pathetic answer I have is that I couldn't keep my hands off of Victoria.

American Racism was inspired by personal friendships and by the years I worked in Harlem for the Welfare Department. All those years ago, *A.R.* was written and, still, I am writing and waiting...

At just about the same time I was forging *American Racism*, there was a young man out of the High School of Bronx Science and Howard University, in Washington, DC, who was also having his thoughts published: *Black Power – The Politics of Liberation*, by Stokely Carmichael. Carmichael called for Black people in this country to unite, to recognize their heritage, to build a sense of community, to define their own goals, to lead their own organizations ...

Carmichael challenged the philosophy of non-violence and interracial alliance that had come to define the modern civil rights movement calling instead for "Black Power."

Stokely Carmichael was born in Port of Spain, Trinidad and Tobago; he came to NYC at the age of 11. Was the main force behind the Student Nonviolent Coordinating Committee (SNCC) in the early 1960s, the honorary prime minister of the Black Panther Party (BPP) and lastly, as a leader of the All-African People's Revolutionary Party (APRP). The global Pan-African movement.

Stokely had a BA in philosophy, 1964, from Howard. Married one of my all-time favorite artists, Miriam Makeba, in 1968; was the fourth chairman of SNCC in office May 1966-June 1967. He was preceded by the prodigious John Lewis. Succeeded by H. Rap Brown. "Violence is as American as cherry pie ... If America don't come around, we're gonna burn it down."

I locked arms, fought beside both of these brave men.

Doris Petty and I saw each other through the winter, and when Julie Burr moved out, I asked Doris to move in with me. "I can't, Robert. I'm finishing up my documentary on

Carmichael this month and then I'm going to move to the West Coast." I didn't hear from Doris again, outside of one holiday card from Conakry, Guinea. I did receive a phone call from Doris in 1994. "I read about your new novel in *Publishers Weekly*. Congrats! Listen, Robert, the reason I'm calling you is sort of awkward. I have nowhere else to turn. I have a daughter, Ariela. She's 17 and has been accepted at Carnegie Mellon. Problem is I can't come up with the tuition ... I'll pay you back. If you wish, I'll sign a promissory note." I sent Doris Petty a check for Ariela's tuition.

One thing Doris emphatically stated was "Ariela is not your daughter, Robert. She could've been." I questioned that. "No, I didn't take any test ... Okay, I'm not sure but ..."

Doris and I told each other we would talk about it when she came to New York. "I have to see some people about ... She didn't come to New York to talk about me being Ariela's biological father. I let it go. Maybe I shouldn't have. But I did. The one thing I am certain of is that Doris Petty prepared me for Eleanor. She has many of my wife's endearing qualities. During the time we were together, Doris must have lost her keys, her credit cards, her driver's license, pens, reading glasses, a dozen times. One time I recollect Doris showing up at my place during a monster Duke/North Carolina bet because she was stuck downtown with absolutely no money on her. She had forgotten her wallet. Another time because she had given her last dollars to a homeless woman and, well, that's why Doris reminded me of Eleanor. Doris was also besieged by sties on the corner of her left eye and cold sores on her upper lip and complained incessantly about her fingernails not growing and her hair growing too quickly. One more way Doris Petty prepared me for my wife. Doris couldn't kill a bug. She'd open a window to let a horsefly out. She couldn't step on an ant or get herself to squash a roach. As for mice that we ran into in her Harlem flat, if I didn't feed them and then find an escape route for them, there would be little affection bestowed. One more thing Doris told me that made me stop my pursuit of Ariela. She was involved with a man who wanted marriage. He loved Ariela and would assume responsibility for her once he was released from a prison sentence that he was serving. "In one year, the two of us are going to reinvent our lives, Robert. Please let it go." I liked Doris Petty as much as I was capable of liking anybody, but timing is everything. Eleanor and I were ready for each other. Doris Petty and I never were.

I realize I took a sharp left turn. I think it's because I don't have any solutions for America's race problem. I feel powerless to do something significant to obliterate it. I just don't have Milo Powers' temerity to face the ineluctable head on. Not any longer. I'm wiped out. Disillusioned. Let someone else try and fix it. I'm going to the Old Timers' Game and taking some applause for my past work. Tomorrow belongs to our young.

Walter Li called this morning. "Your friend, Milo Powers. Have you seen his latest blog? He's off the wall the way he's insulting the President. No man has the right to insult our President the way he's been doing."

When Walter Li calmed down he started telling me his opinion on the Paycheck Protection Program for Small Businesses. "There are thirty million of them in the States. I'll bet you less than a third of the thirty million don't get enough protection to survive." We continued talking. "Robert, of course it's important to keep employees on board, keep businesses viable. That's our goal, isn't it? The question is, when will we be able to open up our cities? When, is the question. When!"

Deaths and more deaths and more deaths are being reported. Hour by hour. I keep forcing myself not to think of the corpses in China, Africa, Madrid, Rome, Florence, Iceland, Alaska, Missouri, Miami, Idaho, North Dakota, South Dakota, California, New Jersey. I keep thinking, why is it most of us never thought of the other fellow till now?

I gazed outside from one of my windows. One solitary bush is blooming with white flowers. Haven't a clue what kind of flowering bush it is. It's the only thing I've seen in a long, long while that makes me feel hopeful. And I am hopeful. So many octogenarians aren't. So many have died. So many more will. So many people who are a whole lot younger than I am are also going to die.

Milo Powers called:

"You just don't understand, Robert. The guy's a racist. With all the Black friends you have, doesn't it bother you? How can you look any of them in the eye? I'm sure they all want him dead. He's the worst president in America's history. If I weren't getting weaker and weaker ... I'm not doing well. The chemo isn't helping. If I were younger, I would…He's the most dangerous president we ever had. You'll see. One day things are going to explode and he'll start doing things as savagely as if he were Hitler. I have to get off the phone. I need to lie down. I don't know if I'll be here much longer. This morning my doctor told me he's going to try and arrange for me to move."

"Move where?"

"You know. Hospice care."

Eleanor's sister called from Dallas. Veronica was excited. She had heard from a cousin that the family had a relative who was a general in the civil war. He fought at Gettysburg leading the New York first volunteers. His battalion was there with the New Hampshire volunteers in a charge against the gray. Here's irony! The New Hampshire brigade was led by a relative of one my past editors, Merle Edison, who has lived his entire life in Pembroke, New Hampshire. When Eleanor brought Duck up to her sister, "He's got George and my vote. He hasn't backed down from one promise that he's made to us."

In the middle of the night I do my best thinking. What leaks out are random thoughts, self-pity, insecurities, triumphs, terrors that have been buried deep, lurking in some mysterious reservoir that is still alive and young. I am writing now. It's early in the a.m. I'm sure I won't be able to capture 5 percent of what has been spilling. My whirl of thoughts is jumbled. Vague. There, there, though as relevant as I am irrelevant. That's what I have become. It's not that Eleanor intentionally makes me feel so, or, for that matter, Reid. It's not even the fault of this pandemic, though this happening we're experiencing is taking a heavy toll. I know it has for everyone. Every soul on the globe is in its grip. As I get up from my typewriter to stretch, I remind myself to think good thoughts, try and remain optimistic. To keep a sense of humor. When I return to writing, what surfaces into my head are Eleanor's lamb chops. The kind she made last night. She's become an expert chef. Our first twenty-one years together, not one home-cooked meal. Now Ely is preparing delicious meals. I smile to myself rather than dwell on what's missing from our lives; on how this virus is traveling across the globe as if it were some radiation from a nuclear fallout. I shake my head. Tell myself to think of something positive. Something that will make me smile. And what comes to mind is Reid. The most delicious news all evening was when our son marched into the dining room and announced, "I just finished the last math test for this semester. I did all right. Now I only have one exam to go. A huge one in physics." An hour later, Reid parades back into the dining room. He's grinning from ear to ear. "I got 100 on my math test," he tells us in a voice that resonated exactly how he is feeling.

My son usually speaks in a foghorn drone, now he's almost on a basketball court swishing jumpers. The fact that Reid will now receive an A in his math course means for certain that his freshman year was a major success. His grade point average will be 4.0 in mechanical engineering. "Congratulations," I shout and rush over to give him a big hug. He pulls away, turns to his mother, begins to discuss his plans for the summer. Then he remembers the pandemic and he begins cursing. When I ask him some questions about the physic exam that he still needs to take, "Ba," he drones, "All I need is a 68 and I'm home free. My average will still stay way above 90 for the semester."

"Does that mean you will definitely have a four-point average for the entire year?" I stammer in the kind of way only an octogenarian dad can muster. Not that I feel my age, it's just that my wife and son, well they highlight my fumbles, think of me as an error at short. I don't exist when the two of them are together. It's as if they are rolling their eyes at everything I have to say, talk through me, around me, over me. I'm sure it's not on purpose. On second thought, maybe it is. I mutter to myself, from now on I'm going to keep everything I have to say inside. Not open my mouth.

I leave my bedroom just about every night. By one in the morning I can't sleep. I toss and turn and, of course, think. I stumble into one of our six other bedrooms, find a fresh pillow, a soft mattress, a quilt that's inviting and cozy. I start counting sheep. Before long I am asleep. The only problem is my mind keeps going. I keep pounding thoughts. Unwritten words, hour after hour. Should I have a notepad at my side? A recorder? I did that once on a novel I penned. It was a lightweight effort in the early '60s. I submitted it to a senior editor at Simon and Schuster. "I like it," she said. "I think it's perfect for one of our pocketbook divisions." I felt insulted. I wanted hardcover. I shopped the book to twenty other publishing houses. It took years for me to acknowledge writers can't be choosers. Now I am at my Smith-Corona. The same machine I used back then. Like me, this typewriter has had six, no, make that seven trips to Gramercy Typewriter Company. Right now I'm feeling more sorry for myself than Jackie O.

did over losing John. I'm not a hero. Not a first responder. Not close. I tell myself I have everything you could possibly want, considering the violations inflicted by this horrific pandemic. I have a perfect son. Reid is decent and brilliant. A good person. On the other hand, I would certainly like my son to be wilder, more robust, a bit more like the kind of boy I was. One that could throw a second pitch. I know Reid's fastball is great but it's straight as an arrow. It's got speed but it doesn't jump. I have the love of my wife. She's everything to me. Is Eleanor everything because I'm old? Would she still be everything if I were 25? 35? 55? I can't answer those kinds of questions without looking in the mirror and seeing that I was nothing but Broadway Bob until I met Eleanor. A Duck-like quack, always putting himself first, having little regard for other people, wanting all the things and glory that all us jerks want. It wasn't until Eleanor came into my life that I calmed down. Matured. Our first year was like Christmas Eve. No one captured my heart like Eleanor did. Eleanor was there by needing what I had to give. Dick would say, "You were burned out. With exhaustion comes perspective." Some would call what I have, "the best of everything." I agree full-heartedly. The past twenty-one years with Ely have been the best years of my entire life. Maybe the closest I will ever get to writing a first-rate novel. Screw writing, I tell myself. Screw sports! Screw theatre! Screw Kiton sports jackets! Screw handicapping! Making money! Screw living life to the fullest. Screw adventure, risk, the dignity of trying. I'm living my life now with peace of mind, tranquility. With Eleanor beside me. What else do I need? I shut my eyes, keep them tightly closed. Eleanor comes into the room, climbs into the bed. Takes my hand. Whispers, "I love you, Robert." I move a few inches closer. Realize somewhere deep inside, as if I am a wristwatch that needed rewinding, I'm an octogenarian approaching oblivion, irrelevant?

Thousands of people dying all over the globe. What was the last count? What just happened in Italy? Who made the decision to pink-slip people over 80? Was it the government? Physicians? Families? It was made. In Italy, octogenarians are not receiving ventilators. Even worse, they're being taken off them! I'm panicking. Shaking like people in New York are who haven't received their benefit checks. I continue thinking. My mind is as alive with these meanderings as my body is betraying me. I can't climb stairs. I can't lift weights. I can't… all I can do is inch over in the bed to the coolest side, adjust my pillow, try and calm myself, think things through. 'I'm irrelevant' keeps coming to the surface. I try telling myself I can still write a halfway decent page. Maybe I can't but I still enjoy pounding on my typewriter. Yesterday I suggested to Eleanor that she watch a play with me on the theatre channel. "Okay," she said. I selected Edward Albee's *A Delicate Balance*. Eleanor watched it with me for perhaps thirty-five minutes, "I like it, Robert but would you mind if I call it a night. I'm tired." I never once left the theatre before a performance was completed. I can still tell you all of the plays I've seen from A to Z. If I can't recall one or one hundred and one, I have my collection of playbills. At least 3,000 stored in my rooftop shed. I have read from James Agee to Emile Zola. I have read Grossman and Oz and most of the other important Israeli and Eastern European and Japanese icons like Abe and Endo and Kenzaburo Oe. I tell Eleanor, "You must read *A Personal Matter*, and after that …" I've read the English and the Irish and the Australians and I've read David Foster Wallace's *Infinite Jest*, too, and I've read at least two thousand or more first-time novelists and the most current rising stars. People like Halle Butler and Chigozie Obioma and I've read the extraordinary Gabriel Marquez and Jorge Borges and Carlos Fuentes and O'Henry and Runyon and Norman Mailer and learned more than I needed to know from Simone de Beauvoir's *The Second Sex*, and was entertained by Judith Krantz and Erica Jong and Stephen King, and I've read my friend, Aliza Ross' novel, *Asymmetrical Woman*, this week. She's pretty darn good. I've read for over seventy years. At 13 I took out of the neighborhood public library a biography on George Washington Carver; from there I graduated to Sandburg's Lincoln. I've read and read and read and I'll tell you right now, I still feel insignificant. All the books, theatre, ballet, concerts, all the Pavarottis and Swan Lakes danced by Fonteyn and Nureyev and you can throw in Balanchine's *Firebird*, and what's it all mean? I'm still as puny as the dollars I've accumulated, as small as the one-night stand erections I no longer pursue. I'm going, going, gone. If this is my last hurrah, what does it all mean? What did it mean? I'm not timeless. I'm a disappearing act. My knowledge of baseball and basketball means nothing. Who cares about George McQuinn and Bob Cerv and Lou Limmer and Elmer Valo and Ferris Fain and Bobby Shantz anymore? Who cares about George Yardley and Joe Fulks and Vince Boryla and Sweetwater Clifton and Harry Gallatin and Red Rocha and Chuck Cooper and Bob Kurland and Al Cervi and Max Zaslofsky and Neil Johnston and the great Bob Cousy anymore? My son is looking through me, my wife is polite. She holds my hand, but she's only, if truth be told, engrossed in her own book, preparing with her editor and her marketing people for *The Calcium Connection* winter release. Eleanor is doing her thing (as I did mine with handicapping) and that's cool. That's what I genuinely want Eleanor to be doing. From the first day I met her until right now, there has never been a minute I didn't want her to have autonomy, her independence. A rock-solid sense of self. Last night, before we went to sleep, I told Eleanor, "When I die, I want you to go on living life. I don't want you to be a recluse. You have at least thirty more vibrant years in front of you. Find someone to share them with. If this pandemic is my last beachhead, it's not yours. Promise me, Eleanor. Don't waste one day. You're still relevant, and, believe me, relevancy is fleeting."

This morning was a fabulous one. The blue was in the sky. White clouds were interwoven like a patchwork quilt. I went down to the kitchen to have orange juice and Cheerios and to slurp my coffee. Eleanor marched in. "Good morning," she chirps. It doesn't take much for a veteran husband to grasp the good from the bad. I immediately realized that my wife was all the way back. That our life together can move on. We shared most of the day. The parts when I wasn't writing and Eleanor wasn't responding to emails. We spent part of the afternoon with Reid. Then we took a long walk. An even longer nap. Soon after, Eleanor started preparing dinner. She cooked enough so I could have two portions. Doesn't sound like much, but throw in the play we watched on TV, "I really want to see the rest of the Albee play, Robert. I was just so tired the other night." Then my wife handed me eight milk chocolate Hershey Kisses. I can't remember having a better day.

For me, the first draft is fun. Ideas and inspirations that will demand rewrites. If I find the original pages have value, I will go to work. One year, two years, I've spent as many as eleven years on a novel. Writing is rewriting and more rewriting until, if ever, the words are faultless. This time is different. I don't have the years it takes to craft, carve, refine and polish my novel. I shall complete this first draft then call it a day. My age, conjoining with Covid-19, convinces me that all I have left to lift off the ground is content. It is definitely not an artful novel. Only farmer's grain.

A BEGINNING: FIRST DRAFT – OPENING SECTION

A LIFE OF SECRETS BY ROBERT SINGER

Much of this part of my life is not known to my wife, my son or my identical twin. It's a life that I lived, am still living, even today, to an extent. I still have the command and the expertise to administer, to control my organization that is as ruthless and financially profitable as I did when I was at my handicapping peak. I will hint at it now and then, show and tell you of some of the savage and brutal aspects, the violence and spilled blood. I will reference men in my life that you're somewhat familiar with to the shadowy extent that I've penned them in my past writings. Now I will go a step further and graphically document these men, more importantly, the person that I must own responsibility for having been. The man I am, that's more difficult.

I certainly cannot answer that one – you must answer that one on your own. Be sure that the men who assisted me up to my sixties to acquire wealth and marginalized status are not make-believe, my fictive imagination. They existed. Just as I prevailed before meeting my wife Eleanor at the advanced age of 62 and consciously forced that Robert Singer to disappear.

Of course, this current version of myself, this bland, civilized, domesticated, venerable Robert Singer I disassociate from my past, but yesterday is deep within me. It is still who I am. Strike a match, I am always prepared to flame, if need be. It's not charming or pretty, it's heinous. More like that sniper is in *Schindler's List* who picks off Jewish concentration camp prisoners from his balcony. You do not have to read *A Secret Life*. Just flip the pages of my earlier books to read about Robert Singer's more conventional life, a true life without preternatural uncertainty or fear, risk or danger, menace or peril or much growth. That, too, is my life's reality. But if you choose to read *A Life of Secrets*, see it for what it is. Don't excuse it as if Robert Singer was some kind of Lone Ranger hero or black and white celluloid gangster. He wasn't. He's me! And believe me, that is not something to be proud of.

Being the son of a cantor on the Upper West Side, I had grown up with cantors! These singers of liturgical solos led their synagogues in prayer. Friends of my father included: Waldman, Diamond, Ringel, Kapov-Kagan, the Koussevitzky brothers, Moishe Oysher, Genchoff, and a dozen more. I had grown up with my dad's RCA Victrola as the centerpiece of our home. Listening to the sublime voices of Amelita Galli-Curci, Lily Pons, Enrico Caruso, Beniamino Gigli, Lauritz Melchior, Franco Corelli, Jussi Björling, Nicolai Gedda. Our gramophone never stopped spinning. I had grown up with my father's two closest friends, Jan Peerce and Richard Tucker. These two spectacular cantors were in our living room, at my father's Steinway, twice a week when my twin brother and I were little, always horsing around, squabbling, scaling, singing, arguing who was the greatest centerfielder, Willie, Mickey or the Duke. When it came to boxers it was always The Brown Bomber, Joe Louis, who was their champion of champions, though my dad brought up the Manassa Mauler, Jack Dempsey, on occasion. It was Richard Tucker who gave my identical and me the greatest bar mitzvah gift of all. Those PM Two Wilson baseball gloves. Dick and I went to bed for month after month with these gloves under our pillows, oiled them daily, had autographed baseballs of Charlie Silvera and Gus Niahos in their pockets.

My mother was a psych professor at Barnard College. My brother and I grew up with her friends: doctors, lawyers, surgeons, Barnard and Columbia professors; jurists, senators, writers; men such as the philosopher Abraham Joshua Heschel; the Talmud scholar Louis Finkelstein; the novelist Herman Wouk. I had grown up unprepared for the likes of Haskell Gold and Isaac Becker. My first impression of these two were the same as my twin brother Dick's. They were cartoon characters. Belonged in a gangster flick. I had as little in common with them as Charles Boyer had with John Wayne. When I evolved into the incipient "Handicapper", I started socializing with these two tycoons; their world became my everyday reality.

More than a majority of you will find this appalling but I've decided to include this fragment to give a clearer insight into my complicated, untoward past. During my 31 handicapping years, years that I climbed to the top of Mount Gamble, I struggled considerably to control my world, as if I were protecting my newborn each day. I had more than one rumpus, not only with law enforcement, not only with Rico agents or D.A.s, or that demented mayor who roots for the Yankees, or malevolent men who placed unsettling contracts on my head, as all of them I considered child's play, or absurdity, in a manner of speaking. For a dollar or half-a-million, those kinds of problems could be resolved and they were. You would be surprised how many individuals would rather collect lucre than have you dead or incarcerated. With the assistance of street-smart Isaac Becker and all-powerful Haskell Gold, I was able to buy my way out of just about every dangerous zone, but then there are predicaments that can't be bought off, that have to be dealt with one-on-one and this, of course, is an entirely different billiard game. There were three such circumstances during my handicapping tenure; conflicts of interest that I could not find a solution for other than by direct profane action.

These three men I had personally condemned without the assistance of counsel from Becker or Gold, or any other fiscal partner. I was personally responsible for having these flesh and blood men maimed or eliminated. One of them, Jason Ressler, a beard that I have written about before, I won't mention again. The other two I possibly will journalize later on. As I now purge this stream-of-consciousness confession, I cannot find one small way to justify my actions. One monstrous felony is more than most criminal courts will tolerate, so I'll leave it here and transform myself into being 62 years of age, ready to begin my domesticated life with Eleanor, the beginning of a beauty and the beast new life.

Before I committed myself to Eleanor, most of the things I did were heavy-handed. As I allow my mind to recall experiences that I am sure are as distant from how I am living today as sand is from water, I dwell on some of them. One of the light-hearted memories is of Vivian and Kim. I had connected friends who owned pole-dancing joints from Scranton, PA, to the Twin-Cities. I made deals with these men – not only by giving them my preferred games to wager on, which they salivated for, but with cash that I earned from these games. Remember, by the time I reached my 42nd birthday, I was as cash rich as just about anyone in the City. As liquid as that jeweler on Canal Street, the one that exchanged under-the-table malfeasant dollars for legitimate diamonds. This silver-haired fellow was always buying legal rocks and giving out illegal currency until he was kidnapped by people I knew. Mr. Silver-hair would never have gotten back to Canal Street, but I called Isaac Becker at the bequest of my pal, the Major, and Becker called two or three godfathers. Before the day was over, Becker had arranged for the jeweler to go home to his wife and children. That's how things were done in 1978. They still are, but now it's with less muscle and noise, granted morality is still relative as is deal-making. Anyway, the incident I'm taking an effort to recollect is of Kim and Vivian. They were two pole-dancers, not hookers, and in those days I, too, made illicit deals for serious cash. My standard proposition with strip-joint proprietors was twenty-five thousand for 5 percent ownership in a lifeless joint. I owned 5 percent of at least thirty of those kinds of dissolute establishments. The dividend was that appetizing pole-dancers were sent over to my 1818 residence. Kim and Vivian were just two of the dozens of women that I enjoyed. Actually, they were two of my favorites. Especially Kim. Both women knew that I was a big tipper and they would have one of my drivers rush them over whenever I called. Usually, I preferred having my ménage à trois at one in the morning on Saturday nights. During the late spring, summer and early fall I'd have them on my rooftop. When the weather turned cold in early fall I'd start having them inside. One thing I discovered was that as many of these mergers as I participated in, I always ended up gravitating to one woman over the other. In Vivian and Kim's case, it was always Vivian who had her feelings hurt as I would end up frolicking with Kim for most of the evening while Vivian brooded on the sidelines saying things like, "It isn't fair. I want to join in. You two are ignoring me." That's how it went. Just about every Saturday night. Then at the age of 46 I ceased engaging in this kind of pleasure.

Isaac Becker came into my life in 1961, the year of Mantle and Maris. I was at Carnegie Hall attending a concert promoted by that fat-fuck, Stickers Bernstein, who eventually brought the Beatles to America. Stickers introduced me to Isaac and his Israeli mistress. In those days, Becker was biding his time to put in a seven million dollar bid to CBS to purchase the New York Yankees. He was also actively engaged in his manufacturing business, producing films, and preparing to do the first million-dollar musical in Broadway history. Isaac was a short, wide, fireplug of a man about town, worth more money and influence than I had the ability to imagine or think existed. And, of course, as far as I was concerned, he was "A Champion Amongst Men." I bought into the I.B. mythology as only an Ortho-dox cantor's son could, and before I knew it I was involved with his mistress, Rachel Mizrahi, who was definitely the most beautiful woman I (and a million other New York men) had ever seen.

I was working for *The New York Mirror*. My desk was next to William Randolph Hearst, Jr., who was sort of a sad character. He was a Hearst, though, and even-tually would follow the path of too many of these trust fund One-Percenters. For some reason, outside of rea-son, maybe by pure accident, I was chosen to do lackey chores for Rose Bigman, who was the right-and-left-arm of Walter Winchell. I started attending all the in-parties in Manhattan. Meeting Miss Universe women, Ford models, actresses, even seven-sister-school intellectual women like Susan Sontag and feminists like Gloria Steinem and Betty Friedan. I had a glib mouthpiece, exceptional looks, could play the Sidney Falco role when needed. So here I am pre-paring, but not overly impressed, by a world that is not open to everyone; that I was, to say the least, skeptical of at first, but if it's there for you and you have a craving to make it, how can you possibly say no. So, after a while, I'm hooked. I put aside my fantasy of writing the great American ... not all of my dream, but enough so that you can call me a prostitute. I begin to leap from my ideal truth to my venal hunger and that's where I am. I join the barbarians. The showy, the fashionable, the scene players, the vapid rich, the cunning, the merciless, and before one year goes by, I'm addicted.

Not all at once, mind you, but by the age of 25, I am with a hook in my throat and the seductive Victoria Lurie and the duplicitous Isaac Becker reeling me in. Victoria's power is fundamental. It's carnal. I just can't stop throbbing. Isaac's is more nuanced. Steak dinners at his restaurant, at the great man's table. It's flattering. It's stroking me where obviously I was also throbbing with vulnerability. I'm meeting every celebrity worth meeting from Sammy Davis to Bess Myerson to Joe DiMaggio to Mickey Mantle. Usually it's enough for a social worker like me to meet the Joe Ds and the Mickeys of the world without needing to be the Joe Ds and the Mickeys, but it wasn't for me. A large chunk of me still wanted to be a somebody and I still had something in me that wanted me to be me. But put that all aside, I was as much of a sellout as a 42nd Street hooker. I sold most of myself on the cheap.

"Wanting to be a novelist is fine, Bobby boy, but I'm going to introduce you to… you're going to have doors open up to you that can make you a millionaire before you hit 30." And Isaac Becker did introduce me to everyone. I did meet everyone. I was attending the right parties, taking out Miss Sweden, Miss England, Miss USA, my fiancé, Sondra Vann. Sondra was wholesome, a breath of clean air, a Tremont Avenue Bronx girl, a graduate of Taft High School who loved baseball, children, me! I was the moron who destroyed what we shared.

Victoria Lurie soon re-entered the picture. With her 165 I.Q. Her pre-med at Cornell. Her allure. Her Ford model, heartless, relentlessness: Victoria was a woman I fell in bed with when the two of us were 18. By 1961, Victoria was not only on billboards and magazine covers modeling for Eileen and Gerard Ford, she was married to some Harvard investment banker and seeing me one afternoon each week on the side. We always had seen each other on the side, through Victoria's first two, no, make that three marriages. I could never get enough of Victoria. I would be turned on by hearing her voice on the phone. I wonder how it would be today with texting.

As I mentioned, I was also involved to a much lesser degree, with Rachel Mizrahi. This Israeli could have been a finalist in the Miss Universe contest, but she was the mistress of Isaac and that meant, his property. She was also my twin brother Dick's love of a lifetime and here I am as inimical as Duck, sleeping with her and buying into, "I need you, Robert. You have big shoulders. I need a man with big shoulders. I must get away from little boys and married men." I kept seeing Mizrahi until my brother discovered my betrayal. Dick cracked up. Had to drop out of grad school. He didn't say much to me. Actually, he just gave me a look that I am still haunted by to this day. I came to my senses. Did an about-face. But I was more guilty than Ethel and Julius Rosenberg were when they were convicted as Russian spies and electrocuted. They had extenuating circumstances. I had sickness. No morality, no ethics, no scruples, only and out-of-whack ego. Who betrays his twin brother? Who goes to bed with the woman his identical is in love with? Who sleeps with the mistress of a man who can have you killed by raising his eyebrow? I was 25, as libidinal, as uncontrolled, as spontaneous, as unthinking as…

❧

Ok, getting back to my engagement to Sondra Vann: At first we had a great time. We went to Yankee games. The Bronx Zoo. We danced our weekends away at the Gotham Hotel. There was a jet-set Euro-club in the hotel's basement called L'interdit and I would take Sondra there. We'd dance The Twist. Before six months went by I was proposing. We had our engagement party at Danny's Hideaway. It seemed as if all of New York was there. I was 26, more content than I'd ever been, with a woman who made me happy by just smiling, who I made happy by being me...

Victoria called. "I'm leaving my husband. I must see you." I made the biggest mistake of my young life. Before I knew it, I was a yoyo between my real feelings for Sondra and my desire for Victoria. Cal Ramsey's mother, Ruth, warned me, "Robert, sex is one thing, being with a woman who will stand by you when it rains and pours, believe me, that's a whole lot more." Desire won out. Sondra said to my mother, "Mrs. Singer, I can't compete with Victoria. She knows everything there is to know about sex. I know nothing." I abandoned Sondra. Married Victoria. Within months, Victoria was screaming, "You must get a real job. Make a living." I left the job I loved with *The New York Mirror*. $48.00 a week as an editorial assistant wouldn't do. The Welfare Department was paying two hundred a week. When your salary is $48.00, every dollar more is more. So now I am married to Victoria, sharing hate-fucks. Both of us are realizing we are incompatible. We despise each other's values. We not only have different takes on what is of value, we both are the kind of people that stand toe-to-toe and swing from the heels defending our positions.

Sondra is gone. Victoria is sniffing around. With her assets it did not take her long to find what she was looking for. I continued pounding a typewriter. Probably the same one I'm writing on today, saying "Black Lives Matter." It was the 1960s. Victoria was hissing "nigger lover!... civil servant!... loser!" Before she stopped hissing, we were yesterday. I didn't know it then but my life would be reinvented. For better! For worse!

It is now December 1971. It's the beginning of the college basketball season. I'm wagering $25.00 on a Western Kentucky/University of Alabama, Birmingham, game. I won. That season I made four thousand three hundred dollars. The next year I started with twenty-five hundred and earned forty-two thousand. That's when I moved out of my parents' apartment. The following year I won one hundred and nine thousand. I paid fifty thousand under the table for the penthouse in 1818 that I am still living in. The manager of 1818, Teresa Quinn, was retiring and easy to convince that her social security checks and pension could benefit from my gratuity. To this day, I think it was the best investment I ever made. I am becoming "The Handicapper." I'm the criminal choice of the month. Isaac Becker and Haskell Gold sniff me out. They join forces with me. Become limited partners. I'm beginning my life of secrets. A life of unimaginable possibilities. Now let me tell you, not everyone has the stomach or vision to go from working in a candy store to owning a fleet of them. Not everyone is a Jeff Bezos or a Chuck Feeney. Not everyone has talent and vision. Before I knew it, I was rubbing shoulders with the big boys. Scheming, planning and criminalizing to the nth degree.

I needed to collect from one of those bookmaker-slime-ball-record-owners who had his office in the Brill Building. The guy owed me seventeen thousand. Isaac Becker's cut was seven. It wasn't a matter of life or starvation to "everybody's best friend," but money is money and accounts receivables need to be checked off. Especially after it gets a suntan in Miami Beach for three weeks.

Twenty-two polite phone calls had been made by me to Miami. Isaac suggests he send Ernie "Beef" Leighton to visit the record exec's office. An hour later I receive a phone call from Leighton, "Singer, this crumb is telling me he can only come up with seventy-four hundred. He says … hold on …" I hear screaming. It wasn't Beef Leighton howling, it was the bookmaker. Beef is holding him by the ankles outside of a 14th story window. Isaac gave his share of the proceeds to his chief of security who divided it up with his security crew. They played craps with the money. Isaac joined the game.

Before I knew it, I was figuring out ways to expand. I certainly had mushroomed. Within two years I had gone from having three bookmakers in New York City to having BMs and beards all over the country. One hand feeds the other. I was making money for Gold and Becker. They were providing me with the assets to expand. Soon I had college kids at several division-one schools feeding me information, each beard getting me down anywhere from five hundred dollars to two thousand. From Paducah, Kentucky; to Ames, Iowa; to Morgantown, West Virginia. That was my strength. Picking winners is one thing. Finding beards all over the country, students who could get me down at the number I needed was everything. That's what pushes you forward. Getting your product on those racks. When I started at my parents' West End Avenue apartment, I never imagined what I was now doing. In those days, if I made twenty dollars, sometimes one hundred or two hundred dollars, it was celebratory. That first year when I started with Western Kentucky, I had no clue of what was to come. I was, as Victoria hissed, "a loser!" Picking games was no more than what Victoria said it was – "Gambling! I was "a gambler!" "A loser!" Now I'm a different person. A new person. An invisible person. With code names, beards, bookmakers who have absolutely no idea of what I'm doing. Where I'm going. Each person I employ I sign up individually. Each person is responsible for one chore. I'm directing traffic. Giving out orders. Doing all the masterminding. These people assisting me to become what most of America calls a winner. I call it a whole lot less.

Before you can spell it out, I was "The Handicapper." I was making more money than I could have ever thought possible. I was using code names, remaining invisible. No one knew who I was or what I was doing. Not Isaac Becker. Not Haskell Gold. Not my twin brother. Not Julie Burr, who had moved in with me. I was living a life of secrets. If you're old enough to have read my earlier novels, you know some of this, but it's worth repeating, even though my wife, Eleanor, unequivocally believes it's trash. How do you climb Mount Gamble? Go from the bottom lands of Victoria Lurie's pessimism to this? Remember, in December 1969 I was thrown out by Victoria, had moved in with my Cantor father and my warm-hearted mom. I was up to my curly, brown hair in debt. I survived because of my parents' generosity for two years. Was only capable of paying off the installments on my Beneficial Finance and Household Finance and Chase and Chemical and Bank of America and Wells Fargo bank loans. I was living on a two hundred dollar a week civil service paycheck. Studying college basketball statistics as if I were my twin brother underlining Beckett, Kafka and Camus. It wasn't philosophers or literary novelists that I was reviewing. I was charting games, researching results, going over rosters, learning trends, evaluating coaches, observing player matchups, exploring the possibility of making it as a professional handicapper. Of course the word "handicapper" wasn't part of my vocabulary back then. Just like "Black Power" wasn't. I was still trying to finish my book *American Racism*, everyone still used the word "Negro," and Victoria was hissing and calling me a "nigger lover." To this day it still turns my stomach that I stayed with Victoria. I have a thousand regrets. I live with them. Back to the moment. "I'll show Victoria I can make money" was the thing that kept driving me. I'm floundering with debt. Begging my best friend, Sam Tronn, "Sam, I can't pay you back one dollar. I'm trying to keep even with finance companies and banks..." "Don't worry, Broadway. If you need a few more dollars I can help." I owe forty thousand and here I am borrowing another two hundred and fifty from Tronn. I think at the time I already owed Ron over four thousand. The two hundred and fifty I had put aside, that was to be my bankroll for the basketball season I didn't have. It went to a better cause than me. A Harlem family in desperate straits. Four children and a mother who needed clothing, furnishings and food. No reason to go further than to tell you my City refused to help them. I had saved that two fifty. My first wager was on Western Kentucky. It's Proustian time. I keep zigzagging. Traveling backwards and forwards. I'm 83. Please stay with me. I'm not the handicapper yet, but I am with an idea, a formula, a plan. I'm going to only wager on games when I find a differential of four and one-half points or more from my power ratings to the Las Vegas line. By then I had discovered that of the four thousand or so games in Division One that Vegas was putting out a line on, one hundred and fifty of them, more or less, had a four and one-half point disparity or more from my power ratings. That I would have won 58 percent, possibly even more when the number was five, six or a seven-point mistake on Vegas' part. I had it down on graph paper. My percentage of picking winners increased the larger the Vegas mistake. I had a business. That was my premise. For 31 years I followed this premise. In 30 of those years I won ... millions!

Victoria was gifted with men. As Eileen Ford put it, "captivating and super photogenic." It's as simple as that. Some people get all the breaks. Deserving or not. Being inimical, being a bitch, not caring about Jesus or anyone else doesn't mean squat in New York. For that matter, America. What matters is something a whole lot more negotiable. Victoria had the physical assets that could be marketed and sold. Transcendent beauty matters! Shrewdness matters! Instrumentalized behavior matters! Cognition matters! Cunning! Victoria moved on. Bankers, hedge fund guys, trust fund millionaires, Harvard men stepped out of their

Ferraris, Mercedes and Jags to kiss Victoria's icy fingers, inviting cunt. As I said, my ex was gifted with men. It's as simple as that. When things didn't work out for me at *The Mirror* and losing a job that pays $48.00 a week is no more than spilt milk unless you're some kind of idiot like me who believed, at the time, that making scenes, writing a novel, dreaming of nothing very real, living with some kind of Hollywood illusion that keeps purring, it was a voice inside that couldn't be removed. Only distortion. "My two little geniuses," my mother would coo to my twin and me every day. Psyched. Programmed to believe that you're the next Hemingway. That you're Rhett Butler in *Gone with the Wind*. Rhett Butler I wasn't. Hemingway ended up dead by his own hand. One thing I did know about myself. I wasn't going to end up one of those literary monks who believed writing a novel that belongs on a dusty shelf is the only reason to exist. I admired several people who didn't read one book in their entire life. They were happy. They were successful. They were enjoying their life. One of Isaac Becker's workmates, "Big Matty" Moreno, that's right, *that* Matty said to me, "What makes you think the only way to live a successful life is to be a novelist?" Dick's confidante, Norman Rosten, the poet laureate of Brooklyn, said, "No one ever twisted your arm to be a novelist. My advice, Robert, is to write if you can't live without writing. If you can, move on." I moved on!

Whoever made money betting on baseball, football, or basketball games? Name one person. You can't. Lem Banker, the California handicapper who looked like Tarzan, made a buck or two on professional football. For a short while, my sources tell. "Jimmy the Greek" promoted the public. Maybe that erudite *Washington Post* journalist, Andy Byers, who had a degree from Harvard, made some cash at the racetrack. But it was only change. All I can tell you is not one person, wise guy or math genius, ever made a living bucking the Las Vegas lines on baskets, football or baseball, college or pro. I was a loser and I knew it, without a friend in the world who would lend me a helping hand. I had used up my quota of hands. Yes, there was Sam Tronn, but my Ivy League buddy was the proverbial rich man's son. As much a misfit as Dostoevsky's Prince Myshkin.

Here I am with the street awareness that in order to win I have to be hurdling "Big Matty" and "Fat Tony," mobsters, wise guys, law enforcement, everyone else who comes into my unfocused picture frame. And they did, and, still, I started winning. At first it was that $25.00 bet on Western Kentucky during the year I was consuming my mom's kosher cooking, grateful for my dad paying all of the rent, walking the Harlem streets, wearing boots and carrying an umbrella so that when I entered the projects and railroad flats I patrolled, I wouldn't be defenseless against rats or junkies. My only other defensive weapon was a black field book that neighborhood people recognized as belonging to a "welfare worker." And that's what I was doing. Knocking on despairing people's doors, trying to provide TLC.

Now I find another four and one-half point differential. Again, I win twenty-five dollars. I continued having kosher food and picking winners throughout that first season. I was on my way. "I'll show Victoria." The last two bets I made that season were for fifteen hundred dollars each. Manhattan College won one of those games against

St. Peter's. Bobby Knight won the other. There isn't a day that goes by to this day, as I sit sunning myself on the porch off our kitchen, that I didn't praise the difference between Coach Knight's skills and those North Carolina, Kansas, Duke and Kentucky coaches who recruit players that can go from high school to the NBA All Star game overnight. Knight's players, for the most part, couldn't play for the Commerce High School team I played for. And if they could make the team, they'd be sitting on the bench next to me. Bobby Knight won with inferior talent. He didn't have Kentucky's Bam Adebayo or Tyler Herro or Devin Booker, and when Calapari had these brilliant talents, they weren't even his prime stars. Knight won with so much less. He found a way. He survived. He bullied, intimidated, cursed, kicked ass, and you know what, maybe I was learning what Leo Durocher said all those years before, "Nice guys finish last..." I wasn't a nice guy. Not during any one of my 31 years of climbing Mount Gamble. I was a whole lot more like Duck than Bobby Knight. Bobby Knight is an honorable man. He didn't cheat. His players graduated. If it had been me, I wouldn't have cared about one player receiving a passing grade. They would have passed and they would have played. Damn, some math professor wouldn't have failed a kid I needed to play. Just transform that thought to handicapping. Imagine what an insurgent handicapper can do who is sociopathic. Not that different than a president. There's always a way.

In business, every problem can be solved. If not one way, then another. You do not have to be Walter Li, Jeff Bezos, or Duck to make important money. It wasn't luck. I used whatever I could use. I win over forty thousand in my second season. Then it's one hundred and nine and

I'm on the freeway. I have enough success to believe I was out of the Golden Gloves, ready for my first pro-fight. A four rounder for sure. Maybe six. Perhaps one day I'll be a Jimmy Herring, a Roger Donoghue, a Sonny Parisi. Oh, you never heard of these boxers. They were real good club fighters. They all had fantasies of one day winning a championship. Just about everyone in our universe has dreams, an ego, aspirations. These fighters did win more than a few fights. They knew about losing, too. I knew about losing. I knew about people being kept in the gutter, not mattering. My public assistance clients: amputees, the blind, the disabled; the aid I was giving out to mothers of dependent children, women without hope; most of the time these women were under 30, already carrying lards of fat that was as unattractive as the fat lady at a Barnum & Bailey Circus. Obesity was a Black woman's plight back then. Think of Covid and the percentage of Black people who are being killed. Think of whitey and his survival rate. These women I visited were without hope, on a trip to nowhere, not only for themselves but for their two, three, four, five, six, out of wedlock children, and if they were in wedlock, their males had disappeared from the home; consistently the Black women I visited didn't have a man in the house. Maybe a few did, at night, but these cats took off, not because of me, but because the truth is, a welfare life is not the kind of life where you want to park your ass. The men split as the novelist Claude Brown said, "for the mean streets." The matriarchal women stayed. Took on the burden of raising the children.

I was a civil servant knocking on broken lives, stepping on rat droppings, fighting off drug-addicted-knife-wielding crazies with my umbrella, having my ass kicked one time by three gang members who were ready to kill for the seven dollars I had in my wallet. To this day I vividly recall the conditions at 52 East 118th Street, a building that was a classic illustration of child abuse, addiction, prostitution. "Hey mister welfare worker, you have two dollars? Give you a blow job," a broken, battered, teeth-missing, emaciated women yelled out at me as I climbed the steps to visit another client who was more than half out of her mind in a stench-reeking railroad flat. I was knocking on the fragile doors of women without lives, education or any idea of how to achieve liberty or equality. Nothing but visible hopelessness for themselves, their half-starved children, from one year to the next, and I'm representing the greatest city in the world; I'm the show-me-the-money "superstar" caseworker who is supposed to turn these forgotten Americans around, when I can't even turn my own life around. And then, out of nowhere, I'm discovering what money can do. That my research, my premise, isn't a sophistry. It's REAL. Hope! Possibility! I mean I knew I didn't have guarantees.

My power ratings could have been a fraud. The Las Vegas Line absolutely correct. I didn't have a Supreme Court ruling. I didn't have squat. Even by the end of my third successful season. I had pissed away the $109,000 that I made. My evaluations, like everything else, came from my gut. My stats were as much intuition as everything else about me. Everything about me came from my stomach. I was Yogi Berra, "You can't hit and think at the same time." I had studied, examined, I did my homework as best I could but what I really believed in was not art or science or math or brain or scribbling down statistics, but in my stomach. I believed in what stirred inside of me when I watched a coach coach. I believed in what I observed: in matchups. I believed in evaluating the strengths and weaknesses of a team. The game. The way it was played. The stats might back me up but the truth is only one thing was all-consuming. My belief that I knew college basketball as well as Charlie Spoonhour, Missouri State, Red Sarachek, Yeshiva, Bobby Knight, all of these teachers, who did something very special with average talent, ordinary players, and still these men built winning programs. None of their athletes were close to McDonald's All Americans. Hell, the only legit superstar Bobby Knight ever coached was Isaiah Thomas. Coach Knight did it by being Bobby Knight. I saw him from the end arena at Madison Square Garden during the 1960s take his Army team and win. Not the game. Fuck the game. But with the sixteen points Las Vegas shorted his Army squad. Never for one minute during the entire forty minutes did his club fall behind by sixteen. Pace, precision, movement, defense, effort, that's what Knight used. Team play.

Las Vegas was always playing catch-up when it came to handicapping a Bobby Knight team. I have written about that and I will repeat it again and again. It was because of "The General" that in 1976 at the end of March or perhaps the first week in April that I was jumping on my rooftop and shouting, "FUCK YOU WORLD, I'M FREE!" My aspiration was a reality. I would never again have to punch a time clock or flash a black field book or put on a pair of boots to keep away rats. There were games to evaluate. Money to be made. Men started coming out of the woodwork in droves to meet me. I was meeting everyone. I was now being promoted by Barney Feldman, a gregarious feel-good salesman of cheap perfumes and cheaper watches. He was my twin's neighbor. Maybe I mentioned Barney Feldman earlier but for some reason I keep regurgitating. Age is one reason. I like to think there are more. One is, what's better than talking about winning a World Series game. The NBA championships. An Oscar. Meeting the woman of your dreams. Nothing! Unless it's the first important money, the first million, you can bury in the dark. Dick and I called Barney "The Major." The Major always had a huge Havana in his mouth. A dumbfounded look on his round face, but more importantly, Barney Feldman was the heavyweight champion of B.S. The Major could talk out of both sides of his mouth, and now he was telling everyone, "Robert Singer is the greatest college basketball handicapper in the country. He started with twenty-five dollars and now he's living in a penthouse on Central Park and betting nickels and dimes. Gentlemen, he's a genius." The Major was telling this to men who were bored stiff with their lives, their wives, their everyday business banalities. Before I knew it, my phone didn't stop ringing. And then I received a call from Haskell Gold. "Sonny, this is my way of doing business. I put up three dollars and you put up one dollar. We split down the middle. That gives you a SEVENTEEN PERCENT ADVANTAGE." No one ever had had an edge on a Haskell Gold proposition. And here I am, Mr. Nobody, with Haskell Gold's financing me, and giving me his bookmaking outs, a chance of a lifetime. And remember, all of my $109,000 was gone. I had paid off all my debts, bought cool furniture, moved into 1818, the penthouse. Paid Mrs. Quinn fifty thousand. So, Haskell Gold certainly came in as a limited partner at the right moment. Then Isaac Becker called. He, too, was ready to give me more than a steak dinner at his restaurant. Becker's investment gave me more leverage. I was on my way. I began to think big.

How does a single proprietorship become a chain? How do guys like Les Wexner, who started with one store, become Victoria's Secret? I realized that I had the opportunity to grow. Organization, management, expansion, vision, never stopping, always moving forward, challenging myself, never forgetting that every dollar matters. That every coin I have is going to war. Every cent is in need of perfect management. Maximizing and minimizing. And most importantly, never trust anyone. Only myself. My own right arm. My own brain. That was my implacable, all-powerful rule. Codes and secrets. Not only secrets from Haskell Gold and Isaac Becker and their cohorts, mobsters like the men you see in a Scorsese flick, only think documentary, real life gangsters, not Pacino and De Niro. I would keep everything a secret. I would use codes, have secrets from every beard, bookmaker, runner, from every woman I dated, slept with or loved. Secrets even from my parents, my twin brother.

Why should Dick have to be burdened with my life? What I was doing. The perils I was undertaking. Dick wasn't built for that kind of life. When my twin brother was at CCNY, I can still remember him making a ten-dollar bet on Whitey Ford and running to the Olympia movie theatre to see *The Ten Commandments* because he didn't have the stomach to watch the game. My twin brother might think he can run a Hollywood studio but in truth he is sensitive, gentle, too honest, too fragile, too intellectual, a pure soul with a greater mission, to write a break-through American novel. I wasn't going to give Dick any distractions or stress, especially the kind that were super-dangerous and corrupt. No one would share in my life of secrets. No one would know the extent of my handicapping business outside of me. I would do all the conceptualizing. I would use line and staff management principles. I would be the man at the top delegating one small incremental responsibility at a time to ten or a thousand people. Not one beard or bookmaker or limited partner, not even my own blood, would ever know more than 5 percent of the sum I was wagering. No one would ever know much else. One man at the top. A thousand underneath. A life of secrets. A business of silence. As "Big Matty" Moreno preached to me from the first day we met, "The only place to look for a helping hand is at the end of your own right arm." FUCK YOU WORLD, I'M FREE. For thirty-one years I lived like that. Outside of three deceptions on my part that led to contracts on my head, everything more or less went smoothly.

Haskell Gold was an underworld star from the 1930s to the '50s. He was an illegal bookie in his early years, running the numbers game and other illegal gambling bookmaking activities in Miami, perhaps the biggest horseracing bookmaker in Florida at one time and owner of several racing horses himself. He is also known for his giant steps into card counting in blackjack in the early '50s and employing the math genius, Adian Getty, to apply theory that could break the casino banks. Gold also rubbed shoulders with Isaac Becker in those days and with Meyer Lansky, the Jewish mob boss who resided at 5001 Collins Avenue, Miami Beach. Of course, when it came to the math brains needed to thwart the house advantage in blackjack, it was his guru, Adian Getty, who proved that the house advantage could be overcome by card counting.

The brainy Getty also developed and applied effective hedge fund techniques in the financial Bobets, was a closet playwright determined to have one of his efforts produced on Broadway; yet at heart, this complex man was an academic with a PhD, teaching at some of the most prestigious universities in America. It was Haskell Gold who staked Getty to a cash amount that I was told by Isaac Becker to be twenty thousand dollars to go to Las Vegas with and test out his card counting theory. It was on a Labor Day Weekend and never again did Adian Getty need or take one red cent from Haskell Gold. Gold didn't care. He owned a chain of parking lots and garages which would evolve into the media conglomerate Gold Communications run by Haskell's daughter, Missy. When Missy got into legal trouble and had to flee to Toronto, Canada, Gould's nephew, Herbert Allen Gold, who eventually became a major producer in Hollywood, took over. Today, Gold Communications is known as The Gold Media Empire.

I was introduced to Haskell Gold by Barney Feldman at the Friars Club, and worked with him when I was in my thirties. Actually, I stood side-by-side with this son-of-a-bitch at a time no one knew, including myself, what a hotshot I would become. I must have impressed or intrigued Gold and his math guru, Getty, because before I knew it, Gold and MIT professor Getty were hounding me daily. Perhaps it was because I was well-versed in theater and opera, more likely because I told them that I had been researching a certain type of proposition bet that I called "the eleven to five teaser" ... "M. Gold, I found a way of beating the odds."

Both Getty and Gold soon started knocking on my door. I had researched numbers on college teasers for the past four years. I was convinced that a super-solid-veteran-backcourt that does not turn the ball over combined with a strong home court, a defensive-minded coach such as Princeton's Pete Carril, and you have a solid shot at breaking the bank with this kind of unconventional wager. "Just eliminate everything else, Professor Getty. Those are the three major factors that will allow you to win the 11/5/teaser." After my unequivocal declaration, both Gold and Getty were at my apartment every Thursday afternoon for the better part of sixteen months. The three of us researched exotic proposition bets and everything else. Adian Getty was a quiet man, deferential and polite, but his soul was money. Professor Getty made several contributions to my business life, teaching me many things that I grasped only after all-night math sessions. Of course, Professor Getty was more than that. He never stopped writing down ideas for his black comedy plays and I continuously made suggestions. His real claim to fame though was as a hedge fund manager. Recently there was an article in one of the financial magazines where it was reported that Adian Getty made an unprecedented 20 percent return for thirty-two years on his personal net worth, that by 2001, it had climbed to three hundred million dollars. Anyway, our time together took place in the 1970s and I respected Adian Getty's modern application of probability theory, including the harnessing of very small correlations for reliable financial gain. I also respected Haskell Gold's satanic knowledge of sports gambling, "Sonny, the first thing you must get out of your mind is that the players are special. They're meat and numbers. That's all they are, meat and numbers." I was in awe of Haskell Gold's perspective. His fiendish genius at the card game, blackjack. Gold was one of the first card counters, or should I say Adian Getty was. For Gold it was one more way to make a killing. Even back then Gold's wealth was enormous. Parking lots, garages, warehouses throughout New York City, Gold Media was evolving into the Gold Media Empire.

Stepping away from business stuff, Haskell Gold was an orphan, rail thin, humpbacked, an eccentric dresser, always with a carnation in his lapel, a crease in his pants. He wore black sandals most of the time and never, and I mean never, left his Park Avenue triplex without a Smith and Wesson 1905 .38 special revolver in his ankle holster and a bodyguard, usually Walter Cooper, at his side. He looked more like a gnome in a Shakespeare play than a flesh and blood man. He had a donkey's hee-haw laugh, and when he cackled, the entire room would shake. He had a demonic streak in him that could surface at any moment. Once, at his Park Avenue triplex, I saw him pull out his revolver and shoot a housekeeper for stepping on his sandals and then demand that the Dominican woman apologize. When the woman refused, Gold shot her again. I witnessed Haskell Gold do a hundred things that I would classify as demented. Once, at my 1818 apartment, must have been during the summer of '73, he was on my rotary phone and started screaming at one of his bookmakers to give him a five-cent line on baseball or he would close him down. And Gold did. Not only close him down, with less euphemism, Haskell buried the BM. And I mean buried.

After Bobby Knight's championship run in 1976, I needed no one. "Fuck you world, I'm free," I was unshackled by debt. Carefree. I soon had beards, bookmakers and information coming in from all over the country. Soon I had the 11/5/teaser bet integrated as part of my working day. It proved invaluable. By 1980, that particular teaser was throwing off to me a guaranteed profit of approximately three hundred and fifty thousand dollars a season. I calculated that that was just about the maximum amount of dollars that I could milk it for without causing bookmakers to quit taking the wager. Everything I did was based on percentages, leverage, alleviating suspicion, keeping a low profile, something that Dr. Getty would have called "The art of gambling with serendipity." I called it stomach. My stomach. I also found ways not to cause hard feelings with BMs...I camouflaged wagers, used dozens of code names; by '82 I had seventy-five beards and seventy-nine bookmakers. I faked losing on baseball games by betting both sides, going for vigorish when the game lost. I did the same with the Super Bowl, betting as much as one hundred thousand one way and ninety-two the other. Most of the time, I ended up going for steak dinners with the guy that thought I lost to him. Like my mentor, Gold, I demanded a five-cent line so my vig losses wouldn't be catastrophic. And remember, you pay vig during the wood season only when you lose the game. I bet the Koufaxes, the Marichals, the Madduxes, the Goodens, the Guidrys, the Coles of their eras. Hardly ever had to pay the piper. Many of the bigger East Coast bookmakers, men like "Big Matty" Moreno, guys who earn 90 percent of their money on NFL football, I would give these baseball bets to, and college baskets too. To their superstar bookmaking offices, it was as if I were Eleanor tossing a nickel into a wishing well. These outfits didn't worry about me, and, of course, I continued covering myself with codes and alternating beards and outs on a weekly basis. I had learned from Gold and Getty the little things. The big things. These two men taught me how to think. "Sonny, think of it this way. It's the little things that get a team to the World Series. Every great team executes the fundamentals. What I'm teaching you are the fundamentals."

As a card counter, both Gold and Getty were ahead of their time. They were counters before Las Vegas switched to two decks, before digital transformed the Las Vegas world of security. Before face recognition. The only thing Adian Getty had to fear from Las Vegas casinos was their managers and dealers spotting his disguises. Today it would be a different ballgame ... For me, I, too, probably was ahead of my time but I didn't think like that back then. Each day I tried to push the envelope further, come up with new ways to break the bank. I tried to stay ahead of the game. Way ahead. Stomach, art, brains, good fortune, or "I'll show Victoria;" it worked. I had beards strategically placed all over the country. One beard of mine was Rob Berg. He was a graduate student at the University of Chicago. He covered territory where Loyola of Chicago, DePaul, Northwestern and so many other significant Midwestern teams are located. He was important to me. Very good at his job. Unfortunately, my first dispute with one of my beards was initiated by Rob Berg trying to screw me. And Berg did for something like thirty-two thousand. He started doing so with half a point. I was consistently finding his games' point spread at least that much more or less than other beards in the area were quoting. After a while, even a dummy like me catches on. Rob Berg is no longer on my payroll. Beef Leighton paid him a visit. That was one problem that was resolved during my thirty-one years. I want to clarify. I handled this problem without much intervention from limited partners. Beef Leighton was not a partner and he wasn't limited. He was at the end of my own right arm.

The other two beards I had stationed in the Chicago area were as true as my son, Reid, would've been. Only Rob Berg was stealing half a point here and there. Half a point is everything. It was easy to spot Berg's larceny as the beards I had at Northwestern, Loyola of Chicago, the University of Illinois consistently would give me early morning lines at one price and Rob Berg would quote me another number. My tendency was to bet shorts. I was always looking for points. I'd say more than 90 percent of the wagers I made were on games where I took points. I always looked for a live short. Always. With Berg, when he gave me a number, it would be half a point off from what was the kosher number. At first I ignored it. Even a second time I gave Berg the benefit of the doubt, but after the third time in less than a month ... "Beef, I have a problem."

Three times in thirty-one years I took affirmative action. I hate these kinds of details. What's worse is I have a strong repugnance to even spelling it out. It makes me feel as if I'm still that Robert Singer. Let's face it, a thug. No better or worse than many of us, when truth is, I'm grateful I'm retired, and that Eleanor and Reid are the sunshine of my sunset. Back to being in the dark. My life as "The Handicapper" and living a life of secrets. Back to Haskell Gold: The senior citizen remained my mentor during those years. The truth is the bastard taught me more about managing money, hiding money, valuing a dollar, picking games, never giving in to a number or price, warehousing outs, laundering green, eliminating bad melons like Berg. "Sonny, you should also eliminate fuckups like Isaac Becker. He's a sucker, Sonny. You want to hang out at his Steakhouse, fine. He's a great guy and all of that, but when it comes to gambling, Isaac's weak. Stay away from the weak, Sonny. They all end up broke and worse than that, they end up costing you dollars. The trick, Sonny, is for you to only have people like Adian Getty in your stable. That's why when it comes to my organization, I only hire MIT and Stanford nerds. What I don't know they know. What I can do for them they don't have the guts to do for themselves. Do you hear what I'm telling you, Sonny, listen and learn."

Haskell Gold would teach me something new each time he visited 1818. "The most important thing, Sonny, is for you to remain as ice cold as a Las Vegas dealer. Never panic. Never steam. Never give in to a number. The number you're looking for is the only number. Walk away from a bet when your piece of garbage bookmaker doesn't growl it out." Everyone needs a mentor. Haskell Gold remained mine to the day he passed. I listened. I learned. It took me a long while but before it was too late I did become soulless. I was 45 when I screamed out for the second time, "FUCK YOU WORLD, I'M FREE." I stood on my rooftop terrace in the freezing cold, stared up at the starless sky, yelled out, "FUCK YOU WORLD, I'M FREE!" I had gone from one million in 1976 with Knight's championship Indiana club to now, and now I had five million in cash. I was liberated from mediocrity, from ever again living paycheck to paycheck, from ever again having to get up at 6:30 a.m. to go to some crummy office job, from living a life without Peter Luger steaks, Ferraris, ménages à trois; free from a life of ennui, a life not worth living. I remember feeling so good that night I grabbed a notepad and started jotting down ideas I had for a new novel and after that, making a list of books that I wanted to read. I even started to write down the kind of woman I was looking for. At the top of my list was one word to describe my perfect woman. Kind... she had to be kind... Let me say this before I continue. Eleanor Caintrell Singer is the kindest woman I've ever known.

It wasn't only my stomach. I had power rated during each of those years and found at least a four and one-half point differential, many times more than that and each half a point gave me even a better winning percentage and the stomach to increase my wagers. Actually, during those five years, if I remember correctly, each time I found a point spread seven and one-half points or more in disparity from my power rated line (as long as my stomach agreed) those seven and one-half or more specials I called Superior Best Bets. I kept finding those games. Not that many, but enough. Of course, I always took Haskell Gold's advice. Each week I won big I took out a percentage of my prof-its and buried it under oak and maple or laundered it, or vaulted it, and counted it, and well, you get the idea. I kept pushing forward, earning all the way through, and now I had five million. As I write this, I think of Robert Singer in the year 2020, with all his scumbag billionaire friends, and their hedge funds and real estate development deals and all the other people I know who did so little and have so much. Most of them it happened for because by some luck or accident they were born into the right family with the right skin color and those people got all the privileges and benefits that that 1 percent of America is famous for, and these people, my friends – I know them as well as I know what Bobby Knight did for me, what I learned from Haskell Gold, how much I love my wife and son, and what I know is this. They aren't one cent better than the men and women on the other side of the rainbow. Those who are homeless, those who are starving, those who are undereducated, those who never got a break ... that's all it is. Ninety-nine percent of the One-Percenters got something for nothing and, believe me, until their last breath they are going to keep squeezing the purse strings of their money trees. Well, what about the kind of people who at one time I tried to give TLC? What about starting even? Starting the race on the ground floor. What about freedom and equality and open doors for everyone? Believe me, the people I know who are in the mansions and penthouses aren't listening to any of this. They're snickering. Telling me I have a screw loose, or worse. Let's keep going with my secret life as I've run out of polemics and tirades.

Five million in cash at the age of 45. Pretty good! And the next year I met Rhoda Cain. And during that year I made a financial jump too, believe it or not.

Again, I was assisted by Bobby Knight. Just a few words on the guy who I never knew who made me, more or less, the man I am. Knight took average players and molded them into a winning team. He could make his athletes play the game the way it was meant to be played. His players became a well-oiled machine, precise at every aspect of his vision. Movement without the ball! Defense! Work ethic! Taking the percentage shot! Most of the time, his club's most efficient shooter was at the spot on the floor that that particular player was most comfortable. And just about every one of his college boys was intimidated by their brow-beating bully general. They were scared shitless to do a damn thing other than sacrifice their egos and bodies for the general. And they did. One thing Bobby Knight was smart enough to know. Don't try coaching in the NBA. Don't try preaching and barking about a perfect union or equality to men. If he had, he would have been laughed off the court or had his ass kicked. But with his college boys, "Yes, sir ... Yes, sir ... Yes, sir ..." was just about all he would tolerate or hear and he got away with it. See both sides of the picture, I always say. I might have made my biggest wagers on Knight, and I did, and I won most of them, but he was as much a "Big Matty," a "Fat Tony," a Haskell Gold, an Isaac Becker, a Robert Singer as any of us, and don't let anyone tell you different.

Yes, Bobby Knight was a winner. But that isn't saying very much when you think it through. Just like all the money I made handicapping. What's it really mean? Think it through. Millions or even a billion and, well, read on and my wealth will reach the sky, but, as I said, it isn't that much when you think it through. But how many Americans think anything through?

On October 11, 1981, for the first time there was a contract on my head. This happened four times in all. On the first occasion, I was extremely fortunate. The powerful mobster who was determined to have me eliminated was indicted and had larger problems to think about. He ended up in Sing Sing Correctional Facility, a lifetime sentence, and that was that. The second contract was scary. If it weren't for Haskell Gold, I would be buried on Benny Stein's farm. I won't go into specifics but I will tell you, it cost me two hundred and eighty-eight thousand to remain alive. That second mediation taught me something I never forgot. If you have one powerful consigliere in your corner, it's enough. I had two. Isaac Becker saved my life on two other occasions.

"Repay me for stepping in. Are you crazy? It was my pleasure, Bobby boy. To think of it, you can do one thing for me. Join me at my restaurant tonight. I'm meeting a real-estate developer guy, needs a favor."

"What do you think, Bobby boy? Should I go into the deal or walk away?"

"Isaac, he and his son can't tell the truth if their lives depended on it. I wouldn't trust them for a second, especially the son."

"You're right, Bobby boy. I hear you. In most cases, I'd walk away from this situation, but they know my reputation. I'm sure they won't be screwing me."

"Isaac, you're wrong. The father isn't the guy to worry about. It's his son."

Becoming soulless wasn't what I wanted. I craved what my twin brother, Richard, achieved. No one gets everything. What I accomplished isn't that bad. Not great... but not that bad. I had gone from a deadbeat husband, forty thousand in debt, a twenty-five dollar wager, to five million buried, owning 38 percent of Walter Li's Global Health company, to giving out seven-figure bridge loans to real-estate billionaires who needed liquid help for their political payoffs. I've now partnered with several quacking ducks and it all started with "I'll show Victoria," and now I am with Eleanor on Justice Lane and the most honest thing I can tell you, these last twenty plus years I have never tired of pleasing my wife. Never!

President Obama tweeted about the deep and real racial inequalities in our country.

My identical tweeted, "we must prepare for a world where the coronavirus is our next-door neighbor. Normal does not exist any longer."

Duck tweeted, "Everything's great. And things are going to get greater."

I made a terrible mistake this morning. Rather than race to my Smith-Corona, I turned on the TV. Every channel I flipped to was reporting on Covid-19. ICUs with corpses. Healthcare workers overwhelmed. Fourth-year medical students biting their collective lips. Praying. Volunteering. Grocery store clerks struggling. Police precinct captains losing troopers. Commentators showing comprehensive charts and graphs on the number of people who have died. It frightened me in a way that I have never felt before. It wasn't a personal terror, it was more as if I were indelibly connected to our entire earth. Then I started dwelling on the individuals I have known and lost. People I have known on a day-to-day basis, people I knew on a first-name basis, people from down the block, people of all ages, all races, all religions, all creeds, and it struck me that my own wife is here on Justice Lane, in our bedroom, and Eleanor was coughing again last night and today has diarrhea. For a while I tried to deny reality, but I can't. My head begins to spin. I try telling myself, this isn't me. I've always been in control, even when I was broke I never felt poor. Even when I was in the middle of a losing streak. Hell, even when relationships with women I loved ended, I realized that the possibility to reinvent my life was inside of me.

I took a long walk in the woods. When I returned, Brian McGinn, our property manager, was doing chores. He looked upset. I asked him what was wrong. "My wife's mother is in the hospital. She's gravely ill. She's on a ventilator. No time table."

I had heard a healthcare professional on TV, "Those who are on a machine for more than ten days most of the time …" I asked Brian if there was anything I could do. He just shrugged.

This might sound inane but what I miss almost as much as picking winners is having Chinese food at Shun Lee. 493 New Yorkers died this month. Two more close friends.

In the past month, I've read five novels, one memoir, *The Color of Water*. I should have said, re-read. *The Fall! Miss Lonely Hearts! The Dwarf! Victoria! Soul on Ice!*

How many friends do I have left whom I can recommend these books to?

I haven't read *The New York Times* or *The Wall Street Journal* or the *New York Post* or the Washington and L.A. papers since March 8th. That's 57 days. I've suspended my subscriptions. Did the same with Spectrum, Con-Ed, AT&T Mobile, Verizon.

Omkar BeHarry, desk man at 1818, if you forgot, just texted. He should be here in 37 minutes. With him are my mail and his one-year-old daughter, Emily Ruby Beharry. Does she have a future? Of course she does. I remain optimistic for tomorrow's generation Who is to say that Emily Ruby BeHarry won't be one of those special people who makes a difference, who comes up with something transcendent.

It is 6 a.m. I've been writing in my head for the past four hours. Now I hobble to the typewriter. I am so "old school" that I haven't learned how to galvanize a computer. It took me thirty-seven lessons with my personal trainer before I was able to master my iPhone. I'm slow to learn in so many ways. Failed the driver's test six times. Though being a hard-core New Yorker, not being able to drive has never been a major problem.

Now it is three in the afternoon. I just finished taking a nap. That is, I tried to take one. I couldn't. My mind kept going. I kept thinking of something that happened in December 1969. That was the time that Victoria and I called it quits. So here I am, half a century later, lying in bed, dwelling on that time in my life. What pops into my head isn't Victoria's producer friend, the one who resided in the same elite building on Fifth Avenue as Isaac Becker, the one who looked like Robert Taylor. No, not him! It was Duck! Even before Bermuda, Victoria was socializing with Duck's sister. Then I think Victoria Lurie was never just a beautiful blonde with big boobs. She was pre-med at Cornell before dropping out to marry husband number one. As for Duck, at 23 he was receiving a million-dollar-a-year allowance from his racist father, and I go on recalling and proceed to think, what a liar and cheat Duck was to friends and associates of mine in the real-estate business and I am soon thinking the same and such for the remainder of the afternoon.

I hope that you realize how difficult it is for me to sustain coherence. I've lost my train of thought more than a dozen times in the past month. Last night I even began to hallucinate. Not dreams. Because making sense of your dream is a good thing. Hallucinating is a whole different ball game. This morning I think I'm lucid. At least a good deal better. I was able to take in the news without cringing. Listen to the latest Covid-19 numbers without shaking. Talk to my wife about Joanie Pryor. Joanie was a dear friend of mine. Social worker, actress, mother of three. She worked in Harlem with me in the early '60s. I also found out this week that Dr. Cohen passed. He would treat Reid and his friends to milkshakes at the Brooklyn Diner. Dr. Cohen died while performing surgery at Columbia Presbyterian. Just keeled over and died.

I spoke to Mimi Zeigler a few minutes ago. I found her on the internet. Actually, Eleanor did. My wife is good at things like that. Me: I suck. Mimi did publicity for me. Also, marketing and advertising and a little designing. I give her all the credit in the world for my last novel being exposed on Amazon, in *The New York Times*, *Playbill*, *Publishers Weekly*, *The Wall Street Journal* and wherever else my book was getting a plug. Not that any of that stuff sells books like it used to anymore, but it is nice to still be in the game. Anyway, I was speaking to Mimi earlier and she was telling me that, like my wife, she never felt attractive enough around men. Mimi is sophisticated, intelligent, self-made, independent, cultured, personable, a real New Yorker, certainly gregarious and decent. Me Too has a lot more work to do.

Why can't we be playing baseball right now? Gosh I miss the game. It's what I think of when I think of America. Not Duck! Not anything close to what's going on in New York. Have you seen the television shots of Times Square? Have you been to the City? Seen the fear of separation between people who are still walking the streets? Hell, you hardly see anyone walking the street. You never hear cars honking or see yellow taxicabs clogging up the lanes. What you see, smell, taste is what we have. The coronavirus from NYC to Gary, Indiana, to Jerusalem, and now the oil-rich Saudis have it too. What am I telling you, not much that you don't already know, but this virus is getting the best of me, just about everything I think is scrambled, like players from different years and eras. It's impossible for me to keep it together. I'm quite sure that Alex Kellner and Preacher Roe played in the 1950s, and then I think to myself, name twenty more pitchers that were southpaws from the '50s and '60s and I come up with Billy Hoeft, Billy Pierce, Joe Nuxhall, Dave Koslo, Hal Newhouser, Don Mossi, Bob Cain, Whitey Ford, Bob Kuzava, Mickey McDermott, Chuck Stobbs, Mel Parnell, and before I know it, I'm thinking, what's wrong with me? How could I leave out Warren Spahn? He won over three hundred games, and I close my eyes and I see Spahn throwing the pitch Willie Mays hit over the Polo Grounds roof. It was "Say Hay's" first round-tripper in the major leagues, and I think for a split second that I'm okay. That if I can still remember that, there are other things I can remember too, and then my mind jumps to Covid-19 and I stop thinking.

If you told me when I was 14 that there were such things as "perfect moments," I would have said the Bobby Thomp son home run that beat Brooklyn to win the pennant, or Mickey or Willie making their debuts or Phil Rizzuto, the year "The Scooter" won the MVP award or Joe D's comeback at Fenway or "Old Reliable" in the World Series when he hit the home run to beat Newcombe 1-0. My gang called Tommy Henrich "The Clutch" in those days, and that's who "Old Reliable" was. Number 15. One of the Yankee players who would always patiently stand outside of the ballpark after the game to sign autographs for us kids, connect with us when the connecting was still forever. Now at 83 plus, I have experienced another perfect moment. Eleanor and I are waking up. There is still sand in our eyes. We're lying on our king-sized bed, holding hands, talking about what our schedules are like for the day. My wife's cough has subsided, her chills are gone, we're just lying together, and I'm breathing in my imperfect perfect wife and thinking how lucky I am. For no reason, maybe every reason, Eleanor fiddles with her laptop. Finds what she's looking for, and before another second goes by, I'm listening to John Legend's "All of Me"! I'm a writer who has strung together millions of words, yet never could I have done what John Legend did. His song is telling our story. I hope.

I've been talking about ballplayers and for most of you who do not know these players it means zilch; so, let's start talking about nurses, doctors, police officers, delivery workers, transit workers, EMT workers, firefighters. The essential people who have been on the frontlines. Let's salute the people who disinfect our subways, our buses, keep us safe from our out of sight foe. Let's speak about the men and women doing the dirty work. Placing their sanity, their lives on the line. Let's talk about our politicians. Men like Mitch McConnell, who is telling all New Yorkers to take a flying fuck. Forty or more years ago I had a partner, a guy who had a reputation as "a champion amongst men." His 800 employees got together on his 70th birthday and gave him a plaque. It said, *To Everyone's Best Friend.* Right now, I have a smile as I think of Isaac Becker. He's still inside my heart and on my mind. Not in the way McConnell is. Mitch McConnell dismisses our heroes, our indispensable workers. He's made life and death into a political game. We/ Them. And NYC is *them*! Doesn't he know that we are all Americans? That New York funds his constituency? Doesn't he know that New York shells out over thirty-seven billion to the Feds every year? Doesn't he know that Duck is pulling his chain? Playing politics is killing everyone young and old and everyone in between.

When I handicapped college basketball, I went with my gut feeling. I tried to have mind and body become one. Handicapping wasn't only numbers, wasn't only an opinion or quantities and qualities and stats. It was my searching for ways to make two and two add up to five. I tried like hell to do that. It wasn't magic. It was taking into consideration all the strengths and weaknesses, all the other equalities and inequities that you can run into when athletes are competing. When I handicapped college hoops, my winning percentage was off the charts. On Best Bets I won more than 74 percent of the time. What I'm saying is, make your wager on our sanitation workers, our nurses, our doctors, on Dr. Fauci and Deborah Birx, on people who are committed to, and know, the game. They are the ones that will see us through.

You think I'm reaching. Maybe I am. Maybe you just don't know how far I've journeyed. The kind of Ducks I've had to go to or war against. When I was handicapping: Making it was everything! I wouldn't let anything stand in my way. I had an organization … beards working for me all over the country. I made deals with Godfathers, stat guys and MIT nerds; squeaky clean college students; corrupt coaches; players who couldn't read; men who were Black, Brown, Caucasian and Asian. All of them never knew my left hand or my right, not even my identical twin did. I had code names and twenty-two phones on my rooftop. I had information pouring into my wires from over two hundred

Division 1 college campuses. All of these people were employed for one singular purpose, to make sure I was fully prepared. They reported to me who chewed gum. Who had a headache. Who turned his ankle. Who was having trouble with his girlfriend or having difficulty with his mother's rent. It certainly wasn't anything like today when I'm rounding third and heading for home. Hell, I'm not even rounding third, I'm sliding into home, holding my breath, waiting for the umpire's decision. Safe or Out. So that's a cameo of who I was and of who I am. And who I am is pleading with Mitch McConnell to do something. Get it done!

Eleanor struggles every day. Each increment of challenge and stress brining on a potential mudslide, yet hour by hour, at the most within a day or two, my wife picks herself up and begins her climb again. Each day I see it. Each day I feel her effort. My wife, whose truth banner is located somewhere deep inside of her, who is in constant combat with her furies, never giving in, rising, overcoming, step by step, upward, onward, regressing, struggling, fighting back to reach an invisible precipice, Dr. King's mountaintop: Consideration! Caring! Thoughtfulness! Generosity! Kindness! "There's a mouse in the kitchen, Robert. Before Eleanor's cat, Mico, could catch it, Eleanor opened the door so it could go free. Robert, please exercise. Please eat less pasta. Please! I love you. I'm here. We still have forever and a day."

I stopped right there. Took a deep breath. Stretched. I had indulged myself long enough. Allowed my full heart to do the pounding. Now I have returned to the mind-body split. I promise myself that it will not happen again. At least not on this dark, gloomy day without one friend alive whom I've been thinking of. With only one solitary chipmunk and Mico, not twenty-five yards from my study, both keeping busy with their own destinies, which are a great deal less precarious than today's political climate, its divisiveness, or the ash and corpses brought on by Covid-19.

As far back as 1961 I was called "Broadway Bob." I knew the City as well as I knew my twin brother. I indulged in razor cut haircuts, Alexander Shields ties, Brioni suits, Denoyer and Jimmy Carrol jackets. As for women, the only ones I went after were nines and tens. My associations – "If you choose to be a criminal, remember the joke's on you," my identical cautioned. I mellowed a bit when I met Rhoda Cain. "I only have one rule, Rhoda. No drugs!"

"That's not a problem for me. I can handle that!" You talk about great decisions. Rhoda Cain and I shared five fun-hearted years until she said, "Robert, we must talk." We remained good friends until last Thursday. Covid-19.

There was one more woman in my life I haven't mentioned. Let's call her "Perfect Picture," as that was what Lenore Engel was from the first day she walked into my life. I opened the door and there she was, responding to an ad I had placed for an editorial assistant. I had already interviewed over thirty qualified candidates to assist me on the novel I was composing, but as soon as I glimpsed Lenore Engel, my choice was made. It proved to be a good decision. I was already

55, Lenore was 26, but that didn't stop my pursuit. In more ways than DNA, my identical and I are similar. I was head over heels, and Lenore Engel was perfect, as perfect as her looks. She was brilliant, talented, and admittedly a prosaic writer but with a somewhat elegiac soulfulness for words and she picked things up as quickly as my son does in a physics course. That connection didn't turn into a relationship until our second month together. It took me at least four weeks to go from an elder statesman with wise suggestions on how best to conduct Lenore's love life in villainous New York City, to being a large part of her love life in mischievous Manhattan. I used all my experience, my sophistication, if you can call it that, let's say wiles, and I sensed it was working. I also tossed in extravagant nights on the town, a gift here and there, flattery on a level that would turn even the most rational somber person – example, my own Eleanor – from a pragmatist to a romantic. I can tell you right now that Lenore was impressed. "How can I not enjoy your company? You're so good to me." But that was as far as the romance went. Oh, we bedded more than once. We shared intimacy on a quarter of a dollar level, but our attachment never reached the point where I was secure, and there were always other more appropriate suiters howling at her heels. Lenore Engel remained an employee for approximately nine months, and during those months I realized that I was falling deeper and deeper in love with her. Damn, even anti-feminist Dick liked her. "Of all the women you've known, Lenore is the best by far," he'd say. She was sort of that perfect girl that we all dream of from the time we get to the starting gate. But Lenore Engel was never mine and eventually I made my Custer's Last Stand. It was after taking her to see the Broadway musical *Phantom of the Opera*. We were having a late dinner somewhere in midtown.

I took Lenore's hand and I asked her to be my wife. "We discussed this, didn't we," she said, almost matter-of-factly. "Anything more would be less." Not being my brother, Dick, I told Lenore less than 36 hours later to finish the week's work in her own apartment, that she'd get severance pay for three months after that, but that I didn't want to hear her voice, see her face, or have anything to do with her ever again. Best decision I ever made as I learned much earlier in life from the queen bee of breaking hearts, Victoria Lurie, that if you don't love lightly you can be destroyed. I was going into the college basketball season about that time, finishing the second draft of the novel I was working on. I'm sort of proud of the strength I had in handling that heart throb. Otherwise, I would have ended up like my twin brother, pining away for a lifetime for what was never meant to be.

Today the only things that matter are: 1) to save lives. 2) to bring the economy back. Eleanor just walked into my study, "My throat is sore. I do not have a temperature but I'm having trouble breathing. I'm going to lie down for a while." Eleanor doesn't know it, but I too am having trouble breathing. When I first met Eleanor, I knew after talking on the phone to her for seven minutes. Ask me how I knew. I don't have an answer. We have been together for twenty-one years. Both of us are having trouble breathing.

Of the 36,000 NYC police officers, 18 percent are out on sick leave. Healthcare workers have paid a larger toll.

Exhaustion, collapse, despair. These people are trying to help people who are dying in droves. When I observe first responders on television, I see the kind of glass-eyed look friends of mine had when they returned from Vietnam. To the day most of them died, it never left their faces. A nurse on television said, "Masks and ventilators we are getting, but gowns are short." What about the fact that we have a workforce unable to function? Our entire population is affected. Eleanor is feeling a whole lot better. "It's not only you, Robert. All of us have been on a rollercoaster ride from hope to despair to hope and back to despair. As soon as we make a little progress we fall back. We make more progress, we fall back again. It seems never-ending." Me! I'm also feeling better. Looking out the window at pocket-sized birds perched on tree branches, and as I do, I ask myself, what the hell am I doing here? I should be doing so much more. Then an impending voice tells me my days are numbered, and at that menacing moment, I have an idea. The homeless in the City are not being cared for. They're on the street. They're suffering. Washington is not helping them. Our politicians mouth off but they're not doing much else. Banks are assisting small businesses with loans. But not the homeless. A friend just called, "I finally got a check. Now I can pay my employees. I won't have to downsize. I can keep going." What about the homeless, I ask myself. Who is helping them? I decided to go directly to my vaults. I'll also be cashing some checks. I figured that I would compile enough capital to start helping homeless people. It's like the old days, I told myself. The days I was in Harlem giving out TLC. Another life...

Did I mention the week in my life I was one of the homeless? It was when Victoria Lurie threw me out. I refused to move in with my parents. Pride, ego stubbornness. I didn't have a dollar. I moved into the Nassau Hotel. A rundown violation on East 59th Street. Sounds like a swell location but, like all of NYC, it was and it wasn't. After one week I ran out of money. Ended up on the street. I didn't have the character to make it back then. Self-pity and middle-class softness were my calling cards. I was broken over losing Victoria, feeling my life was close to over, gave in and finally telephoned my parents. That night, after taking a steaming hot bath, having a lavish kosher meal, I went into the twins' room and collapsed in bed. Thanked someone up there that my father had a good heart. My mother was my mother. It was that night that something inside of me changed. "I'll show Victoria I can make it. Be someone. Do something." I didn't know my ass from my kneecap what it would be but "I'll show her," I muttered to myself. A minute or two later I was fast asleep.

Now fifty-one years later I'm going to give out Franklins. There are 40,000 homeless people on the streets of NYC. Children and mothers, sick people and physically challenged people. I'm wearing a mask. Gloves. I have a shoulder bag filled with cash. I phoned up one of my One-Percenter cronies: "You're looney tunes," he said. Then he started lecturing me on how the banks will be making 4 percent on those small business loans they've been handing out. "That's a business," he said. "What you're doing is crazy."

On Monday, I visited New York City, stocking up on three-hole paper, perfumes, soaps, stamps, battery-driven toothbrushes, and typewriter cartridges. While I was in the City, the only people I saw on the street were homeless. I spoke to dozens and dozens of souls. One man I spoke to was in his late seventies, "I was a pretty good musician in my day. Then my hands got the stiffness, and it was all over for me. See Sarah over there," he said, pointing to a one-armed lady sitting at the curb. "She was lead singer in Beau Bernstein's band." Sarah smiled, then started singing. Her voice was palsied, cracked over and over again. Before leaving the City, I located homeless people uptown, downtown, crosstown, distributed cash. In a way, it reminded me of my father feeding pigeons. Every week after my dad retired, he took a brown paper bag with a loaf of stale white Silvercup bread to Riverside Drive and fed pigeons. When he returned home, my mom, who in those days was still feisty, would berate him, "Kalmen, you got bird doo on your shoulder." My father had been a cantor for forty-nine years before retiring. Singing liturgical melodies every Sabbath. To me, from the time I was 6 or 7, he always sounded off-pitch. To his congregation, he wasn't. They'd flock around him when the services were completed. Shake his hand. Laud him on his magnificent voice, then, like most people, would return to their homes and commence with the mischief and temperate activities of the day. My mom would attend the synagogue on those Sabbath days. She'd sit in the balcony with the other women, listening attentively, not believing every word, yet posturing, rising and genuflecting when it was appropriate, yes, a large chunk of my mother remained a non-believer like me. Two of my dad's dearest friends were nonpareil tenors who performed at the Metropolitan Opera House. Till the day my father died he regretted that he didn't.

After three weeks I started cutting my visits to NYC to every other Tuesday. I could say it dawned on me that I had been giving away too much money. That wouldn't be the truth. I do have my limits, but that wasn't the reason. Eleanor said, "You're too old for this. Come home where it's safe." Reid said, "Ba, you're decrepit. Going to the City is like making a best bet that you won't be getting any older. And, Ba, did you bring back that signed photograph you have of Muhammad Ali?"

I knew Ali during a period in my life that I was partnering with Becker. Ali was joyous, kind, giving, sincere. Everything he said, he meant. He gave up his best earning years. Certainly, his best fighting years, almost his career, for principle. For people. For a belief that was a whole lot larger than any one religion or color. One Monday night Ali and I were having dinner together at Isaac's steakhouse and I was telling Ali about my marriage with Victoria. He started to cry. Muhammad cried a great deal. Even over Joe Frazier. When it hit him how much he had insulted Joe and his family with the "gorilla" taunts, Ali silenced his mouth and started crying. He apologized to Joe Frazier before he died. I mention this because I think it's important. You know what kind of person this man from Louisville was. Something simple. Something deep. Something all of us should strive to be. Ali was a human being. Sure, he was flawed. Ask his wives. His nine children. Yet, Ali was special, as human as Marlon Brando in *On the Waterfront*. But Ali was not playing a role. He was not an actor. He lived real.

That night I called on several of my One-Percenter friends to set up a fund. Some made lame excuses. Some scoffed. The majority of them invariably said things like: "I would need to talk to my lawyers and my tax people." Walter Li chuckled, "Robert, stop kidding around. I know you better than that!"

The next morning, I walked around my acres. I walked over rocks and boulders, some gravel on the roads. There I was peering out at the woods, listening to the tweets of goldfinches, cardinals, hummingbirds, mourning doves, hiking on land that is not traversed by anyone other than family. Here I am limping along, loving my wife, my life, yet sort of forlorn as I keep thinking not of a new book to write, a new company to invest in, a wager I lost or won, but of those homeless people in New York, like the musician who lost the use of his hands, like one-armed Sarah with cracks in her voice. The next day I received an email from Walter Li that informed me that one of my investments had benefited greatly from the two plus trillion-dollar bailout the government provided. A split second later I was admonishing myself for not having done enough. For being decrepit and old.

I'm making a concerted effort to stay away from statistics. We've been here in North Salem for just about two months. It's the first week in June. Each day has been indistinguishable. If it weren't for writing this book, I probably would be going out of my mind. And now I'm worried about my son. All of his exams have been completed. What will he do now? "I'm going to make dinner tonight for you and Mom. I'm also going to do some housekeeping. This house is a mess."

People are leaving their living quarters. "First time I'm out of my apartment in six weeks, no, make that seven," Patricia Coleman told me. Over the weekend New Yorkers flocked to Central Park, Van Cortlandt Park, Prospect Park, all the public play areas the City has to offer. People all over the country are starting to move again. Will it continue, is my question. It's seventy-three degrees. Perfect weather. It's springtime. People are still dying. Six feet of separation is still necessary. The numbers are staggering. I sit in front of my Smith-Corona. I pound the keys. Gosh, I miss live theatre. Last night was a good one. Eleanor and I watched Chekhov's *Uncle Vanya*. It's still hard for me to comprehend that today, people who graduate from the very best schools America has to offer, people who not only graduate but graduate with honors; people more educated than I ever was, that their only concerns are digital. They are digital. Chekhov and Ibsen and Shaw and O'Neill and Williams and Miller and Moliere and his majesty, Shakespeare, and so many other immortal playwrights these digital people are missing out on. Eleanor loved *Vanya*. I knew she would. Chekhov is always a joy. The first time I saw *Uncle Vanya* I was on a double date. My friend, Walter Li, was with a 19-year-old, Patricia Coleman. I was with Victoria Lurie. Patty lived in Woodmere, Long Island, back then. Now she's a New Yorker. She has brought up four daughters. Lived with an abusive husband for ten years. When she finally found the strength to rid herself of him, she began to forge her own career. She used her will. Her resolve, "My motivation was simply to survive." I spoke to Patricia earlier in the day. She couldn't recall seeing the Chekhov play.

"How could you forget *Vanya*?!" I exclaimed.

"I'm cooking, Robert. Who gives a darn about your silly play? I do remember your friend, Walter. He was sort of materialistic." My way of living is gone. I'm sounding like Uncle Vanya.

Reid received his final test score for the year. He received a 92 on his physics exam. That grade, with all his others this semester, add up to a 4.0. Sounds great. My ass! You know what my son told me last night… "Your writing means less than nothing. Who's going to read you? People today are much more concerned with what mommy has to say."

After three arduous years of incredible effort Eleanor is finishing *The Calcium Connection*, her book on discoveries that she's made concerning heart disease, diabetes, Alzheimer's, Parkinson's and a flock of other illnesses. It's impressive. I mean sufficiently impressive that a renowned scientist is writing the preface. This PhD has embraced my wife's book with such enthusiasm that he's presenting her to several colleagues, distinguished All-Stars in his scientific community. Besides that, both of them are talking about joining forces to further fund his medical research company. The company is located in St. Paul, Minnesota, and will be announcing some exciting breakthroughs it's made to defeat Parkinson's Disease before the end of the year. Eleanor's excited. It's Monday night. Covid-19 is still with us. Major League Baseball isn't. My focus is once again blurring. I've returned to my typewriter to get away from today's coronavirus statistics and from thinking about what else is missing. Today, 299 more New Yorkers have died.

Now Reid has that 4.0. He's so much more. It's beginning to feel as if I have my son back. This time he's not a boy, he's a young man. It's actually the first time I'm getting the chance to know Reid since he was fourteen. That's when he went off to boarding school. "Ba, I want to get out of the

City." The same could be said for Eleanor – "We must buy a house that is halfway between Choate, Rosemary Hall and our apartment in the City." Little did I know that Eleanor would fall in love with the house that we acquired. I'm a City guy. Love everything about New York. Always did. Always will. Eleanor never loved New York. She promised me. "I want to live your kind of life, Robert. It's exciting. It's adventurous. It's what I want."

Oh, you're getting confused. Eleanor did reside in that walk-up on the Upper West Side, but when she became pregnant, she moved to Dallas. She stayed with her sister, Veronica. I'd visit regularly. Call every night. Eleanor never fully forgave me for letting her leave. To this day, when her back is arched, I hear how I broke her heart. How things have changed. since that moment.

I'm also getting to know Ely again. She's been living on our North Salem property for the past five years. I mostly stay in the City during the week and come up to Justice Lane on the weekend. Since the virus, it's been different. I'm getting to know my family again. I'm learning that my wife is stronger than she's ever been. A whole person. Living life, her life, assertively, confidently, and well, Eleanor has certainly come a long way. As for Reid, the truth is he has become a man. His posture is straight. His concerns, "Ba, if one day I decide I want to take advantage of our resources, I'm warning you, it will not have much to do with making money. It will have everything to do with elevating people who are disadvantaged."

For the first time, I believe my son, my wife, no longer need me. If I go tonight, it's okay.

"I know it sounds naïve, but when your dad goes to the bathroom, if he stays there for more than five minutes, I start to miss him," Eleanor tells Reid.

Patricia Coleman's daughter just phoned. Patty is on a ventilator at Lenox Hill Hospital.

I'm almost sure that I mentioned that Walter Li and I have more than a few things in common, one being an avid interest in theoretical economics. We both minored in macroeconomics analysis while attending NYU and had some of the top men in the field as professors. One was Baron Tessler, another Levi Goodwine. Another economist who comes to mind is the aforementioned "Mr. Bowtie," Julius Bachman. Bachman was a charming man with extensive humor that bordered on Jack Benny. He was also somewhat unkind – as when he posted final grades, he didn't take into consideration a U-shaped curve. Only one of the forty-three students in our class received the "immortal A." It was Walter Li. Walter and I have our chats now and then. We usually agree on most things outside of politics. I'm a dunce, as I readily admit, when it comes to the ins and outs while Walter Li is what I would label a modified categorical imperative. Whichever party provides a better platform towards his tax situation is what he's for. Right now, he's spending a small fortune contributing to the party of Lincoln and Duck. I told Walter that the Republican Party is falling apart, "Too many of them are scared shitless of losing their seats. Too many of them only know how to play follow-the-leader, and just about all of them relate to Duck as if they were schoolboys and he was Bobby Knight."

After that effortless harangue, it only got worse. Walter started mouthing off on how delighted he was that his son, Gary, had taken over one of his companies, and how well the company was doing. How Gary had increased sales and efficiency and the result is an additional profit of seven million this fiscal year. The conversation started to make me nauseous and, after a while, I interrupted, "Walter, you do realize that if you had ten children, three of them would be capable and successfully running one of your companies, but not one in a thousand could start a company from scratch. Not Gary or any other 'Gary' would be able to go from poverty to powerful." Walter snidely retorted, "Not everyone can take a 250 dollar bankroll and turn it into a million a year for thirty-one years. I don't deny that, Robert. But running one of my enterprises is no small achievement."

I had had enough. "Being custom-fit at Exeter, getting an MBA from Harvard and having you as a father doesn't hurt either," I said. Walter Li hasn't called me this week. And just to get the record straight, in one of those thirty-one years of handicapping, I broke even.

I don't want to offer an apology, but I do brag too much of the time about things that are unimportant. I do things for show. I have lived my life "my way" without regret. When I was a professional handicapper I was obscenely calculating. "Making it" was gnawing away at me as if I were starving. In a vulgar American way I was successful. I mention this not to toot my own horn but because I think it fair that you get to know all of me. When I tell you that I'm the luckiest guy on the planet to have met Eleanor, I mean it. Just as easily I could have ended up like those clowns in Scorsese's movie, *Casino*, six feet under. This story is not only about how I am living my life, it's also about how I lived it. I could go on and on about climbing Mount Gamble! Disappointing women! How dehumanizing fame is! Venal corruptions! Nefarious Godfathers! Disillusioned friends! All the people that at one time or another I partied with, stepped on, hurt. I could acknowledge my strengths, have my identical spell out my weaknesses, but when Richard talks of me, he becomes like Saramago's allegorical blind people, he only sees darkness. I could resurrect my worldly friend, Isaac Becker, have him speak about me, but his limitations were profound – "Don't worry about that guy, Bobby boy. How much does he owe you...I'll talk to him...Bobby boy, did you hear about what happened to that beard that was causing you grief?"

I learned from CEOs as pathological as Duck. I've learned from men who own giant companies, funeral parlors, parking lots, whorehouses. I learned from "Big Matty" and "Fat Tony" and Victoria Lurie and, mostly, I learned from Isaac Becker, just about everything I know.

It is too simple to call Duck an asshole. Everyone is doing it. The media, friends, neighbors, people I've never met. I've tried to stay away from it. I've made an effort. Every minute we spent together I wanted to scream, "Duck, you asshole!"

When Duck telephoned me this morning and said he, like his father, always tried to turn away Blacks from his buildings...

"What did you call me?"

"You're a fuckin' racist."

"Look, Singer, I got nothing against Blacks. It's just that there's something inside of me that knows we'd all be a whole lot safer with less of them around."

I was fresh out of college. Just beginning to shave. Still living with my parents. My world was my mother's home-cooking, my friends who were young, optimistic, talking about the girls they were meeting, the jobs they were beginning. Good days. My social investigator job gave me all the money I needed. Enough to go to NYU and Knick games. Before entering the old Garden, I would buy two hotdogs at a Nedick's tucked into the Garden's corner. It was there I first met Rodney Parker.

"Shine. Best shine in the City."

Rodney and I hit it off.

"The Knicks don't suck, dude, but they won't be much until they get themselves a center that ain't six feet five. Shoulda drafted that dude out of San Francisco or if they were real smart, they'd go after Wilt."

Rodney Parker didn't stop talking. I had been 18th man on my Commerce High School team. Coach Herman Wolfe gave out 17 jerseys, the team manager job to the 18th man. I got to scrimmage with the players. Go all over the City. Watch some of the best basketball I'd ever seen.

"The great players come out of Brooklyn. That point guard out of Jefferson."

"You mean Nurlin Tarrant. You're right about him, Rodney. He could play with Bob Cousy right now."

"Sheet, he's not the only one. What about that white dude from Erasmus, Johnny Lee, and those two 14-year-old dudes in junior high. One of them has the prettiest jump shot in the whole damn country. And the other one's a monster."

"You mean Tony Jackson and Connie Hawkins."

I had found someone who loved basketball as much as I did.

"I have an extra ticket for the NYU game. Why don't you take it and meet me inside? It's a great matchup. Cal Ramsey against West Virginia's Jerry West."

Rodney didn't show. A week went by. I spotted him in front of the Garden scalping tickets.

"What happened, Rodney? Why didn't you meet me?"

"You gave me a new profession, Dude. From now on I'm a ticket engineer."

Rodney Parker went from shining shoes to helping more boys in trouble get out of nowhere than anyone I knew. What did Rodney have to overcome?!... Rodney Parker began his life in a Bed-Stuy project overrun by gang killings, the death of his father to heart disease when he was 6. "I had to steal Borden's milk bottles for my siblings before I was 7. At 12 we didn't even have pencils. The ones we had I broke in half, shaved them with a razor blade and made sure my sisters and brother took them to school." Rodney not only climbed the American success ladder, he was victorious not because of the money he earned, that's the least of it, he helped people, especially teenage boys who had little or no chance. Rodney Parker made it his calling to make sure that these boys didn't take drugs, become gang members. He made sure they earned high-school equivalency diplomas, got into junior colleges, and Division 1 programs if they had a gift for basketball. At least two dozen of Rodney's boys played Division 1 basketball and at least eight of those boys played in the NBA. That is why I think Rodney Parker was special. Now that he's gone, I miss him as much as I miss Calvin Ramsey. The Hawk and I were friends since the two of us were 15 and shooting hoops together at Commerce High School. In those days, Calvin was already chiseled, but he'd brick layups, play the game as politely as if he were playing for a prep school. It took his entire sophomore season for him to toughen up. Once he did, it was obvious that he'd be going somewhere, and he did, not only as a basketball player, as a man. Cal Ramsey was one of my closest friends for sixty-six years.

Cal Ramsey always said I was the kind of guy that would wear a three-piece-suit at the beach. Truth is, Duck made me feel grimy. As if I just came home from one of those scorching days on the shore. First thing you want to do is take a shower. Wash the sand off. I did call Walter Li. I knew he'd be interested in what Duck had to say. Walter Li is as hungry today as he was at 17. He's always looking to get bigger.

"I'll listen to Trump's proposition. You're not mad at me are you, Robert."

"You're a big boy, Walter. Do whatever you feel is right. I'll tell you this, Walter. Duck is panicking. He'll pull all stops to get re-elected. You can probably make a deal with him that will open new Bobets for Global Health. Just make sure that if he fails to win the election, you've covered yourself on five sides."

When I finished speaking to Walter Li, I needed to get some fresh air. I've learned the hard way that it isn't

pineapple juice or apple or cranberry or Tanqueray London
Dry Gin that gets me through a rough day. It's doing some-
thing positive. I reached out and called an old friend, the
former Knick, Freddie Crawford. He's a co-founder of the
Rucker Pro Tournament. It's an adjunct to the Rucker Pro-
Tournament International born in the summer of 1965.
Eleanor was born in 1965, but that isn't what's noteworthy.
Nineteen-sixty-five was the year of the march on Selma.
The assassination of Malcolm X. The passing of Holcombe
Rucker. Rucker was a playground director in Harlem for
the New York Parks and Recreation Department. He was
someone Cal Ramsey thought highly of and I think I came
up with an idea that can honor my friend. Cal loved playing at the Ruck. He played against the greatest players of
his time: Joe Hammond, Dr. J. Connie Hawkins, Roger
Brown, Wilt, Jackie Jackson who could jump so high he'd
snatch a coin off the top of the backboard, Clint Roberts
and Cleo Hill (they were as good a backcourt tandem as
Wanzer and Davies). Every player from Brooklyn to Philly
played at Rucker. Cal Ramsey is the only player to be voted
MVP in their college division and their pro division.

"Freddie, my brainstorm is to have a game that we call
The Calvin Ramsey game. It will honor Cal and help kids
in the Harlem community."

CALVIN RAMSEY

A lifetime friend. We'd been close since we were having lunch together in our high school's cafeteria. What I remember about "The Hawk" is just about everything. At 12, Cal came to New York with his mom, Ruth, from the segregated South, Selma, Alabama. They did so to escape Jim Crow. Brought with them just about nothing in worldly goods, everything in resolve and intelligence, and Ruth Ramsey's work ethic. Mrs. Ramsey never stopped working or caring or teaching her son accountability. "Most people have problems, Calvin. Just remember everyone needs a helping hand." Mrs. Ramsey's efforts were not in vain. Cal Ramsey was the exact opposite of Duck. Give me an antonym for a person who was never witless, inane, odious. Never with a message of division. Never an asshole! That person was Cal Ramsey. He was All-City at Commerce, broke nineteen school varsity records while playing basketball at NYU; represented the Knickerbockers with super class as a player, color analyst, community leader. His commitment to people was one he made for his entire lifetime. The Knickerbocker Organization honored Cal a few years back. The entire Madison Square Garden stood as one. Cheered and clapped as his picture flashed on the giant screen. It wasn't nearly enough.

Cal Ramsey was a person of impeccable dignity. He lived his life like he rebounded the basketball. "Mr. 19.6" we called him when he set an NCAA rebounding record while playing for NYU. 19.6 outdid Wilt Chamberlain and all the other stellar backboard gladiators of the day. I can recall the birthday parties we celebrated, the marches on Washington we took, his Knick debut, the dinners at my parents' home, but what I remember best of all is our conversations in the end arena at the old Madison Square when we were 15, 16 and 17. We would meet in front of the Garden, use our GO cards, pay something like seventy-five cents for seats. We'd sit together, watch the great college players of the time. All-Americans like Tom Gola, Lasalle; Sihugo Green and Dick Ricketts, Duquesne; Ed Fleming, Charlie Hoxie and the toughest point guard of his time, Larry Costello, play for Niagra. We'd both go a little crazy when Guy Rodgers came into the arena for the Temple Owls, and completely berserk when Maurice Stokes took the court for St. Francis of Loretto; yet what I remember best is our conversations during halftime: "Rob, I realize your dream is to write an esteemed novel. I also have a dream. Mine is to play for the Knicks. I know that sounds as crazy as your writing an important novel, but I have another dream that I know I can make happen."

"What's that, Cal?"

"It's to do the kind of work Dolly King and Holcombe Rucker do in Harlem. They work with kids in the community. Make sure the kids get a shot at the American dream. You know what my mom is always preaching, 'Colored or white, we're all the same.' I just want to help kids in my neighborhood get their chance." Then Calvin's brow would wrinkle, and he'd frown as if he knew how difficult his goal for equality would be.

The Hawk lived his life as he went for the basketball. Full throttle. He risked his body and sacrificed his knees. It finally caught up with him. Cal's knees ended up destroyed. His body poisoned when a knee operation went awry, and a staph infection almost took his leg. For years I watched my friend become more and more crippled. First using a cane, then a wheelchair, and during his last year, confined to a bleak room at The Riverside Premier Rehabilitation and Healing Center on the Upper West Side where several of his closest friends visited him till the very end. There was Earl Monroe, Dr. Dick Barnett, John Starks, Tom Hoover, Carl Green, Ernie "Nes" Morris, Michael Linton, Dick and I, a few others. Each of us stayed an hour or two, trying to cheer Cal up by talking basketball, bringing up his glory days, such as when he scored thirty against Jerry West in college, other special games in which he dominated, one in particular against a number one ranked North Carolina Tar Heel team featuring All-American Lennie Rosenbluth, and the game he got twenty against the Big O... "I held Oscar to forty-seven that night," Cal would say with a grin. That was Cal Ramsey, a humble, gentle, unperturbed, soft-spoken man with a ferocious commitment to teaching kids right from wrong. Near the very end, whenever Cal awakened from a deep sleep, I would speak about our days in high school, and his mother, Ruth, who was also a great friend of mine, "You should marry the girl that you like as a best friend, Robert. The other kind don't last." I didn't take Mrs. Ramsey's advice. During those last days Cal would open his eyes every now and then, ask for a glass of water. I'd fill up a paper cup with ice and a straw. Calvin was so weak by then that I'd have to hold the cup for him to take a sip and invariably as soon as he did, he'd begin to sink back into a coma. I loved Calvin Ramsey, and I can take an oath from the time we met in September 1952 to the day he died, March 25, 2019, he didn't stray from his commitment to people, no matter what color.

Dick and I sat on a hard bench in front of the guest house. I was saying how the past three months have been great for me. "I've never had this kind of quiet time in my entire life. I think I'm doing better work now than ever. I have no distractions. Am completely focused. It's without sports, theatre, friends, restaurants, accoutrements, a million and one other things to distract. This place has provided a haven. As a writer, I couldn't possibly ask for more. I feel guilty for admitting this. Should I?"

My twin didn't listen to one word I said. His response was, "This Covid virus is the spiritual death as well as the earthly death of America. Trump personifies our country's death. He's Covid incarnate."

For the past seven days and six nights Eleanor has disappeared. My kid is minimalistic. He always is, now he's not saying one word to me. Forget about hugs and kisses, he has stayed in his basement accommodations. I haven't seen him in three days. For a while we had all been eating together as a family. That was new for us as we've always been on different schedules or in different parts of the country. Now it's as if we're in different worlds. Eleanor goes into her study, works on her calcium ATPase book, makes contact with her entourage: discusses marketing, advertising, publicity, media appearances, design, branding, whatever else she is consulting a multitude of professionals on. Not me! I'm left out as I am with just about everything else in my wife's life. When Eleanor makes personal calls, she makes sure her door is closed. She has been avoiding me for days. Dinner has gone from a feast to throwing leftovers and a can of corn or peas on the kitchen table. Breakfast is a box of Raisin Bran. I'm feeling as if our life together is over. I've felt that way for the entire week. Now it's well past midnight and I'm feeling more sorry for myself than I have since my first wife screamed, "Get out, you loser, you gambler, you!" and, then, out of nowhere, Eleanor slips into our bed, lies down next to me, takes my hand, "I love you, Robert. I'm sorry. I just have been feeling so bad lately. It's not you. I've been feeling like I did when we first met."

When I first met Eleanor, she had crying jags that lasted days at a time. Silences that lasted weeks. I held her, stroked her, tried to love her the best I knew how. I had never felt that way before. The one thing that has remained completely true for all our years is that I've always wanted to protect Eleanor. Help her in whatever way I could. Now we're back on track. Helping, protecting and holding Eleanor's hand is what's most important to me, and my wife climbing into bed and whispering I love you, Robert, is everything.

It was 5:18 in the morning. I couldn't sleep. I had so much in me. It had to come out. I was flooded with appreciation, gratitude, the good fortune that I had in finding Eleanor. My wife is on top of everything. She continues to watch over me like a hawk. Now it's "Please, Rob, don't go to the City. It's too dangerous." As much as she loves me, she worries about me even more. I feel like waking Ely up. I need to talk about my twin brother. He's been driving me mad. Twins are opposite sides of the same coin. Chicken and egg, that's who we are. It's certainly more than okay with me that my identical receives the kind of recognition he has. Short-listed for two Pulitzer nominations… He deserves it. He's paid his dues. His entire adult existence I've been screaming at him, "You're living half-a-life. You're an idiot. There's more to life than Kafka, Beckett and writing a novel. More to life than underlining books, scribbling footnotes in the margins." Even yesterday when Eleanor and I went to the guest house to bring Dick his laundry, before either one of us could open our mouth, he was pontificating on Kafka, "Destabilized world, that's what Kafka was talking about."

"Everyone knows what Kafka's contribution was. You've said the same thing for sixty years!" I shouted.

"Eleanor hasn't heard it said the way I'm saying it now. She's interested."

Sometimes I get so mad it sounds as if I don't love my twin. It's because I do that I sometimes go crazy. As soon as he takes off on one of his literary rants I get triggered off. What it does is remind me of all that he's missed out on. He thinks I don't get what he's accomplished. His novels, his ideas, his avant-garde contributions to the canon. I get it. He's created a new form to convey today's motifs. To him, George Eliot and Flaubert are obsolete. Dostoyevsky should be edited down to two hundred pages. Tolstoy should be cut by two-thirds. Those giant novels of yesteryear – just words, words and more words, he will tell you. Zola and Jane Austen, even Proust and all the others. "Those writers are boring... boring... boring..." As soon as I hear Dick start to take off on one of his diatribes, I see red. It's not that what he says is wrong. On the contrary, I think he's correct. I mean, I saw those NBA players in the '50s. Don't tell me you can't see the difference between George Mikan and Giannis Antetokounmpo. It's the price my brother has paid for being who he is. It's a terrible price. He's a man without. He's denied himself real love, real relationships, to taste anything close to meat and potatoes. When I tell him the best time in my life was the twenty-five minutes I spent taking my son to school, Dick doesn't have a clue on what I'm talking about.

Each morning, from the time Reid was four till the time he left for boarding school, "Ba, I don't want to go to school in the City. Please, Ba..." It killed me when Reid left home at 14. Now, with hindsight, it turned out okay. My son is much more mature and independent than most of his peers, especially when he's not around his mother or me. Reid's doing just fine. Better than that. His head is on straight. Getting back to my twin. He isn't. He still thinks I'm a loser for wanting a wife, family, children. "It's pathetic the way you've always needed someone in your life," he roars. "You're living half a life," I shriek back. "I'm all for Dick writing the great American novel. Committing himself to a life of the mind. God knows it's a whole lot more than making money. But just think of what he had to give up."

I'm pounding all of this out not because I don't love my twin, but because I do. Because it's too damn late for him to change. It makes me sad. It makes me crazy. I can't help myself from yelling at him as soon as I see him.

It is now 8:30 in the morning. I'm opening the fridge. Taking my first break from writing after three hours straight. I'm pouring some cereal. Dropping in prunes and an apple sliced into small chunks. The milk comes last. As I'm doing this, Eleanor walks into the kitchen wearing one of her real jazzy silk pajamas. A few minutes later Reid walks in. I gaze at them. Eleanor begins to make coffee. She's still half asleep. Reid isn't. He has to start studying for some summer class quizzes. "I need a hug," I say. "I do too, Ba," Reid says, trotting over. Eleanor smiles and brings steaming hot coffee to the kitchen table. She gives me a kiss. Dick has his glowing reviews. His awards. His breakthrough novels. Two sides of the same coin. Why can't any of us put it all together? I ask myself that question all the time.

It's May 10, 2002, Mother's Day. Early in the morning, Brian McGinn (what would we do without him) brought over Sunday brunch: lox, bagels, cream cheese, tomatoes, onions. It's for Dick and me. Reid sleeps till one. I prepared a Mother's Day card. Affable Brian brought over a planter of flowers for my wife, which I forgot to ask him to do. Brian manages six other properties besides ours. This week ours took priority. He had his crew work on the air-conditioning unit in the garage and on Dick's ant problem in the guest house. Reid had his demands too, "Mr. McGinn, can you put on my wall the autographed uniform my dad got me of Michael Jordan? And can you get me a few more KN95 masks? I'm going into the City this week."

There's always something to do around here and it's always Brian McGinn or my wife who has the brunt of the burden. "Eleanor, I have the laundry you asked me for," Dick said when he came over, handing Eleanor a pillowcase with a month's worth of dirty underwear. Another bag with filthy clothes.

"I need one day to myself. You will all have to fend for yourselves." Eleanor's voice was shaking when she said this. I know my wife. She's ready to collapse. Stress, pressure, responsibilities 24/7. Eleanor's fragile. She's been working overtime since we arrived. Actually, she's been doing more in the past three months than in all the years that we've been together. You might think it no big deal, that all moms do it. But Eleanor is Eleanor is Eleanor. For her to make sure I take my meds every day, bring into my study the oximeter, measure my oxygen level – "Your saturation rate should be between 92 and 98, Robert, it's 89." My wife takes my blood pressure – "It's over 170!" she screeched earlier this morning and freaked. "You must take your blood pressure pills." The problem is Eleanor is always right. I hadn't.

Eleanor is unnerved. She's tired. She's exhausted. She's not built for this. It's true Eleanor finished Yale at the top of her class. Her friends would tell me, "When we were at school it was Eleanor who got us through."

"Eleanor, since you were in first grade have you ever got less than an A?"

"I don't think so."

My wife is who she is. Fragile and brilliant. Brittle and strong. Disconnected and connected. Dysfunctional and productive. Benevolent and meager. Self-sacrificing and deficient. The woman I love, 24/7. Even my self-absorbed twin is beginning to admire her. "Eleanor's definitely taking more pride in her appearance. Lately she looks great." For Dick to say something like that means something. At

brunch today he said, "I can see why my brother loves you."
Yes! My identical is definitely beginning to appreciate how
lucky I am!

Dick and I were already eating when Reid walked into the
kitchen. "I'll be right back guys. I want to finish writing the
Mother's Day card I prepared for Mom."

When Reid returned, we put our heads together and
finalized our plans to give Eleanor one day off a week.
"Let's give Mom today off too. I'll do the dishes. You
only rinse. They need to be cleaned. And for one day,
please, Ba, remember to take your meds without mommy
having to remind you. I'll also help you with your band
exercises."

Giving Eleanor one day off a week (I know I said it
before – this time I mean it) allows her to be free from both
of us, to read Dürrenmatt, call her friends, all of them the
kind of women I'd never have known if not for Eleanor.
I was moronic Broadway Bob sleeping with models, pole
dancers, wannabe actresses, living a cool New York life,
and then I reached an age when my body started to let me
down. Blood pressure out of whack, energy depleted. I felt
burnt out. Ready for the junkyard. And out of nowhere my
life turned around.

That night, when I crawled into bed with Eleanor, the
first thing she said was, "You shouldn't have written that
Mother's Day letter. I loved it but now you've put too much
pressure on me to live up to it."

The real problem is not that Eleanor said this; it's that
she meant it.

Today I was ambitious. I decided to go down to the pool, which is located on our lower tier. To get there you have to step down over twenty-two ledge boulders, each one descending an impressive depth. What makes it somewhat easier for me to do so is that I had Brian McGinn build a redwood railing on one side of the path leading down to the pool so that I could hold on for dear life as I take the trek. Finally, I get to our pool. Believe me, it's only a big deal to the decrepit me. Reid, Eleanor, even Dick, just about anyone in relatively good shape would never mention it. To me, everything is beginning to be a big deal. I lay myself down on a chaise lounge chair, grab a book to read, lather myself with Coppertone. I'm ready to enjoy this perfect day and then, out of nowhere, a wasp comes along … settles on my left shoulder. I bolt. The wasp stings me on the fleshy part of my left arm. I curse it out. I soon accept the throbbing pain and continue with my reading. Then, two more wasps show up. One I eliminate with a beach towel. The other one gets me pretty good. That's the end of it, for sure, I think. It wasn't! Before I know it, twenty wasps are coming at me as if they were dive bombers. I'm pretty bitten up right now. Vicious bites on my left hand, right leg, my arms, chest, even one nasty welt on my neck. Eleanor had to give me three Benadryls and use some anti-bite cream. First time in years anyone, including Eleanor, made a fuss over me.

All the junk I left in NYC doesn't mean squat to what I've found here. I've learned a lesson these past months from the woods to the dirt on the road, the smell of fresh cut grass, observing eagles, hawks, deer, even a brown bear and so much more of what I've never experienced before. Quiet time, a life without frenzy, gut-wrenching wins and losses, emails, texts, phone calls, scarcely any at all. I have time to focus and write, read a book, reconnect with family. Walter Li said, "You don't know how lucky you are. You can write your books on toilet paper. Do you know what it cost me to run my companies?" What did I need to go through all of it for? A simple life, a mind that works, family. I wish I was smart enough to have known that sixty years ago.

My iPhone rings, "Singer, it's me. Do you know someone named Milo Powers? The police found him parked in front of the FedEx store on your corner. He was amongst a dozen homeless people they were clearing out. In his wallet was your name, address, and my private phone number. The one I gave to you. Don't know what any of this means, but your name's linked to mine. My security guys thought it was suspicious. Do you know this Milo Powers? No matter. He died on his way to the precinct. Are you coming into the City this week? Could use some of your pineapple juice… Don't worry about that Powers guy. Just one more crazy bastard. He doesn't matter."

I have to get away from this pandemic. Every time I put on the TV the statistics get to me. All I hear are how many died. I promised myself I would not think about Covid-19.

At that moment, Reid walks into the room.

"The next two weeks are going to be brutal, Ba. Not only in NYC, all over the country."

Eleanor enters the room. "In 2015, Bill Gates warned us after Ebola that the next pandemic was around the corner. All of us need to plan forward. Most of us won't."

Eleanor listens for a few moments to what I have to say about Duck. "It's not only the president who messed up. It's the entire Republican Party. But he's an easy target. We need someone to blame. Sour grapes is part of our DNA."

Reid jumps in, "Trump might be putting more value on reopening the economy than saving lives. I don't agree with him, but either way, we're screwed!"

Eleanor sighs, "I would be so much happier to get back to your father criticizing your Uncle Dick for living half-a-life."

Here is something that doesn't sound like lines from an Off-Off-Broadway play.

Reid has volunteered to assist a food pantry in Bridgeport one day a week. He will be distributing food parcels; doing whatever he's assigned to do. He'll be wearing protective equipment and when he returns home, Eleanor will check his temperature.

I must remember to wake Reid at six in the morning for his drive to Bridgeport. I must also remember to remind Eleanor that she has two important phone calls to make. One at two in the afternoon. Another at five. The first concerns her book, *The Calcium Connection*. Eleanor has received a forward for the book from the top person in the field. Eleanor's also agreed to talk about calcium ATPase at several prestigious medical schools in the fall. Eleanor can do just about anything she sets her mind to do. There's a reason I call her "Kafka."

The second phone call I have to remind Eleanor to make is to Dr. Michael Schapiro, her therapist when we first met. My wife was in love with Dr. Schapiro. You must have heard the theory of transference in the shrink/patient relationship. Believe me, it was more than that. It was as much my doing as it was Dr. Schapiro's. I'm the one who screwed up. When Eleanor was pregnant, I told her, "Go to Texas. It's the best thing for you to do, Eleanor. Your sister can take better care of you than I ever could. What do I know about pregnancies and raising newborns? I'll provide you money for a full-time nanny. I'll send Veronica whatever she needs for expenses. I'll fly down to be with you as much as I can. I'll call you every night. But when a person's lack of esteem is as deep-rooted as values … when a person's sense of self is tenuous … when a bridge has a fracture in its middle – so, as soon as my wife stopped believing that my love for her wasn't unconditional, well, borderline cases like Eleanor's, they don't come back all the way. Eleanor returned to New York, she started holding back. I can whine and tell you Dr. Schapiro caused some of this, which is probably true, yet all I will say right now is that during their sessions, Dr. Michael Schapiro would break all the traditional rules. He would cradle Eleanor in his lap, rock her, sing her lullabies. Enough said.

That evening, while reading my manuscript, Reid recited one of the pages where I wrote, "When I didn't win a game, I felt was a sure winner, I felt it wasn't me. I had checked off all the boxes. Went over every detail. Followed every one of my checklist rules. It was only hours after I received the results of the game that I was first able to calm down. Remind myself that with all my preparedness, all my management skills, all of my cunning, research, and strategy, with all the hours, days, weeks of homework, once the game hits the floor it's in the hands of the Gods.

"Reid, I am fully aware of what I accomplished. College basketball gave me a whole lot more than seed money for the life I have, but, still, a part of me also realizes that handicapping was as much an art form that I mastered as a science that I practiced. I'm grateful that I beat the odds, but there isn't one day that goes by that I don't tell your mother that if you wanted to follow in my footsteps, I'd break your head."

ISAAC BECKER

I wanted to write about the man I consider the most important influence in my life. Isaac Becker. He would be 105 years old today. He died in 1989. Yet Isaac remains as alive to me today as when he opined half-ass opinions all those years back. I was 24 when I first met him. He was a jewelry manufacturer, a theatre producer, a man-about-town. He was above board and below. A sportsman, a philanthropist, a statesman, a gangster. A New York character in the truest, street-smart sense of the term. He grew up in the Bronx. He started with nothing. "Bobby boy," he would tell me in his guttural rasp, "I didn't know I had nothing because no one had nothing in my neighborhood." He stayed in high school because he could play basketball. He was a point guard for his high school team and one year his team won the city PSAL championship. "Best year of my life, Bobby boy. My proudest achievement," he must have told me once if not a thousand times. And this was coming from a man who went from working on a jewelry bench for six dollars a week to advising presidents. His forty million disappeared, but not the man. To me, even when he went belly up, he was still "A Champion Amongst Men."

I loved him till the day he died. "Take it easy," "What's doin'?" "I'll rip his ears off," I can still hear him holler.

Everyone who knew him would tell you, "Isaac Becker was everybody's best friend."

People would line up in his office for a handout. People would call him a dozen times a day. "Isaac, I got a problem!" "... I can solve just about all of them problems, Bobby boy. At least all of them that aren't terminal." I loved that man. Still do.

"Don't worry, Eleanor, I'm not going to write much on Isaac Becker. I've covered that territory before."

When I first met Isaac, I thought I was doing God's work, giving TLC to public assistance recipients. I was so naïve, so innocent, and then I started handicapping college basketball and a few years later, I was partnering with Isaac. Somewhere along the way, between there and here, I made enough dollars to provide bridge loans to billionaires, have dinners with CEOs, invest in twenty-eight top-shelf enterprises. Once you have money, it gets a whole lot easier. As for Isaac Becker, "Bobby boy, I have six million left. I'm going to invest it in a telecommunications company in Russia. I think they got something. It's all new frontier stuff so I'm not too familiar with it, but it sounds as if it can become the biggest thing since AT&T." You can't steam! You can't mismanage! You can't chase! You can't be a degenerate gambler! You can't go into business with Donald Duck! You just can't! Isaac did. He went belly up. He went from being "everybody's best friend" to having only me.

My wife stepped outside. Walked into the woods. Shouted out to the maple, oak, locust, and ash trees. To deer, to hawks circling above, to a bald eagle flying by, "Please! Please stop this!"

We need more hand durable blades, more medications to put virus victims in comas so that our medical people can do their procedures. We need more of everything.

Extraordinary times! I do not have to tell you that. It sounds banal, even patronizing, as I pound paper. What is amazing, at least to me, is how fast all this has happened. How resilient we all are. When I think of how my family is living. How I am living. I feel guilty. What I'm saying is, why should a retrograde like me be so blessed with all that I have? My pal, Andy Gee, has spent the last fifteen years incarcerated for a crime he did not commit. The D.A. had it in for him. Gee's the one person I would want in that proverbial foxhole with me. Andy Gee was reputed to be the biggest bookmaker on the East Coast. He was on one side, I on the other. We thought of it as a civil war. Did you know that Abe Lincoln thought it would be a three-month war? Is Covid-19 going to be that kind of war? Not two hundred thousand of us, but coming back again and again and... I'm not thinking straight. I've been writing since four a.m. I'm so damn tired and disgusted with people dying. With this virus-war. I must try and get some sleep. I tried. I couldn't sleep. I went outside a little after dawn. There was Brian McGinn mending the corral fence. Eleanor loves Brian McGinn, this large, beefy, wide-shouldered, good-natured family man. He's a great father to his four children, a devoted husband to Annie, whom I never actually met, but I'll make a wager that she's as genuine as Brian. McGinn's dad was a police officer, patrolled in East Harlem in 1958 and 1959. We probably crossed paths hundreds of times. In those days, that 'hood was nowhere to be. Yet Mr. McGinn and this college boy, 21-year-old Robert Singer, were there. I don't know about Mr. McGinn, but as a social worker, I helped a whole chunk of community people. I can remember a few. There was Mr. Rivera and his family. Thirty-five years later, one of Mr. Rivera's sons tracked me down. "My father and mother still talk about you, Mr. Singer. I'm a principal of a junior high school. My sister, Jenny, is a nurse. Louis became an entrepreneur. He's the rich one in our family."

Another family was Hana Brockington's. Five abused children. When I entered their lives, they were starving. They were so wounded that they didn't even realize how wounded. I found a way to help. I was a person who thought he would never be poor, maybe broke, but never poor. It never occurred to me until my first wife drilled into me that money is a necessity. That all of us must make a living, pay rent, that writing a novel is not close to the answer. As, of course, Isaac Becker taught me, "First you make your living, then you live your life." Well, I learned the hard way. I went from being a joke to – well, to who I am today. It's been one hell of a journey. One more thing concerning my casework days in Harlem – I was mugged three times. Once, I had to fight my way out of a project building with an umbrella when three gang members trapped me on a stairwell. Another time, I was walking with my field book on 117th Street and Third Avenue where this little boy with his big brown eyes and a bigger smile was skipping along. He was wearing a shiny Mets jacket and, out of nowhere, two older boys appeared. "Give me your jacket," one of them said. The little boy wouldn't. He held on to it for dear life. The older boys tried to pull the jacket off him.

The little boy held on as best he could. It all happened in a matter of seconds. The next thing that happened was something I never forgot. One of those older boys pulled out a gun and used it. The little boy was paralyzed for life. He's still alive. Billy Harris called me last night. Wanted to know how I'm doing.

I am a bit zonked. Benadryl really knocks me out. I'm shaking my head, splashing my face with cold water. Waiting for Eleanor to get off my iPhone so I can call Abigail Wexner in Truro, Massachusetts. When I reached Abigail, we discussed how I would need her to line edit my novel and convert it to a digital format. Abigail is just about the only one who can read my manuscripts. I'm behind the horse and carriage when it comes to high tech. I need her to modify my pages in the form required by agents and editors. Editors do not read paper anymore. As for my last book, it's still selling as an eBook or for Kindle. Not so much in print. My publicist, Mimi Ziegler, who in her own way is as smooth as Duck, said, "You told me you just wanted to have fun writing your novel and getting it published. I think you had fun. Your publisher is pleased with the results. Stop making me feel bad! It's still selling. I know you really wanted a hardcover hit, but eBooks and Kindle are selling more copies these days."

Well, with this novel I'm now writing, I'll expect nothing for my efforts except a digital presence.

I'm losing it for sure. I can see it when I read my pages. One after another belongs in the trashcan. I'll have to be ruthless with my cuts. Less is always more. Or, as Abigail Wexner would say, "The first draft is for you. You can have fun. Then comes the hard work – to transform your venting into a novel."

DRAFT – FOR SECOND SECTION

A LIFE OF SECRETS BY ROBERT SINGER

Some readers who enjoy page turners would insist on more hyperbolic graphics concerning the violent incidents in my life. I, for one, always believed it a done deal that if you live by the sword you have a good chance of dying by the sword.

The third contract on my life took place outside a small town in upstate New York with appropriate casting, unidimensional men, three of them, a driver of a locked-door Buick, two grim-faced, long-haired, foul-mouthed assistants who had kidnapped me from Elaine's restaurant. They had stabbed me in the neck with a needle. That's all I recall until I woke up in a green-treed woods with scary red ants and deer dung. Fortunately for me I awakened in time to plead my plight. "One phone call, guys. That's all I'm asking." That phone call to Isaac Becker led to another call and then another and before thirty-six hours had passed, a Ford truck was driving up the road and Beef Leighton was delivering a briefcase stuffed with Franklins. An hour later

I was still in a fugue state so I'm reporting only what Beef told me. "Singer, I have to tell you the truth. You continued to bite your lower lip and whimper. And you continued whimpering all the way back to the George Washington Bridge."

That was one of two times that Isaac saved my life. I find it embarrassing, actually painful, to talk about these things as they reduce my life to some kind of ugly American gangster cliché. That kind of life has been glamorized more than John Wayne Westerns and, damn, that's exactly what I'm trying to avoid.

It was during the 1983-84 season that I stopped burying cash under maples and oaks. I started visiting the Caribbean, the Cayman Islands, Europe. "The trick is to have money to launder," Haskell Gold always cackled. I certainly did. I was earning over three mill tax-free dollars a season. Now I was even more secretive, more dehumanized, less inclined to care about people. More and more capable of executing a business plan that made me more and more and more. Strategies, vision, and the execution of that vision were my entire life. Then one October day at an East Side watering hole I met Rhoda Cain. She was sitting by herself at the bar. When I got into a skirmish with Mr. October, a flamboyant loudmouth who was never as good as his five hundred and sixty-three home runs suggest, Rhoda noticed. She waved to me to come over, and I did. Almost immediately she said, "I'm 21, I'm dyslexic. A high-school dropout. My boyfriend has a bad drug habit. I'm here to try and hustle up money for us and some more money so I can have my teeth fixed. Can you help me?" Rhoda looked like a Holocaust survivor. She couldn't have weighed 105 pounds. She was wearing a sack for a dress. Had a mop of hair that looked like it belonged on a soaked poodle. For some reason my stomach said, "I like this girl." I gave Rho my card. That same night she called, "Robert, my boyfriend beat me up. I'm on the street. I have nowhere to go."

"What happened?"

"It was my fault. I couldn't stop talking about you when I got home. He got jealous."

I told Rho to grab a cab, "I'll meet you in front of 1818." At four-thirty in the morning, Rhoda moved in. Happily, she stayed for five-and-a-half years.

During that period, I became the poor man's version of everybody's best friend. Not bragging, just stating facts. I was having the Carnegie Deli deliver Thanksgiving Day turkeys all through East Harlem to my old clients, to their children, their grandchildren. I was giving Franklins to ADC moms who needed the kind of help public assistance wasn't providing, I was arranging for winter galoshes and coats for as many people as I could, sending Catholic Charities gobs of children's books and young adult novels, and with Rhoda at my side, visiting soup kitchens, temples, churches, handing out not only the day's soup but Rhoda's home-made pies. No, I wasn't all bad, that's also a fact, but I was as split down the middle as Donald Duck or Hermann Hesse's Harry Haller. That's the truth.

I had a checklist of rules, codes, an anonymous presence. Isaac and Haskell knew I was making money. It was for them, they assumed. Both men couldn't fathom, wouldn't believe, that I was an independent thinker. The days of my having an allegiance to morality and ethics were over. I wasn't anybody's best friend. I was relentless, unidimensional, in pursuit of the almighty dollar. Doing everything I could think of to eliminate the kind of mistakes I had made in the past. Trying to follow a protocol that I had learned from the cannibalistic Gold, the streetwise Becker. Every night as I hit the pillow, I vowed to myself – never again would I place myself in the position where I would be a loser! Hopefully, I had puked the flaws of a lifetime out of my system. Cleansed myself of everything from god-fearing religion to patriotism, to a weakness for companionship. After Rhoda left, women became T and A … they were only in my life to celebrate with after winning a big game. After losing a huge bet, I would hole up in my apartment, pace the rooftop, curse out the world. Sometimes I would place a phone call to one of my Jersey strip-clubs. Have one of my partners send over a young lady, or two, to alleviate some of my stress. Those days, stress was always building up in me. It was like air in a balloon, the pressure needed to be removed. I had become someone that I didn't know existed during my prison time with Victoria. I was a changed man. Beginning to see myself as one of the 1 percent that own this country. "Own," that's a good word for someone who was as faulty as a punctured tire. "Money is what counts, Sonny. Having it, the power of it, the glamour of it. The more the better. Whatever it does for you, Sonny, it does, but it's a trip that only very few of us ever experience. Make sure you are one of them." Gold kept drilling this into me. Unfortunately, I was becoming one of them. The same greed. The same gnawing hunger. The same disconnection from decent people.

Every Wednesday morning from 9:15 to 12:45, during the seventeen-week college basketball season, I would spend going from bank vault to bank vault just to count and drop off money. Bank of America, JPMorgan Chase, Citigroup, Wells Fargo, Chemical, Capital One. I had stashed in each bank vault two hundred thousand in liquid cash. Later on, when the amounts of Franklins became unmanageable, I started using other hideouts, other ways to hoard and launder. It was the year after Rhoda Cain left me that I began to seriously invest in real estate. I didn't buy Tiffany or Cartier diamonds until I became ultra-sophisticated. I hate that term. There wasn't a day that I wasn't learning from Haskell Gold. "Tell me about 1918, Mr. Gold." "The Spanish flu was a killer, Sonny. I think six hundred and seventy thousand or more Americans died. All that people were concerned with was loss of their jobs, their children not going to school, having food on the table. For a time, I was one of them people, Sonny. Yeah, I was as lame as everyone else. Worried about the ABCs of life, but I'll say this – it didn't take me too long to wake up. By the time I was 15, I was working with Meyer Lansky and Longie Zwillman. Where were you at 15, Sonny? Probably whining because your twin brother grabbed one of your kosher lamb chops off momma's table. Am I right, Coop?" he'd cackle, turning to his bodyguard. Outside of Adian Getty, the only person Haskell Gold trusted was Walter Cooper. A Tuskegee airman from WWII. Cooper, the story goes, had been invited to the White House by Eleanor Roosevelt, but for years now the fact was he had been employed by Gold for all sorts of butchery work. By the time Walter Cooper was part of my life, he was over 70, in poor health. He would anchor himself in Gold's Park Avenue triplex, read a newspaper, do a crossword, sit in a corner on a Hollywood Regency antique chair, rarely stir, but he'd pop up when Gold needed him to take care of something. Things like visiting hits on people who lived as far away as New Zealand. Nothing more to tell you about Walter Cooper other than he was always polite, minimalistic, a chain-smoker – Lucky Strikes – taller than gnome-like Gold, and even more disconcerting.

I was … I was! I would like to say we were, but the truth is, it was never "we." I could never understand it but Walter Li and Adian Getty and Haskell Gold and the dozens of other implacable friends of mine, all those One-Percenters who were in real-estate development and high finance, running hedge funds, these men who were taking their families to homes in the Hamptons, Aspen, planning their vacations on European beaches, in Monaco, these ostensibly law-abiding citizens who were living the good life, a life that most people never sniff, they were giving away nothing outside of what their lawyers and accountants told them was the smart play for tax purposes. I could understand it, but I couldn't understand it if you understand what I'm saying. As bad as I am, I promised myself that if I ever made real money, I would help people, not "posture" good so I would look good, but how could you not? Before Rhoda vanished, she didn't look at me with disdain as Victoria did. Rhoda really saw me. We shared five fabulous years together. When she developed strong wings (she went through therapy, earned a high-school equivalency diploma, acquired 103 credits at Hunter College, good teeth, and a solid bank account), Rhoda had the strength of character to announce to me, "Robert, we have to talk. I hate leaving you. I know you need me. You know I love you but it's time. I want to stand on my own two feet. And let's face it, Robert. You don't want children." Rhoda looked at me. I stared at her. What else was there to say...

I dived into my work. I made a wager on Villanova/Georgetown game. It was a monster bet. A superior best bet. My stomach loved the game. I lost the wager.

One biblical truth I genuflected to during those pregnant years was that when Bobby Knight lost a game away from Bloomington, Indiana, let's say in Madison, Wisconsin, when he got that Badger team back at Assembly Hall, the price on the game could have been nine or twelve, even twenty-two points. Whatever the number, it would never scare me away from wagering on Indiana. It just didn't matter. I would power rate this a "revenge game"; call it "Knight's Vengeance"; lay the twenty-two if I had to. It just didn't matter. Bully Bobby would have his players foaming at the mouth. The final score would end up being something like 92-62 or close to that kind of carnage. A whole lot of my millions came from Knight revenge. And never did Las Vegas linemakers ever catch up with 90 percent of my "Big Games" or with Bobby Knight. And I mean never.

Not even when Knight was banished to Texas Tech in Lubbock, Texas. Bobby still won more than his share and so did I. Knight did it with mirrors in Lubbock. With his fire and brim energy and his brain. What did I do it with? I did it, that's all that matters.

Talking about revenge and no mercy. That was how I was conducting my handicapping business. I was acquiring something of a shadowy reputation. I remained invisible yet certain individuals from New York to Costa Rica were beginning to whisper, "It's The Handicapper's game." Professional gamblers were starting to follow my games. They were reading the winter winds or wires. Jumping on games I was wagering on. Through my early moves in Canada, London, Costa Rica, Las Vegas, New York. As soon as a hoop line came out, I would get first crack at it, but an hour later, these wise guys would follow my lead. Of course they would be laying anywhere from one-half point to two and one-half points more than I did. Bookmakers are pragmatic, bottom-line men. They know what they're doing. Guys like the Vaccaro brothers in Las Vegas and Mel Hall and his wife in Costa Rica are two pros who move a line as well as anyone. As soon as I or one of my beards made their move, other no-nonsense men would move the game a half point or more. And I repeat, every half a point is worth a certain percentage of winning or losing. It's worth killing for. Wise guy handicapper or asshole, no one can make a living giving away half a point. No one. It's the difference between paying your rent or being handed an eviction notice.

I remained invisible. No one knew the equivocal things I was doing. Such as, "Past Posting" by twenty-eight seconds, sometimes as much as fifty-eight with a sloppy runner.

Camouflaging. Appearing to lose significantly during the football and baseball seasons. Each noisy loss designed to make me look as if I were some kind of degenerate Isaac Becker, sucker gambler wagering on the entire board when what I was (intentionally) doing was investing pennies to protect my capability to function at optimum efficiency during the coming hoop season. I know I said these things before but when you make millions doing them, you do develop a kind of hubris and it certainly isn't false pride. It's "FUCK THE WORLD, I'M FREE!" I was tossing away pennies to ultimately make millions. That last thing I wanted to hear from a bookmaker was, "Let's stay friends, Singer. Lose my number." And believe me, as much as I tried to protect myself from BMs dropping me, once the college basketball season commenced, many veteran BMs did drop me after two or three weeks.

I discovered real quick that there were adversaries as sharp as me. A ton of them. I did the best I could. I succeeded. There for the grace of my brain go I… There by the grace of accident, contingency, Godot or whatever you believe in, go I. Some people pray, and when their prayer comes in, they'll say it was the almighty hearing their prayer. I say there by the crimes in my brain and all the absurdity there is in the world go I. A dedicated schoolteacher who spends his life illuminating youngsters earns a yearly salary of what I earned on a Bobby Knight special in two hours. Absurd as it is, it's the world we live in. Join it or be a schoolteacher. FUCK YOU WORLD, I'M FREE.

I took advantage of everything. What do you do when your parents are deceased? When your first wife is a shrew like Victoria, when your identical remains in a state of denial, "Robert, I'm begging you, stop gambling! You'll end up broken and broke. Do you need me to pay your rent?" I must have heard my twin cry out to me more than I had heard Victoria's "Gambler! Loser! Get a real job, Nigger-lover!" Never did I tell Dick what went down. Never did I tell one soul. I worked alone. Didn't confide or trust one single individual. What I told everyone, whether it was a chatty friend, a snarling bookmaker, a runner, partner, relative, was only what they needed to know. Beards knew what number I was searching for. The kind of information I wanted like... "East Tennessee State's Center is out, he tripped in practice and sprained his ankle... or the point guard on Princeton is all fucked up. His girlfriend is sleeping with his best friend." If a beard was to get me down one thousand dollars, he knew my law. It was only at the number I was searching for. I'll emphasize this to the day I die. In thirty-one years, I never gave in to half a point. I never steamed. I maximized and minimized. Watched every dollar. Do you hear me, Joey? Let the losses go. There's another game tomorrow. If there isn't, go to a movie, take out your wife, find some young thing to shack up with or just read a book. Yeah, read a book, Joey.

As for never giving into a number. Remember, I had BMs and beards all over America. I had the ability to shop for the number I was looking for. Get the information I needed. Most of the time I succeeded. Sounds supercilious. It wasn't. I was putting my limbs on the line. My life.

One more Haskell Gold detail. I always placed Franklins on my desktop in the amount of the wager I was making. Whether it be two thousand or the ninety-two thousand that I wagered on that Indiana/Wisconsin game in Bloomington that I referred to with dots and dashes not too many pages ago. It's always going to remain dots and dashes. I just can't take the chance of spelling things out. RICO ... ambitious D.A.s ... Mayors – like that Yankee-lover. Police Chief ... Wise guys ... Competition ... I'm sorry but I must take the fifth.

On my Chinese desk, I would stack minted green. It was an old Haskell Gold's ploy. "Sonny, it's smart to see, smell, touch the currency you're wagering. Money isn't make-believe. It's real. See it. Touch it. Smell it, before you call in your bet. Take a few moments to allow that brainy stomach of yours to digest if it's worth the investment you're making. Sonny, you know who you're beginning to remind me of?" Haskell Gold said to me a week before he died. "Me! That's who!"

On second thought, the last detail I should comment on isn't the money I spread out on my desktop before calling in a bet, it's how Haskell Gold died. It was because of a proposition bet. His past posting was exposed. For once in Gold's life, his larceny was challenged. Ironically, it was Beef Leighton acting at the command of Isaac Becker who paid 88-year-old Haskell a visit. "Singer," Beef said to me at Isaac's steakhouse two days after Gold was put in the ground, "Isaac might be a sucker but it's only when he's having fun. Understand what I'm saying."

Did I tell you how Haskell Gold was killed? I don't think I can. Right now, I want to mention Beef Leighton. He would call me boss, or Singer. We fought together, side by side. On two occasions Beef was wounded defending me. Once shot in the neck, another time two bullets penetrated his chest. I, too, had a few close calls. Once I was stabbed two inches to the left of my groin, another time I almost lost my right eye, but other than that, both of us survived. Beef would always clean up whatever needed to be cleaned up. For him, the chore was difficult. Beef was squeamish about blood. As tough as he was, Beef would just about faint at the sight of red. Especially if it was his own. We always ended up having milkshakes and pastrami sandwiches when the day's work was completed. Beef Leighton was the only adult I ever knew who loved milkshakes as much as I did. We had one other thing in common. In Beef's living room, the one thing he had there that I found endearing, was a life-sized oil painting of his departed wife. Each time I'd visit I would sit quietly on a sofa, old Hickory Tannery, in front of Molly's painting with Beef and he would stare at Molly, pear-shaped tears would come to his beefy buffalo face. It always made me think of the oil painting I had of Victoria when she was an Eileen Ford model at the peak of her powers. How many times did I peer at that oil and cry like a child? With Beef, I would put my arm around his massive shoulder and try and console him. Many times, our evening would end with me taking him to Carnegie Deli for corned beef and pastrami and chicken noodle soup. On occasion I would cook dinner for him.

Now I'm dwelling on my third year of handicapping. The year I made 109 thousand, the year Barney Feldman, Dick's neighbor, came into the picture. The Major was terrified of his wife, "Mona, what makes for a good marriage is to enjoy your own company." The Major made me laugh. He made a buck by selling cheap perfume and cheaper watches as a young man. Now middle-aged, Barney was peddling Rolexes, Patek Philippes and Audemars Piguets at a tremendous discount to well-heeled businessmen, wise guys, and Russians. For a high-school dropout from Morris evening school, The Major was impressive. Expanding exponentially when he started leasing helicopters and small jets. Barney Feldman had the verbal gifts of Duck, "Mona, a woman's voice should never be heard above a whisper. It's offensive to a man's ear." The Major started telling everyone at the Friars Club, the Metropolitan Club, The Town Club, that I was the greatest college basketball handicapper in the country. The result was pear-shaped businessmen, lean card-playing loners, were coming out of the woodwork. Several pleaded with me to take them in as partners. It seemed as if the entire City wanted a piece of me. My deal was a simple one. These men would put up their cash. I'd take half the profit. Within three years, I didn't need "OPM," OTHER PEOPLE'S MONEY. I cut these leeches from my balance sheet. I had learned when you take in partners, you can benefit from their money but when you do this, you have to listen to their two cents' worth of ego and opinion. Within thirty-six months, I didn't need that kind of irritation. I only kept my alliances with Gold and Becker. These two outlaws could watch my back. I was fully aware by then that I was in bed with mobsters.

Eleanor just called. We discussed the sorrowful death of RBG and the exquisite timing of Duck coming down with Covid-19. Pooooor Duck...Come on people. There's not a thing Duck says or does that isn't a self-promotion. He's my buddy in a world of pimps, or as Isaac would say, "You don't have to go to bed with Haskell Gold to benefit from knowing him. Play the game, Bobby boy. Just remember it's a game."

As I pound away at my life of secrets, here's one that I haven't revealed. In my thirty-one years of climbing

Mount Gamble, of acquiring, there was only the five years that I shared with Rhoda Cain that were blessed. Julie Burr proved as insincere as most One-Percenters, in fact, more so, but Rhoda, a waif, a spiritual spirit. I enjoyed each day, every day. Five delightful years Rhoda Cain lived with me and when I close my eyes and have some quiet time, I can remember Tuesdays at twilight, during those hoop seasons. I would walk into our bedroom and toss industrial garbage bags onto our king-sized bed. Crumbled twenties, fifties, Franklins would spill out of the bags. Those that didn't tumble, I shook out. Then I would tell Rho to start counting, and as she did, I would kiss her ears, cheeks, her neck, her breasts, her hips, her vulva. Rhoda would lose count. Had to start over. I continued picking winners, stashing important money, but after Rhoda left, it wasn't half as much fun. One year after Rhoda, Isaac passed. Haskell Gold died two years later. My mother and father were also gone by then. And my twin brother, Richard, he was still doing the same things he's doing right now in our guest house, underlining Kafka, Beckett, Pessoa, Max Frisch, David Bobson and writing his novels, living his life; as I said, in a million years, my twin brother would never have believed the life I was living. Only my left hand knew what my right was doing. And on many occasions, it didn't. I continued to make a living. Sharing my life of secrets with no one. No one!

The End

Reid and I had lunch together. I had a bowl of soup, he had sushi. I told him about the moment I fell in love with him.

"Your mom and I went to Dr. Rotardier's office. She showed us your sonogram. Right then, Kiddo, I knew."

After lunch we walked out on the porch adjacent to our kitchen. Reid stepped to the front.

"Ba, come here," he whispered.

I walked over. A fox was on our lawn with three of her kits.

In the early afternoon I walked down to the guest house. I was a bit concerned, as, for two days I hadn't heard one word from my twin. With some difficulty I climbed the steps leading to the second floor where my brother has his desk and writing tools. He was hunched over his laptop.

"You're out of breath," he shouted. "You're thirty pounds overweight. You don't watch your diet. You're killing yourself with the way you eat." Dick does thirty push-ups every day. I can't do one. He meticulously watches his diet. All my life I've indulged myself with super-rich foods, enjoyed milkshakes, pastries, ice cream. Before I could get one word in, he was asking, "Now why did you come down here? I'm writing."

I took off. Sat down on a bench located in the back of the guest house. It's where the mid-afternoon sun is strongest. I closed my eyes, dozed off for a while. When I opened my eyes, the first thing I noticed was two chipmunks not fifteen feet from where I had been snoozing. I remained there awhile, gazed into the woods, saw more trees than I'd ever seen before. I started counting them. As I did, I heard birds chirping, many other sounds that you don't hear in the City. I'm so fortunate, I thought to myself. Picking winners did it for me. You might think it plain stupid to stake your life gambling on college basketball games, but it worked for me. More importantly, at least on that glorious day, I stopped dwelling on Covid-19.

My identical receives the kind of respect for his literary fiction that I never will. He's lauded for his prose style, honesty and originality. I stick to my own life experiences, which most of us share.

Speaking about "honesty," for Dick's latest novel, he's receiving more credit than he deserves. All those men of letters who are slapping him on the back for creating a one-of-a-kind character. The truth is, that quirky figment of my twin's imagination is Richard Singer. For four years he did hang out at Holman Hall while attending CCNY. He did ogle a co-ed he was totally in love with, without uttering one solitary word to her during those four years. He did fall in love with a 19-year-old Bulgarian girl when he was 57. He did crack up because this girl would only relate to him as a father figure. He did fall in love with "A Face!" when he was 24. When it didn't work out, he was so hurt that he had to drop out of graduate school. For the next six months I stayed up with him every night till four in the morning, the time it would take before he would finally stop sobbing. As for The Face, the moment Dick started expounding on the phone to her about Nietzsche, Kierkegaard, Schopenhauer, Sartre, de Beauvoir, and all the other thinkers he was enamored by, you guessed it – she was asleep. To this very day my twin believes that The Face was the love of his life.

The first sentence out of the Fox newscaster's mouth was, "As we reopen, we're expecting the numbers to rise exponentially." I went into my den, started writing checks. A whole batch of them. People I know who live paycheck to paycheck are still waiting for benefit checks to kick in. When I finished, I made some calls:

MANHATTAN: "Did you hear what happened in the City? People stood at their open windows, on their balconies, their terraces, in the park, the streets, wherever they were, and they clapped and cheered. We were all cheering for these wonderful, brave, angels of mercy.

HARVEY, LOUISIANA: "I'm okay. Now! I did take sick. It started with the runs. Then I was nauseous for a few days. Then I fainted. Must have been out cold for ten minutes or more. Now it's three weeks later. I'm okay."

SANTA MONICA: "I'm fasting. Going to church every day. I've become a Coptic Christian."

DALLAS: "We're going to the ranch for the weekend. Taking our granddaughter with us. Eve reminds us so much of Reid when he was that age. She's beautiful."

1818: "Hi, Mr. Singer. Just watered your terrace. Everything's looking great. Thanks for the check."

PARIS: A friend who at one time was making important contributions to the world of letters. "It's all gone. Gone!"

GERMANY: "I don't have a dollar left. I haven't even enough money to buy writing paper. Not even a ballpoint pen. My girlfriend left me. I've been laid off. There are no unemployment benefits. And there's no Donald Trump to give me twelve hundred dollars. You must help me. Please!"

Duck says our economy must reopen. We will come out of this greater, bigger, stronger. I keep hearing from my octogenarian friends that they do not expect to make it. If it goes on much longer, they feel for sure they'll get struck down by Covid-19.

"The viral contagion is still out there, Robert. Someone can breathe on you and you'll be upended."

Today something hit me. I'm feeling the kind of anxiety that I haven't felt since I lived with Victoria and was gambling case money bets. When I was "The Handicapper," I wasn't afraid of losing. I took my swings. Even when contracts were placed on my head:

"Look guys, just one phone call. That's all I'm asking."

On three different occasions I telephoned Isaac Becker.

He worked out my problems with whomever it was that I had figured out a way to beat for too much money. I had a brutal, immoral, ruthless, street-smart partner in Isaac Becker. We made real dollars. Now I'm an old man.

I know I'm not doing enough. The first responders, the healthcare professionals, the essential workers, these people are all doing something. People like me who just write out checks, eat gourmet dinners... Eleanor has purchased enough Omaha Steaks to feed an army. Not for a week or a month but for an entire year. "What if," she says when I tell her it's going to be over a whole lot sooner than that. "We will have sophisticated medical treatment plans. We'll probably have a vaccine..." Eleanor won't listen. She doesn't even hear me. She's terrified like most of us. Whenever I speak to people, all I hear are stories about their loved ones, friends, neighbors, workforce buddies who have come down with the virus. Those who haven't resolved it and those who have died from it. My question remains: What if we beat the virus this time and then in two years, no, let's say five... What if...? Is it always going to be part of our "new normal?"

Our children's future? Will our kids ever have peace of mind? Ever again feel secure? Ever live one day where they feel completely safe? Safe, that's a word that should be eliminated from the dictionary. Where am I going with this? Where is there to go with this? I'm calling Duck tonight. Not for answers. He doesn't have answers. Just to talk.

"… Thanks for leaving a key for me, Singer. When I walked through your lobby, I saw this man and woman there. They were going jogging in the park. She was built like Marilyn Monroe. He looked like he had just gone broke."

"Oh, that's the Laurens. Hillary's a model and Joe's in finance. He went broke last winter. He overextended himself in the commodity Bobet. When he told Hillary he went belly up, she freaked. They're still living together but there's nothing left of their marriage … Yes, of course you got a shot with her. The last time I spoke to Hillary she said that she was going to vote for you. She said you keep every promise you make. The Bobet, tariffs on China, standing up to Kim Jong-Un."

"I told you, Singer, white women love me. It's the Black women I'm worried about."

I had a life before Eleanor. Some of it romantic. Some of it adventurous. Some of it obscene. Most of it just plain dumb. Don't ask me why but right then, as I was pounding the typewriter, I started visualizing climbing up the stairs to the end arena at MSG. Sitting there with Cal Ramsey and watching Robin Freeman and Bob Zawoluk and Togo Palazzi and Bill Russell when they played college ball. I recall Bob Cousy and Max Zaslofsky, and before I stop typing, let's talk about Wilt. There was never anyone like Wilt. Even with today's players he'd still be one-of-a-kind. And I saw Bob Kurland and George Mikan and Joe Fulks and Wally Choice and Sugar Cain and Paul Unruh and Pistol Pete and Hondo and Frank Selvy and Bevo Francis and can time-travel all the way forward to Zion and a thousand more. I would never leave out Kobe or Michael or LeBron – they belong, and so does the one guy that I would still tell you is my all-time number one. It wasn't Larry or even Magic. Nope, it's not any of them, not to me. It's "The Big O"...what he did, when he did it, with his economy and consummate game, well, if basketball were in the hands of Rembrandt, he'd have painted O...Oscar Robertson was the blueprint on the way the game should be played. He's the big point guard that changed the game. Helped it evolve to what it is today, where seven-footers like the Greek Freak can do it all. Of course, the game is still evolving, but as I said, it all started when Oscar Robertson replaced Bob Cousy and Bobby Davis and Slater Martin and Dick McGuire and showed us things that we couldn't even imagine from those end arena seats in the mid-1950s. Not back then.

"Over two million cases worldwide! More than one hundred thousand people dead. Italy is rebounding!" Eleanor reiterates these facts as if they were a Burl Ives folksong. "Italy doesn't have any tears left. That's why they're not crying." …

"We're up here, Robert. We're out of it. Hospital mortuaries are packed to the brim."

"Did you know that the mean age in Italy is ten years older than in the States," Reid chips in.

Eleanor adds to the eulogy, "They were slow to lock their country down."

"We were not exactly an express," Reid contributes.

Eleanor sighs, "One of the tragic truths is this illness separates people from their families when they need them the most."

My wife stares at me. Just stares.

What flashes into my head: I took for granted that Eleanor would be at my side at the end. I can't ever remember being like this. I always thought, if not of immortality, of at least a million tomorrows.

'Ba, look out the window. In front of our house was Reid's Volkswagen. Brian McGinn had arranged for one of his crew to fly to Athens, Georgia, and drive the vehicle back to Justice Lane. "I'm planning on taking it apart, Ba. Learn every part, including its motor."

"No sweat, Kiddo. Whatever you want."

Reid also has a blue BMG. A silver Porsche. Nineteen years old, three cars, while spastic me has never even learned to drive.

"Ba, do me a favor. Remind me to thank Mr. McGinn for having my car delivered. I texted him but I still want to thank him in person."

My son's entire life he will never have a money problem. I don't know why but I think like that. I think of my father who every night walked around our West End Avenue apartment shutting lights off before he went to bed. My dad worked from the time he was 8. He would sing Yiddish melodies on the streets of Brooklyn. By 10 he was touring the country, earning seven dollars a week. Every one of those dollars went to his parents. "I was the oldest. Your grandfather couldn't find work. Your grandmother was an invalid. Your uncle Tommy was 3. Your Aunt Clara, 4."

Not one day in my father's entire lifetime did I ever make him proud. Now I dwell on how difficult his life was as a boy, traveling from one city to another, frightened and lonely. Never once did I tell my father that I loved him. The things you live with. The things you regret.

My mind jumps to Duck, "Instead of worrying about your re-election you should be tearing down slums and building cleaner, more affordable housing."

"Singer, sometimes you amaze me. That's the most stupid thing I've heard in years. Real estate isn't charity. It's bottom-line profit and loss. Let me give you some advice, if you're thinking of investing in real estate, invest in me."

My mind returns to my twin. He never took one dollar from our dad. He paid his own way through college. When he recovered from "The Face," Dick didn't go back for his PhD. He reinvented himself, ended up being a first-rate novelist. Amazing how tragedies and accidents shape one's life.

With me it was a whole different ballgame. My dad paid my tuition to go to NYU. In those days it was twenty-five dollars a credit. Eight hundred dollars for the entire year.

"I can't afford it," my father would cry.

"You don't have a choice," my mother would tell him.

Now I'm shelling out over sixty-five thousand dollars a year for my son to attend Georgia Tech.

"Hey Ba," Reid just yelled out. "Want to go for a little drive to Harvest Moon? Ma asked me to get her some flowering plants. I have a mask for you to wear."

PART THREE

EVERYBODY'S GOT
A MOMMA

I rushed to my Smith-Corona not knowing what I wanted to say. My brain feeds me a line. "The candle burns at both ends and will not last the night." I stay with it, hoping it will be a catalyst to fill up my blank page. While I am praying for inspiration, Eleanor walks into the room. She scans my manuscript. "Rob, you're repeating yourself again. You said these same things earlier in the book. Why don't you write more about Dick?" Then Eleanor grazes my shoulder and leaves the room.

My twin brother has always refused to take one dollar from me. He's never earned enough money to live anywhere other than in a tiny rent-controlled studio on the Upper West Side. He's always been honest to a fault. When Dick signs a contract with one of his publishers, he always tells his lawyer, "Make sure it's fair. Not for me, for them." Dick never contrives or bullies, nor has he ever done one thing that I would classify as hurtful. My brother is unselfish, generous with his time. True, he never stops complaining about the digital culture, incessantly howling about the price he paid to write the novels he has. "If my publisher sells one thousand books, I'll be elated," he says. Still, his novels have a chance to endure. This is not coming from me. It is said by literary scholars. He's always been the good twin. Washed the dishes. Went shopping. Studied like a fiend for our bar mitzvah. My mother told Dick, "Your father's colleagues will be attending. His professional friends. They'll be coming from all over the country, including rabbis from Israel. Over one thousand people will be in attendance at the temple. . . . Darling, I can't talk to your brother. You know how he is. We're counting on you."

Dick did everything. I stood there, mute as my twin chanted, thinking, *what the fuck am I doing here?*

The only intimacy my brother has had in his entire lifetime he's had from his treasured library of books. And to conclude this brief biography, Dick has always helped me: through my obsessive gambling days, my Victoria wars, my days with gangsters, and now, actually for years, he's been cursing me out, "With a brother like you . . ." and his second gripe is, "I wasted my life. I should have gone to Hollywood. I could have created the kind of high-concept films Spielberg does . . ."

"Dick, you never took movies seriously. You're a great novelist. That's more than enough."

"My kind of life doesn't exist any longer. The literary culture is done. I was a fool. I'm obsolete," he tells me every day in a sad voice. A mournful face.

I'm walking on a gravel road down to the guest house. I have Dick's laundry in one arm, a shopping bag in the other. Eleanor's prepared a roast duck that she asked me to bring to my twin.

I knock on the door. My identical answers. He's had a bad day. Sore throat. Coughing. Difficulty with his breathing.

Dick quarantined himself for twenty-one days. He's better now. We think! He was never tested. He could have been a carrier.

I climbed into bed after taking two Benadryls to help me sleep. Eleanor started yammering, "I've been thinking how the two of us got together. I guess we bought each other at discount prices. If you had been younger, you would never have looked at me. If I hadn't been so damaged, I would never have settled for a 62-year-old man."

"Timing is everything," I say.

Eleanor smiles. Takes my hand. "We were both ready."

At three in the morning, we were still jabbering. At least I was, "If the virus hits me and I don't make it, you must promise me…"

"I'll never replace you Rob, Eleanor says, beginning to sob. Eleanor turns away. "Let's not talk about this again. Why upset each other until we have to."

It was one in the morning when Duck telephoned, "My week has been an absolute disaster."

We arranged to meet at my apartment at 6 a.m. Monday morning. At 5:45 I opened a secret compartment in my desk drawer to get some cash. At 5:45 Duck was at the door. Within minutes he was slurping pineapple juice.

"Don't drink hard liquor much, was never partial to wine. I'm not even a smoker, but since I was a little runt I loved juice. Got to go to your restroom. Be right back."

When Duck returned, he began rattling off people he needed to escape from. "Poor people and Black people have health issues, vaccine or no vaccine."

"I'm sorry, he said a few minutes later. "This shit is getting to me more than it should." He took a long swallow from his juice glass. "I'm going to be campaigning soon and I'm really starting to worry. Not about Joe Biden."

I made a comment.

"I know his favorability numbers are even better than Clinton's were. I think his are 51-41. Clinton's never were more than 51-46. You're not the only one telling me that it's not 2016."

He stopped. Took another sip. "I can still turn it around. Did it with Clinton and I can do it with Biden. In the Midwest there are plenty of African Americans that I can still get. Maybe not in places like Milwaukee and Detroit, they hate me there, but that's okay. I know what I need to do. In the suburbs I can still get my share of educated women. I don't think I've lost as many of them as the pundits are predicting."

I had given Duck the key to my apartment for a specific reason. I asked about Hillary Lauren.

"I screwed up there, Singer. You know how the media's always saying I never admit a mistake. I'm admitting this one. I couldn't keep up with her. She not only jogs three miles every day, she works out two. Hillary's 32. I'm past 70. What's worse than that is that I lost her vote."

"How did things work out with Walter Li? Did you two come to an understanding?"

Duck squinted. "He's a hard-ass. Couldn't get him to budge on key issues. You know me, I never like criticizing our senior citizens, but Walter Li is an old man, and he's stubborn. I'm sorry, Singer. No other way for me to put it. I tried real hard to work something out. I really wanted him to join my team. God knows I tried to accommodate him, but he left me out in the cold."

Eventually we settled into a less toxic conversation.

"... Singer, you must admit I've done some good things too. Covid-19 patients in hospitals have declined dramatically. According to the latest reports, by July, 90 percent of the hospitals will be empty."

I brought up police violence. A problem that had been looming larger and larger. "In my opinion, it needs to be addressed," I said.

"Police violence is not an issue. I can handle that one."

"What I'm trying to say is that you must show empathetic leadership."

"If that's your point, you sure are saying it in a serpentine way."

It was incredulous to me how much Duck knew. The economy this, the economy that. He started to throw out stats. It was as if he was "The Handicapper" and I his neighborhood bookmaker.

"Those people making less than forty thousand a year in salary are the people that are hurting the most. And then out of left field, 'We must help each other through this.'" I am sure Duck meant it. At least when he said it, he seemed sincere. "I'm going to have to flood our country with three trillion dollars. Our Central Banks... We must start printing currency. You do know the Federal Reserve can only lend money. It's up to Congress... Those bastards have more authority than I do. They control the purse strings." A second later, "We're spending more than we're taking in." He gulped down some more juice. "This isn't going to go away without a vaccine. Our economy has shrunk. Millions have lost jobs. Even during the Great Depression only 25 percent were out of work. And who gets the blame." He paused, took another gulp. "It's my job to keep workers solvent. And I'm going to do just that." Then Duck started on one of his pet peeves. "Obama," he spit out. He shook his head. "People snicker when I call him grossly incompetent. Give me a break."

He tried to calm himself by getting some air. He walked onto the rooftop for a few minutes. Paced to the rails. Peered at the Park. Returned inside somewhat calmer.

"People make a big deal when I speak about borders. I'm not talking about borders any longer. No borders can be protected. No amount of money can prevent this virus."

It was as if he were having a breakdown. Still, a large part of me was wary that he wasn't. What I concluded was that he was as disconnected as I was during my handicapping years. Pressure gets to you. You might not be aware how it's destroying you from the inside out. But it is. Long winning streaks, surprisingly enough, at least for me, were worse than long losing streaks. I dreaded them. Always felt I had to keep going. Not lose a game. I guess it's something like Eleanor when she said that I had placed too much pressure on her to live up to my compliments on the Mother's Day card I gave her.

Duck kept going on and on. Sometimes ranting, sometimes fudging issues, sometimes avoiding them. At other times becoming almost incoherent. "All my wives told me that my children were intimidated by me. It's true. I can be intimidating, and I do take advantage of that. But never have I ever brutalized my kids. I'll swear to God on that. What do you think?" he asked, looking innocently at me, taking another swallow of juice.

"I would say that your kids are what they are, who they are, because of you." I hesitated before adding, "And that's not necessarily a good thing." Duck's reaction – another swallow of juice.

"Anyway, I didn't come over here to discuss my children. I have a country to run."

A few minutes later he laughed to himself. More of a snicker. "You know what I recall like yesterday. Becker placing hookers in all our rooms at the El San Juan hotel." It was when we went to Puerto Rico. Both of us had been invited by Isaac. He had factories on the island, made trips there on a regular basis, not only business trips but to enjoy the casinos and women. "I was the guy who told Becker that night that you were partial to women with inverted nipples."

As soon as Duck said that, a cloud burst. Victoria had inverted nipples. That son of a bitch. He slept with my wife.

By the next morning I was laughing at myself. Victoria was one hundred years ago. True, if I'd found out back then about Victoria sleeping with someone, I would have gone crazy, but now I realize I was the one who was the screwup. "Gambler! Loser! Get a real job!" Hissing nigger-lover at me is not that different than what half of America is doing right now. The world that I envisioned as a young, idealistic writer is not for everyone. It's predominantly for people who are already human beings. If you're not, all the words, all the books, all the conversations in the world aren't going to influence you one damn bit.

At dinner last night, "Reid, I haven't been watching much TV lately. Haven't been keeping up with the news. What's been happening?"

"Everything's fucked up."

Reid stormed out of the dining room and disappeared. Eleanor too has been acting strange lately. She's been spending more time than ever in her study. I realize all of us are a bit stir crazy. The cumulative toll this virus is causing. I try to get back to writing. My mind jumps to the pandemic. I think of New York; Brazil; Italy; Fayetteville, Arkansas; Gary, Indiana; Truro, Massachusetts, where Abigail Wexner is confined to a hospital bed for the past seventeen days. I step away from my machine. Open a desk drawer. Pull out a batch of blank checks. I've now written one hundred and eighty-seven of them. I will now write some more. To 1818 employees: porters, deskmen, handymen, doormen, to Karina Lopez, our housekeeper in the City. Karina didn't ask for one. I did tell her to text me if she had a problem. She hasn't texted. So far the largest check I've scribbled has been for seventeen thousand dollars. The smallest, a buck fifty. Eleanor just walked into the room. She's worried about me. She wishes I was younger, stronger, less feeble, more adroit. I can't blame her. I feel the same way. For a few minutes we speak, "I'm concerned about Reid, Eleanor," I say. "He's been avoiding me. He just doesn't talk to me anymore."

"He's sixty-four years your junior. You two just don't have that much in common. Besides, you've been spending all your time on your book. Don't worry about Reid." With that said, Eleanor disappears. A feeling of irrelevancy envelops me. Both my wife and son have been ignoring me more than ever. Doesn't matter what the conversation is about. They rarely include me. They don't hear me, listen to me, care what I have to say. If I try to include myself, I get nowhere. They just keep talking to each other as if I'm not there. One thing Eleanor did say last night. She was speaking about her calcium ATPase book and then she told me that her publisher is bringing out new editions of Ibsen's *Enemy of the People* and Martin Buber's *I and Thou*. "He's going to bring out those books next year, Robert. I thought that's something that would cheer you up." There was a time my wife would hang on my every word. Now it's as if she's heard it all before. As for Reid, he's always been high tech. When he was 3, he would play in his room with gadgets, tools and wires and he'd know what he was doing. I'm sure I lost my son once he started boarding school. Never got him back. All my married friends tell me that he'll come back. I don't have that kind of time, I tell them.

"…Reid, stop being so negative. We will come out of this pandemic. America will once again thrive. We are a land of exceptional people with entrepreneurial skills. We can improvise. We will improvise. We will create. Will come out of this with our independent minds, our brains, with new companies. We will…"

"Ba, you sound like Trump."

Lying, untruthful, dishonest, deceitful, mendacious, false, dissembling, insincere, duplicitous, hypocritical, fraudulent, double-dealing, two-faced, perfidious, out-of-whack-ego, self-satisfied smile, modern-day robber baron. You probably think I'm alluding to Duck. I'm not! I'm speaking of myself.

My identical's novel, *The Nihilesthete*, "It speaks with a singular honesty, power and eloquence about our spiritual diminished modern world. It is as important and original a novel to have been written by an American author in a generation." About my last novel, "If *Robert Singer* were a song, it could only have been sung by Frank Sinatra." These are direct quotes from critics that reveal all so poignantly the difference between twin and me. Dick knows his narratives, his characters, his moves, every move, before he begins his novel. I have a blank page when I start my book. If I'm lucky, the plot finds me. If it doesn't, it usually stays that way until my last page. It's the difference between a quacking duck and Toni Morrison. For my entire lifetime I've lived with it. Hopefully, with little envy. Certainly, with as little bitterness as possible.

On the other hand, my twin brother is a contradiction. When he goes to his neighborhood movie theatre, he walks. I mean for an hour or more in the middle of winter, in the snow, in the summer during New York's blistering heat waves. My twin is not going to spend money on a taxi. Not Dick! Now he's up here at our guest house having his groceries picked up and delivered every two weeks by Brian McGinn. He's paying Mr. McGinn one thousand dollars a month for this miniscule chore. Is this the kind of inconsistency all of us share? Are we all contradictory? Live life as if we were a Hoyt Wilhelm knuckleball.

The general manager of 1818 telephoned. Seems the building needed access so that their roofers can fix a leak on my rooftop. I continued chatting with Mrs. Hill. She brought up Norman Chesky, a tenant in the building for as long as I can remember. Chesky studied creative writing at Columbia with Herman Wouk. You know of Wouk, not Chesky. Norman took sick six days ago. He's now at St. Luke's on a ventilator. Mrs. Hill also told me of the death of Katherine Burns. She was a working actress her entire life, but she was more than that. Katherine Burns was a big personality. Exuded a Southern belle's flair. She was born in Alabama. We argued about everything as well as about nothing. During those days, we insulted each other each and every time we were together in the elevator. Before I journeyed to North Salem, we really went at it. We almost came to blows. "The last movie you were in you weren't acting, you were playing yourself. A Southern woman in love with Jefferson Davis. No wonder you're squawking now about taking down Confederate statues. You're as much of a bigot as George Wallace was."

"Mr. Singer, where is this anger coming from? I don't deserve such wrath. Mind your manners."

"You're from Alabama, aren't you? I'll bet you never questioned Jim Crow."

When Cal Ramsey was a boy in Selma, he was forced to drink from the "for colored only" fountains; use the "for colored only" toilets; ride at the back of the bus; go to a segregated school. Cal's mother, Ruth, told me a thousand times the kind of sickness they experienced. Even today, all these years later, you scratch the surface and you still see the same kind of ugly truths revealed.

That last outburst took place not long after Cal Ramsey died.

"I needed someone to talk to. It's been a rough couple of days."

"You mean Nancy Pelosi?"

"I shrugged it off when I first heard her say it, but now it's beginning to piss me off. Do you think I'm obese? Tell me the truth."

"Well..."

"It's my metabolism. It's slowed down more than it should have. Besides, I think I look pretty darn good for a man my age."

"You certainly don't look like you did in 2016."

"It's all this garbage I have to deal with. People think everything bounces off me. Most of it does. But when Pelosi said morbid obesity, I got to tell you it..."

"You've said a whole lot worse about people."

"They either deserved it or it was politics. Pelosi's like John Lewis. She really means what she says. That woman has the biggest set of balls in all of Washington."

"What about your balls?!"

"Tell me the truth. Do I really look that bad?"

"I told you. You're definitely showing some wear and tear."

"I know...I know...I know..."

A moment later Duck's mercurial nature came to the surface. His mood changed. "Remember West 52nd Street? Some of my best memories are of that block between Sixth and Seventh. I loved going to Jimmy Ryan's jazz club and Ronnie's Steakhouse. And there was a hat-check girl at Weston's that I was mad about. Could never get anywhere with her but just the same I never stopped trying. Talking about women, Becker's mistress was the hottest woman I'd ever seen."

"My brother had to drop out of grad school because of her!"

"She certainly was the kind of woman that could do that to a man." He paused. "What about Jimmy Wynn's girlfriend. When he owned the Harwyn Club." A second later *that* Duck disappeared. Became invisible. The next words out of his mouth were on Walter Li and his campaign.

A few minutes later he steps onto my rooftop. He has a glass of juice in his hand. He takes a swallow. He squints at the view. He peers at the Park. At Harlem. He mutters to himself. For a split second I think I should say something about how he's pitching this racist crap to his majority. Calling Black people thugs. Protecting our heritage. His hatred of immigrants and foreigners. How he's dividing America by race. His "My People..." and all the rest of his triggers that have a supremacist tone. Instead, I keep my mouth shut. I'm completely aware that my silence is immoral. My son wouldn't keep quiet. Why am I such a coward? In all of a split second that's what goes through my mind.

Duck shakes his head, 'I'm confident that my decision to reopen was the right thing to do."

"Most people are saying you did it because you're panicking. The election getting closer and your numbers..."

"Screw them. I always think first of our country. What kind of lowlife President do you think I am?"

Duck takes another swig from his juice glass.

"You know, a month or two ago I insisted my own son pay a one thousand dollar fine for not obeying Cuomo's law."

"What law is that?"

"You know, on social distancing. I told Junior, 'Cuomo was right. He didn't want your money. All he asked for was your compliance.' Junior just doesn't care a plug nickel about anything. He never listens to me. And that daughter of mine. She and her husband texted me at four in the morning. They got a new idea for a business. They want me to find them forty million. That princess of mine. She's almost 40 and she still thinks money grows on trees."

"When you were young your father staked you to millions."

"Everyone thinks that but the truth is my father gave me no more than a few bucks to get started. It certainly wasn't ten million. More like five."

One hour later:

I switched on the TV. A reporter was talking... "There's anecdotal evidence, not rigorous studies that..."

Duck interrupts – "There's no magic bullets right now. I know that. The whole world is struggling to get this virus under control. I did something. I had to do something. Most of my people are telling me that we have a tough month or two ahead. That in the fall it's going to get worse.

I don't think so. I think we've flattened the curve for good. Don't quote me on that but it's my opinion. I think from now on things are going to get a whole lot better. And that's what I told Fauci. He didn't agree. The prick."

Duck channel surfs. Lands on a channel where they're speaking about the Hasidic community in Brooklyn.

"Those people should have been put in jail. None of them gives a damn about anyone outside of their own kind. They disobey our laws. And let me tell you, they're rude. They gather at funerals, have weddings in their homes, in their temples, they don't follow our social distancing rules. I've talked to some of them. They're rude … rude … rude …"

I ask Duck, "Would you like to help me with my garden? I find it therapeutic to water, plant, fertilize."

"You must have a trillion things to do when you have three thousand feet of rooftop." He smirks. "I bet you have a million stories on the women you've had up here."

"Do you want to help me or not?"

"Sure, I'll help. Do you have a pair of gloves I can put on?"

"In the shed there's a pair you can use."

Duck runs off to get the gloves. It's as if he were Reid when my son was 3 or 4. I told Reid at the time, all three feet of him, to help me plant some impatiens. "I'm going with mommy to the park to play." I thought it was adorable. I was wrong. Not being stern certainly cost me a lamb chop or two. The other night Reid ate all six. Didn't leave me one.

Duck comes out of the shed, "I have a problem I have to deal with. Another police officer screwed up. I got to be leaving."

"Before you do, I want to say something. You asked me to make some suggestions on how to give your campaign some momentum. Let's get real, Donald, right now Biden is the front-runner."

Duck peers at me. "What are you saying? Sleepy Joe is senile. He can't remember his wife's name without using a teleprompter."

"Just the same, Biden is leading in all the polls. In 2016 you got lucky when Comey's outburst on Hillary went public. If it hadn't been for Comey's integrity..."

"Don't start giving that prick any medals. He wanted me dead. The only thing was he didn't have any balls. Instead of doing things from his gut, he got caught up in the fancy ideals he espouses – Patriotism...Honor...Truth...Guy like James Comey I eat for breakfast."

"Maybe so, Donald, but you asked me to make suggestions and I have one. I've been thinking out of the box. It's pretty radical."

"No, that's what I want, Singer. Remember, I knew you before you became civilized. Give me something you would have done when you were The Handicapper. Christ sake, you partnered with Haskell Gold and Isaac Becker, two of New York's great felons." Duck squints at me. "If you have an idea. Shoot!"

I hesitated. I knew what I was about to say I could never mention to Eleanor, she would never understand. But a part of me did want Duck re-elected. Even now as I write this it sounds sick to me. But the truth is I could live with Duck having a second term. I would be able to take advantage in so many murky financial ways. I won't go on. All I can say is, as civilized and content as this octogenarian is, there's still a breathing miscreant deep inside. I'm not close to dead or the man I want to be. It's always a war.

"I know how you think, Donald. As soon as RBG is gone you're going to nominate Amy Coney Barrett for the Court. You're licking your chops, praying that Ruth Ginsburg dies before the election. Barrett would give the Court a six to three conservative vote. And that's what you're masturbating for. No more legal gay marriages, no more Roe-Wade, Barrett would kill the Affordable Care Act. Damn, you would have the clout to strip healthcare from one hundred and thirty million Americans. You're probably having wet dreams every night thinking of the things that you can do if you get Amy Barrett on the Court."

"You're dead wrong, Singer. I'd rather think about micro than macro. It's more exciting."

"Stop the bullshit, Donald. Get real. It's my opinion the only chance you have of winning the election is to establish a sympathy vote. You must show the country that you are vulnerable. I have an idea."

"I'm listening."

"You fake having Covid-19. Make the public believe you're dying. Go into Walter Reed Medical Center. Spend two weeks there. People will see you as human. That's what you need. To change your image. The public will start crying for you. Lighting candles. The lawns of the White House will be flooded with thousands of people praying for you. They'll be standing at the gate and praying. Carrying get well placards I guarantee you, Donald, you do what I'm saying, and you'll have twice as good a shot at winning the election as you do right now."

"Singer, that's a great idea. Great. You're a genius. Why didn't my people think of that? Look, I got to go but I'll call you later. You know, Singer," he half smiles, "you're just about the only friend. I have."

I stared down Duck. I wasn't a coward. At least I didn't think I was. But here I was at the same time equivocating. I knew I wasn't intimidated by the fat fuck. It was just that I wanted to keep our relationship intact. What do you call that, covering your own ass, as his cowering GOP does? Anyway, I felt ashamed of my dishonesty. My ingenuous glibness. My inability to spit out what I was really thinking. And then, for some inexplicable reason, don't ask me why, I thought of my father's brother. My Uncle Tommy. Did I ever tell you about my Uncle Tommy? At 18 he joined up to fight the Nazis. He was a combat soldier stationed west of the Rhine, near a French village. He saved fourteen French lives. Killed twenty-seven Nazi soldiers. He was wounded twice. Came home with two Purple Hearts. The Bronze Star. When he returned to New York he met, at a soldier's dance, Kitty Pollen. They played tennis a lot and then he became a professional fighter. He sparred with Rocky Graziano and was in the ring with the great Sugar Ray. "I lasted four rounds with Robinson, Robert. I'm proud of that. The referee, I think it was Ruby Goldstein, stopped the fight with me ready to collapse, my arms draped over the ring ropes. I had nothing left. Ray came over to me and gave me a hug. He said, 'You got a hell of a right hand, buddy.' I think it was the proudest moment of my life."

After my uncle's boxing career ended, he married Kitty Pollen. They continued to play a great deal of tennis and my uncle ended up the manager and bartender of his father-in-law's deli in the Bronx. The deli-bar was located two blocks from old Yankee Stadium. I think off Jerome Avenue and 163rd Street. One afternoon, after the Yankees beat the Saint Louis Browns in a game, Vic Raschi out-dueled Ned Garver two to one. Dick Kokos, the Brownie outfielder, hit a solo home run over the 344-foot sign in right field. I wasn't there but you could ask me about any Yankee game that season and I could tell you more about it than the sports columnist Jimmy Powers or, for that matter, the voice of the Yankees, Mel Allen. Later that afternoon, at Pollen's Deli and Bar, two Black guys walked in with guns out. My uncle, in his white apron, jumped in front of two female customers to shield them. He took three slugs to his chest, one to his groin. My uncle still came at those guys. They panicked. Ran out of the deli into the street. My uncle ran after them. He collapsed in front of the deli. Was taken to Harlem Hospital. The two men got away. They disappeared, blending in with the crowd leaving Yankee Stadium. That day there was a doubleheader and the second game had just ended. My Uncle Tommy died the next morning at the hospital. That's all I want to say about my uncle other than that, when I was a boy, I had heroes like Mickey Mantle and Dr. Bobby Brown and then I had a real hero, my Uncle Tommy.

Now let's get back to Duck. I'm staring him down. I'm no coward, as I said. I'm glowering at him as he steps over an antique end table, reaches down, picks up the *New York Post*. Duck stood there not three yards from me, still look-ing as mad as Lear. I was about to tell him that with his attitude and weapons he could ruin the electoral process. How wrong it was to encourage divisiveness. How his kind of thinking was un-American. His rage increased when he heard me utter "Black Lives Matter." I was fully aware that POTUS was cognizant that he could lie and distort as much as he wanted. That is until free harbor time sets in. That was when his lies would become a criminal act. The law and the Constitution protect all American citizens from that moment on. My Uncle Tommy, I like to think, fought for that. Duck stood in front of me, oblivious to right from wrong. As clueless as he was when I told him how I felt goosebumps and butterflies the first time I called Victoria up for a date. You know what Duck said to me? "The only thing I ever experienced with a woman was my prick throbbing." He didn't even smile or smirk when he said this! It was his bottom line when it came to females. Duck is without a doubt, categorically, inimically, self-absorbed. A one-of-a-kind odious leader. A POTUS who is completely, *completely* indifferent to everything but his own needs and wants. Duck reached for the *New York Post*. On the front page in bold print the newspaper was exposing a Catholic priest who committed several sex abuse violations against a 9-year-old boy. Duck squinted at the front page. Then, without as much as a blink, he said, "I'm going to win the election." He exclaimed this once, twice, a third time. His voice unwavering. Determined, perhaps a trite hysterical. He then glared at me in defiance, as if I were the enemy. He glanced again at the *Post* headline. Uttered to himself, I would rip the cock off that Catholic priest. I responded by commenting that it wasn't only Catholic priests. It was everyone. Anyone, that when I was a small boy, almost ten, I, too, was sexually abused.

I remember the date because it was the day the legendary Josh Gibson died. The iconic catcher for the Homestead Grays in the Negro League. Josh Gibson had hit over eight hundred home runs and had a lifetime batting average of .359 playing in the Negro Leagues. And was probably as great if not better a player than Babe Ruth. It's not far-fetched to think that Gibson was at least the equal of Ruth. Yet, Gibson died at 36 of alcohol poisoning. Eaten up inside because he never got the opportunity in the Major Leagues. "Black Lives Matter, Duck," I cried out. It came out of nowhere. Out of everywhere. It wasn't only me crying out; it was so much more than me. And then I started to talk about Rabbi Steven Seif and how he abused me. It was at my father's shul. The services were about to commence. It was early morning. My twin and I were seated in the first row on the right side of the synagogue, where there was a private exit door that my father the cantor, the head rabbi and the assistant rabbi, Steven Seif, the sexton and some of the high and mighty wealthy donors had the privilege of using to get to an inner sanctuary to go over the class schedule or relax and chat or, if need be, go down the hallway where there was a toilet and urinal. I had left my seat in the temple to use the urinal. When I got there, I unzipped my fly. Rabbi Seif barked out, "Freeze! Young man," he commanded, "on Monday afternoon when your Hebrew classes are over, I want you to come to my office." Rabbi Seif was in charge of the Hebrew School. "Come alone. Don't tell anyone. Not your father or mother or your twin brother. Do you understand my instructions?" he barked.

On Monday after Talmud classes I showed up at Rabbi Self's office with my Hank Greenberg Louisville Slugger baseball bat. You might not believe it but even then I could swing that heavy lumber pretty damn good, especially if I choked up six inches. When Rabbi Seif asked me to open his fly I swung my bat at him, bruising his knees and shins. Then I darted out of his office. I felt as mighty as Josh Gibson must have felt when he hit that baseball that was alleged to have left Yankee Stadium, traveling over the left field roof. It's an impossible feat but I believe if anyone could have done it, it was Josh Gibson. I believed it for years. What do you think?

When I told my father what had happened in Rabbi Seif's office, my dad grabbed my hand and ran with me the twenty blocks from our home on West End Avenue to Rabbi Seif's office at the Talmud Torah. The cantor looked as berserk as Duck does at times. At the rabbi's office, my father didn't wait. He started flailing his tender fists at Rabbi Seif as if he were the Manassa Mauler and the Brown Bomber all in one. Two days later Rabbi Steven Seif was dismissed by the synagogue. Looking back, the Trustees should have had Rabbi Seif put in prison, but they failed to do so. They never brought criminal charges. To this day he might be working at a Hebrew School. Of course, he'd be over one hundred years old if he were still alive so it's unlikely. But Rabbi Seif could have worked at another synagogue or Hebrew School for at least another thirty years and abused countless more children. My point is it wasn't only the Catholics that protected their own. It was all of us. And it still goes on. Even my own father and the head rabbi buried what happened to me. They all swept it under the rug. Things are changing but multitudes of these wounded offenders got away with hurting children. Of course, at the time it happened, I was elated by my father's actions. The way he confronted Rabbi Seif. I had never seen my father that irate. Never would again. But that winter day he was my all-time American hero. By the time evening came, my dad had calmed down. I recall him coming into the twins' room and telling my brother and me, "It's not Catholics or Jews or Protestants or Germans or Blacks or Whites or Hispanics or Asians or poor people or rich people, it's all people," he said. "Most are healthy, some are sick. You must learn to distinguish one from the other and you must stay away from those that are sick. Of course, if you or your brother wants to go into medicine, become physicians, I would like it very much. Yes, if you or Richie wants to study medicine to become a physician, I would like that very much."

I glared at Duck. He didn't utter a sound. Then, rather than comment on what he read in the *New York Post* or on what I told him had happened to me in '47, he abruptly changed the subject. First, he said something that to me sounded incredulous. "The only thing my dad ever advised me to do was to go into business. Make money. In our home, that was everything. Making a buck." Then he shouted, "I hate to lose. And I'm not going to. I know what I need to do to win. You can wager every dollar you have that I'll be doing just that."

After that, Duck sort of cleared his throat and returned to a calmer demeanor. "Singer," Duck said, "there's no such thing as a false narrative. All that garbage that Black lives matter, that law enforcement targets Blacks, the B.S. being said by Democrats and liberals that I'm not paying attention to Covid-19. Screw all of it. The first thing is I got to win this election. That's all that counts right now. The other stuff don't mean a thing unless I win. That's the only thing that counts right now." He stared out of the window at Central Park for a long while. "Nothing will stand in my way. Nothing!" he uttered.

Ten minutes later Lear was gone. Caesar was back on the throne and things returned to almost normal. At least back to what they had been. And then Duck asked, "Did you really get goosebumps and butterflies when you called Victoria that first time?" He paused for a moment and said, "I guess a part of me envies that."

I really miss going to Porterhouse, the upscale steakhouse in the Time Warner building. Having a cowboy steak, B.S.-ing with Bruce Willis, cavorting with the billionaire crowd. Men like Mr. Hudson Yards and Lloyd Blankfein. Men who seem to always wear a half-smile of attainment and slight contempt. Even more than them I miss The Grey Eagle, Tim Brown. Tim's the manager of the restaurant. Of course, "The Grey Eagle" was Tris Speaker's moniker. Speaker was before my time, though I did meet him once. I must have been all of 13. He was coming out of a midtown hotel where many of the Hall-of-Famers of yesteryear had gathered to celebrate something to do with Cooperstown. It wasn't an induction ceremony. Anyway, when I read in *The New York Times* that these Hall-of-Famers would be at the hotel, I hustled down there and waited on the street; it was a bitter cold winter night and I waited and waited and waited for these iconic men to finish their food and drink, come back into the freezing cold. I remember I was unable to speak when Ty Cobb appeared. All I could do was hand him my autograph book, nod at him to sign. Players like Babe Ruth and Mickey Cochrane started spilling out into the snow. Then it was Jimmie Foxx and Mel Ott and Lefty Grove and Jim Thorpe. Jim Thorpe really got to me. I had heard about Thorpe my whole life. He was my dad's all-time favorite athlete. When Thorpe appeared on that bitter cold night and took the time to ask my name, shake my hand, tell me, "Boy! Whatever you do give it the best you have to give. This is America. Anything's possible!" Well, that's all it took for me to believe …

It must be 49 years now since I gave those autographs to my parents' cleaning woman's son. I should have kept them for Reid. No, my son wouldn't want them. He has little interest in baseball. He's not interested in so many of the things that inspired me. Eleanor explained it to me, "Kids don't idealize or hero-worship any longer. Reid lives in a different world than the one you grew up in."

It was four in the morning. I was pacing around. One of those nights when I couldn't sleep. Been having a lot of them lately. I ended up near Reids's bedroom. He was on Snapchat with his brainy buddies. They were playing some kind of game. Each of them particularizing ways they would assassinate Duck.

The thing is, Reid is minimalistic. At least with me he is. If he utters twenty words in a day to me it's a lot. And here he is at four in the morning, alive, alert, voluble, spelling out Duck's death. It sounded as if he and his robotics team pals were having at least as much fun doing so as I did when playing basketball for my Commerce High School team. I mean these teenagers are nerdy, bright, overly rational, high achievers, wired tight. Maybe they are disillusioned with the way things are going but... I've read enough books, seen enough movies to know that... when I hear Reid say, "The president is responsible for sixty thousand deaths by taking Covid lightly. Now he's reopening. He's defying the experts." And then I hear one of his pals say, "He's not the most detailed policy person. I know that it's hard to separate policy from..." And then Reid says, "He's like my dad. He's all Me!... Me!... Me!"

Sometimes it is difficult for me to open my eyes, to brush my teeth, gargle with mouthwash, start the day. Today was that kind of day. I wanted to stay in bed with Eleanor. I didn't. What am I doing here? Living life in a blur. Watching the days peel by. It already feels to me as if I've been here for a lifetime. As for my twin, it's the first time Dick is out of the City this long since he went to the Frankfurt Book Fair with me in '76. At the fair, we were introduced to Max Frisch, Gunter Grass, Peter Handke. I wasn't tongue-tied with any of them. Dick didn't go mum either. Both of us felt we belonged. Now I know the truth. Dick belonged. I didn't. When I dwell on that I become real weary. I realize that I'm not only atavistic but also without possibility. In today's digital world, who actually cares about writing a novel or even reading a novel? Doing good or even bad work? Perhaps it's indulgent of me to put these thoughts on paper, especially now when I should be concerned with Reid. My son has been on my mind for days now. Should

I continue to bring up what he and his friends are discussing? Is Duck in danger? And then I place these thoughts in the same place I've placed so many other dilatory mishaps of mine of late. I file them for another day. More than ever, I do. I sneak looks at Reid, though. He has a nice face, a good face. He doesn't have a cynical smile, nor is he a born salesman. And he doesn't prevaricate. The more I try and put these thoughts together, the less I can think it through.

While we've been in North Salem, Wednesday nights have been theatre nights. We've been watching several classics, from *Long Day's Journey* with Katharine Hepburn (she stole the show) to *King Lear* to Oscar Wilde's *Ernest*. "Ugh," was Reid's reaction to Ernie. Eleanor quietly left the room. Tonight we watched a more earthy English prototype. John Osborne's *Look Back in Anger*. Reid seemed to identify with Jimmy Porter. He stayed alert from beginning to end. When it was over, I tried to talk to my son. I was as feeble as ever.

"Ba, I believe everything can be scientifically proven. If not now, one day!"

I couldn't help myself. You might even say I was compelled to quote Hamlet. "There are more things in heaven and earth than are dreamt of in your philosophy."

As soon as I uttered those words I knew I had erred. Reid stared at me. Then he rolled his eyes and marched out of the room and that was that.

When my son was little, I would tell him, "What's important is to stand on your own two feet. Find out what you love. Follow your own truth. Not hurt anyone. Know in your heart what's right from wrong."

"Ba," my son would say, "I know all that."

"Ba, did you hear what Trump is saying? ... 'You must go to church. I'm ordering it. America needs our prayers.'"

"He's slipping with his evangelicals. He must do something."

"Ba, his identifying houses of worship as essential is dangerous. He's more of a Sunday golfer than a church-goer. Ba, I forgot to tell you. I quit the robotics team. I just couldn't get along with those guys. They just don't see things like I do. The truth is I think they're closet Trump guys without the guts to admit it."

At today's Sunday brunch Dick told us of Margaret Kerr. "When I was 32, I met Margaret. She was a friend of Kevin Lynch. Remember Kevin? He was one of my gay neighbors. He worked for Sotheby's. A great guy. Margaret would come over to his place all the time. That's how we got to know each other. She was Seven Sister School to a T – a debutante, in the Social Register, yet for one reason or another she liked me, and I sort of fell in love with her. I got more serious on each of our dates. Then when I finally had the guts to tell her how I felt, she said, 'Dick, I have to tell you. I've been raised for one kind of life, one kind of husband. I'm sorry but that's who I am. You're an artist. A writer. You want to create meaningful fiction. You'll never compromise your values. You'll get bored with me as soon as I turn real.' I went back to my dance clubs with my friend, Mr. Popper."

It is not until after my first draft is finished that I start thinking about run-on sentences, grammar, syntax, repetitions, begin paying attention to detail. That's when my words will be typed on a computer. The draft will need proofreading, line editing. This entire manuscript will get a whiff of some expensive perfume. Dick just barged into the room. He's upset because I read his manuscript and told him it should be called, "The Man Who Never Grew Up."

His response was typical, "Robert you're not a writer!" he exclaimed. You never put in the effort. You're a coward." You must understand my brother. Never once has he acknowledged my handicapping prowess, never thought it was anything more than my way of avoiding meaningful work.

Here's a page I wrote all the way back on April 27th: New York might be turning the corner. Numbers reflect a leveling off. The Naval hospital ship, COMFORT, has reported one of its sailors has tested positive.

Here's a page from April 28th: It's a direct quote from a registered nurse at Harlem Hospital. "We're terrified to get up in the morning. We know where we are going. What's in store for some of us. Many colleagues have called in sick. Many have already died. I'm still going to work. Each day I start counting twenty-five more before Covid-19 manifests itself... Each day I start counting to twenty-five."

Workers at Walmart, Trader Joe's and a thousand bodegas have died. I went to my desk and wrote checks out to "No Kids Hungry." "Community Pantry."

Some countries have been successful in flattening the curve. Others haven't. In Brazil people are dying in the streets. Two who died were cousins of our housekeeper, Karina Lopez. In London, Prime Minister Boris Johnson received oxygen. It's now two months later. He has recovered.

In Florida the number of cases reached … Like Italy, it's one of the oldest communities in America. Walter Li called last night. He's visiting friends in Palm Beach. "Why aren't people following the law? They must wear face masks. It's a crime not to and this crime will have serious consequences. It will cause other people's deaths."

Took a forty-minute nap in the middle of the day. Most of the time forty minutes will suffice. Now I'm refreshed and ready to write. The truth is, I haven't been feeling like myself lately. Can't expect ten more years any longer. Five is probably stretching it. Don't tell Eleanor. She'll start to sob.

When I first sat down to write, my mindset was to say something on the way Duck has been dealing with African Americans. Then I had second thoughts. I realized it's not worth commenting on. Everyone with a pen is doing it. Duck is losing it and if you don't agree, you should have heard our conversation earlier this morning. No, I'm not going to speak about that either. What's the sense? I've said enough about Duck's lame character. The one thing that nobody's commented on is his hideous hair.

Today I took a long stroll on our property. Unbelievable how I am noticing things that I'd never been aware of before. Pebbles, rocks, boulders, a small brook. I ran into three deer. They weren't startled by me at all. During my walk all I saw was beauty. All I heard was the tweeting of birds. It was more impressive than all the noise being bellowed by all the Ducks. That's what impressed me most of all. I gazed up at the trees, so tall, so majestic. It was as if I were discovering a rainforest. For me it all came together. It was the kind of experience all New Yorkers should have. Nature is so much more than accomplishments, celebrity, glory, trinkets, power plays, the deals we make, accumulations, ego. I felt some kind of obligation to run back to the house to tell Eleanor how I felt. The first thing out of my wife's mouth was, "I signed the contract with my publisher. It's official – *The Calcium Connection* is going to be published this winter."

Eleanor is definitely deserving. She gave her calcium ATPase book four years of superhuman effort. I couldn't be prouder of my wife. It was only after hugging and congratulating her that I asked her if she wanted to take a walk in the woods with me.

"I'm much too busy," she said.

I'm expecting a visit from Omkar BeHarry today. He's driving up from the City to deliver one of my reconditioned typewriters. More important is that BeHarry is bringing my mail from 1818. That means a fresh supply of blank checks. I've already used up the ones I have here.

I can continue helping people. So many friends, building workers, acquaintances in need. Writing checks I realize is a whole lot more important than pounding. As I tap these keys to register this point, I think of a time I failed to help – a friend of mine, Ralph Evans, who desperately needed my assistance. It was college basketball season. I was too involved with my own bilge to care. I couldn't hear or see or give a damn about Ralph Evans; couldn't give a damn about anyone but me in those days. Everything was me. Everything was "making it;" everything was dollar bills; climbing Mount Gamble; collecting and winning and collecting and winning more…more…more…I was famished, empty, blind. I just didn't have anything to give Ralph Evans. He'd been a friend of mine all the way back to Public School 54. We had grown up together, yet when he knocked on my door, so terribly in need, I had nothing to share with him. To me he was just one of the anonymous servicemen coming home from Vietnam. Ralph Evans had nowhere else to turn. He was as hopeless, as powerless, as reeking with misery as so many of the other Vietnam veterans were at the time. As much as so many people all over the globe are today. Despair and hopelessness, people are powerless from New York City to Ho Chi Minh City. Yes, it's different today than what Ralph Evans went through. But not that different. Things change and stay the same. Things change and don't always get better. Possibly my checks can help a few. At the least, giving them out is making me feel a whole lot better.

"…You got such a terrible break. The virus, the Blacks, the police, the economy, the election coming up. It's an impossible situation. No one could deal with it. Of course, you're going nuts."

"You're one of only two people that understand. If I didn't have you to talk to and Edna, did I tell you about Edna? She's a 97-year-old woman I have coffee with every Wednesday. Edna was my nanny when I was a child. The one person outside of you that I can talk to. Without you two I'd be going bananas."

"Poor Donald," I said, patting his head.

"…No one saw me. I wore a mask. A Green Bay Packer cap. I used the key you gave me. I just had to get away."

Duck's visit came after two WNBC analysts had been pretty rough on him. Eugene Robinson was one of them. Robinson is a fellow I've admired for years. He's grounded, thoughtful, extremely intelligent, thinks before he comments, struggles to be fair. Robinson said, "Duck is a hyperactive Twitter troll." Steve Schmidt is a political strategist. "The United States has never had a president who has performed this badly in a crisis of this magnitude…"

Reid is also furious. "Ba, don't you realize he's causing fatalities because of his stupidity. Wearing a mask protects others. Do you realize how many people will say, if the President isn't wearing a mask, I don't have to, either."

According to the latest studies, Duck's not wearing a mask could cost as many as thirty-six thousand more deaths.

When I returned to Justice Lane, the first thing I was going to tell Reid is that Duck wore a mask. No, I won't. I haven't told my family about these clandestine meetings with Duck. Besides, Duck only wore a mask today because I insisted.

'Thanks, Singer, for meeting me today."

"I see you've put on a lot more weight. Look at you. You can't even button your jacket."

"I didn't come here to be insulted. I know I've put on a few pounds. It's not only you. Edna, too, keeps reminding me to watch what I'm eating. This stuff is getting to me. It would kill a lesser man. I'm not going to let it kill me. The way I figure it, Singer, is it's a war. I'm the number one target. Did you ever see those old boxing film clips of Joe Louis and Max Schmeling? Not the first fight... the second. I've always thought of myself as Joe Louis in that fight. Schmeling never had a chance. Louis took no prisoners."

"Joe Biden isn't Schmeling and you're not going to knock out the coronavirus without a vaccine."

Duck and I had been spending more and more time together. We've been jabbering a great deal. I even showed him some of the pages I wrote that put him down. You would be surprised at how much the President can take if condemnations are presented in the right way. He is not always defensive. Sometimes he reminded me of Reid when my son was nine. I'd let Reid have his temper tantrums then I'd step in and give him some love. Patience and stroking do the trick. Is the President really that different from any of us?

"You should come over here more often. Tend the garden. The only one you'll have to avoid is the night porter. Wear a mask. Your Green Bay cap. Camacho will never know it's you."

"What the hell do you think I've been doing? I hate masks." Duck paused, "I'm not worried about the night porter. It's Hillary Lauren I have to avoid. She's trouble! As for gardening, I told you, I enjoy yardwork. I find it relaxing."

There wasn't one word that I said that wasn't hollow. You can say I was fawning. I certainly took advantage of Duck's pathological need for flattery.

"One thing I've always envied about you," I said more than once, "you've lived your entire life by dominating the less fortunate and these people obviously survived by allowing you to dominate." Most of the time, Duck would look at me with a smug curl to his lower lip.

Later on, I became more direct. "The night we ran into each other at Eden Roc, I left Victoria for a minute or two. Anyway, my question is, while I was gone, did you come on to Victoria? Victoria said you tried to feel her ass."

"You asking this man to man?"

"I wouldn't hold it against you. I did a whole lot worse. I'm curious. That's all."

"Your wife was a beautiful woman." Duck paused. "Listen Singer, as far as Victoria goes, she came on to *me*. She kept telling me what a loser you were. She said all you did was bet on ballgames. She begged me to rescue her. That's the truth."

A few minutes later we started to discuss Joe Biden.

"I told you I don't have to worry about Smokey Joe. I got the podium, not him."

"I know Biden can't get out there with the same volume as you but the things you have been doing of late. They're costing you."

"My base still loves me. Besides, you know what I've discovered my greatest strength is? It's that I'm unpredictable. Those media assholes will never figure out the best way to attack me. I'm like a great dancer. I'm there and then I'm not. I'm all over the place."

I thought of two subjects I would have liked to bring up – assault weapons and the right to choose. I didn't. I knew it would be futile. We continued conversing. Most of the time, Duck either skirted the issues or made light of them. It wasn't because he was defensive. I think it was because the nature of things is such that you can only cover so much territory. I brought up, "You've done nothing to expand your base." And then I hit a nerve, "U.S. deaths have gone over one hundred and fifty thousand."

"I've done a great job!" he shouted. "I've held deaths under five hundred thousand. In my opinion, that's doing a great job." He took another long swallow of juice. "That's what people just don't understand."

Duck seemed hurt when I mentioned that if he had taken action just one or two weeks earlier, he would have saved…

"Singer, do me a favor. Pour me some more juice and do you have a bag of peanuts? I want some to keep in my car."

I was surprised more and more on how on top of certain facts he was. No doubt he had a sharp brain. I told myself there is something human in Duck. He can make you laugh or cry. I realized that this election was going to be close. Duck had his base and more than likely there was a strong possibility his base could grow.

Duck glared at a photograph on my desk. "Who are the Black guys with you?" he asked in a judgmental tone.

"That's Cal Ramsey and Satch Sanders. They're friends of mine."

"Boy, Singer, you really have a thing for Blacks."

I bit my lip. Tried to hold myself together.

"Come on, Singer, don't get pissed. I have nothing against Blacks who play professional sports."

Here's where I found my balls. "I won't be seeing you again."

"Why?" he sputtered.

You're a fucking racist," I said.

Duck looked at me with the kind of shock a man has on his face when he's told without warning that he's been fired. He was!

"… Donny was always an insecure child. From the first day I cared for him, he was difficult. He wet his bed, he made in his pants, he had temper tantrums, there wasn't one day I had it easy."

I was speaking to 97-year-old Edna Litwos, the former governess of Duck. I was astonished when the President showed up the next day with his former Nanny.

"I thought you would like to meet Edna and she was determined to meet you. Hope you don't mind, Singer."

The hunchbacked woman had hennaed hair with massive spots of scalp being exposed on the front of her dome. Her tufts of bleached hair were cropped as short as the crewcut owned by Moose Skowron when he played first base with the New York Yankees. The old woman had several teeth missing in the front of her mouth – yet was still more than capable of making herself understood. Once she took off the faded, lime-green, cloth coat, her mottled arms were exposed, which seemed to be eaten alive from within by some unknown fungus; but this ancient chalk-white woman in my suite seemed to be having a great time with

Duck and me. She answered question after question that I brought up concerning Duck, "He was a handful alright, Mr. Singer. When Donny was 5, his mother called him into the bedroom. He was having a playdate at the time, in his nursery. Well, little Donny tracked into his mother's bedroom with this 5-year-old child and he says to the child, 'let's play…' Then he tells the little girl to climb on top of his mother's bed and when she does, he jumps on top of her and starts rubbing himself against her. It was right then that I knew what type of man he was going to be."

Edna grinned. Duck beamed. It was obvious that Edna Litwos was the one person in the totality of "Duck world" that he allowed himself to feel vulnerable with. Before I knew it, Edna was in my kitchen pulling some deli out of the fridge. Duck took it as matter-of-factly as if he was still a child. Edna seemed more than happy to serve.

I hadn't been in the proximity of a 97-year-old woman in seventy-two years. The last time I recollect was when I was still working for the Welfare Department in 1958. The client was Helen Treetop, a Native American woman who was a descendent of the Apache tribe. Helen Treetop had been in a teepee with the Indian leader, Geronimo, 1829-1909. She told me that the Indian warrior was a terrible lover, that he was cruel and always in bad temper.

Edna said, "I was 18 when I left Warsaw for America, Mr. Singer. My parents and I were real close to the Warsaw Ghetto. They hated it. I despised it. Those Jewish people were dumped on us and who wants to live near garbage?" I bit my lip. Duck didn't react. On Edna's brow you could see blue veins bulging and imagine certitude, bias, narrow-mindedness pouring. She was a woman who combined the kind of animal strength and non-reflective instincts a draft animal has to keep going. For the way Edna Litwos related to Duck, it was as if she had been an employee of his firm for thirty, forty, even fifty years, and now felt as if she had titled ownership. Nothing about Duck being POTUS phased her. To Edna he was still little Donny.

A few minutes later, Edna Litwos and DT passed the kind of quick look my twin and I have shared a million times. The kind that says, "I know…what do you think? Do you agree that we should allocate this private moment to a stranger…?" Duck and Edna apparently agreed to: "When Donny was 13, I was, let me count…" On her knobbed fingers, Edna computed. "I must have been 37. One night Donny knocked on my door. It was well past midnight. In those days, I slept without any clothes on, not a stitch. Donny opened my door, stood there. I remember it as if it were yesterday, Mr. Singer. I asked him, 'What's the matter, Donny? What is it?' He just peered at me. I was under the covers, mind you. He just stared and I knew what it was. I might be an uneducated woman, but I know that look. I peeled off the blanket I had covering me. Donny slowly approached my bed. I reached out for his hand. Hoisted him in my bed. That was Donny's first time. Wasn't it, Donny?" I turned my head towards Duck. He had a look on his face that almost seemed to me as if he had regressed to being 13. Duck stood there gazing at Edna. Then tears came to his blue eyes. "Edna," he whispered in a husky voice. "Edna, Edna." That's all that he rasped. Edna smiled and quietly walked into the kitchen. Duck wandered to the terrace and a moment later disappeared as he paced the rooftop. Approximately fifteen minutes later we entered my study. Edna matter-of-factly went on doing several banal chores that had occupied her before this story was unveiled. I left it there. It was obviously a powerful experience that they had shared. I felt it awkward that it had been revealed to me. To this very day, I can't fathom why Edna Litwos chose to mention this intimate moment or why Duck allowed it, but I'm glad I have become privy to that adventure in our president's history.

As I said, Edna returned to the kitchen and soon started making more deli sandwiches for Duck and me. It didn't seem to me as if this woman ever stopped keeping busy. She was one of those people who always can find something to do. Furthermore, it seemed as if she expected to keep doing so for another 97 years.

Edna Litwos and Duck stayed for another hour. I continued listening as Edna told baby Duck stories one after another, several of them worth repeating. Later in the day, after Edna Litwos and Duck left, I was still feeling sort of privileged that I was confided in to the extent that I was. I also felt a bit queer as it was clear to me now that Duck had been in good faith in the way that he had related to me while I was the one in bad faith, betraying Duck as if I were a Judas. I was the one using him.

Today I started writing at five in the morning. Reid says it's nuts. "I have to start early, Kiddo. My mind conks out by three in the afternoon."

Now that I've completed my day's work, I'm having something to eat – some leftover steak, 25 percent of an overripe cantaloupe. I'm following Eleanor's orders. She's demanding I lose weight. After the steak I put on my gym pants and Nikes. Eleanor is also insisting that I exercise. I did ten minutes of pedaling, five pushups, lifted 10-pound weights. Then my wife and I walked to the guest house, sat down on a bench in the back where, from the porch, you can see the woods, the corral, our basketball court. Eleanor remained with me for a while, then she returned to the big house to do some chores. Now I'm waiting for chipmunks to make an appearance. Have cashew nuts in my pocket. They never showed. It was the first day that the weather went over ninety. Chipmunks prefer staying under rocks and boulders when the weather turns torrid.

I'm still learning little things, big things. I'm still making an effort to move forward.

Now I'm writing checks. Paying my 1818 rent for July, August, and September. I'm also writing a check for Geraldo Camacho. He's been watering my terrace, pruning the greenery, doing other odd jobs when necessary. Later today Omkar BeHarry is delivering six pair of socks; ten ballpoint pens; 3-hole paper; some red, black, and blue flair pens; twelve bottles of rubbing alcohol; two bottles of iodine; my lime-colored summer slacks; a pair of swimming shorts for Dick; several of Eleanor's summer dresses; Reid's certificate of title for his Vox. Eleanor is rewarding Reid for his 4.0 by trading in the Vox. Purchasing an Alfa Romero for him. BeHarry is also bringing up a reconditioned Coronamatic 7000 that he picked up for me at Gramercy Typewriter Company, then he's returning to the City with my Smith-Corona 8000 that broke down this week. "Don't forget to get some typewriter ribbons and to wear a mask," I reminded BeHarry when we spoke earlier. I also spoke to Ralph Evans' granddaughter, "Don't think of it as a handout to pay off your student loan. It is to honor your grandfather's service in Vietnam." Life is pleasant and unpleasant things, dealing with disaster. Eleanor is here. Reid is here. Dick is here. They're all safe. Am I lucky or what?

If I learned anything during my lifetime, it's that 1 percent of this country has too much. 99 percent have too little.

The vision to make it large is something few people have. The situation we find ourselves in might define most men, but I still believe a man can reinvent his life. Sadly, most people stop dancing, dreaming, singing their song by the time they reach 30. People learn to settle. If a man has a modicum of good fortune, he'll find a wife that will probably bore the life out of him, no less than he will bore the life out of her. This is reality. There are variations on the theme, but very few that are foolproof.

One person is dying in America every two minutes. Stay inside; stay six feet apart; don't think Black, Brown, White, Yellow or Red. Think we're all in this together! Maybe that's our one comfort zone!

I'm worried about Eleanor. She has had bad days before, at various times she's retreated into herself, within three or four days through, she's always returned. Now I'm terrified that this engulfment is too much for her. Her nerves are raw. She's irritable all the time. She's taking walks by herself, avoiding communication, going to bed by seven. I would like to rationalize her behavior by telling myself that all married couples go through difficult stages.

"Eleanor, I realize that you're feeling overwhelmed. That you need some space. Why don't I go into the City for a few days?"

"You can't do that. It wouldn't be safe. All this would have been wasted."

Whatever I suggested was knocked down.

"I'm just tired. I haven't been sleeping well. Last night I was up all night. It's the unpredictability of our situation. The fact that we could be stuck here for the next three years. I will not be seeing my family. I have not seen my friends. I've stopped working on my book. All I'm doing is cooking dinners, cleaning the house, taking care of Reid and you. You're not complaining. Why should you? You're oblivious to all that I have to do. You spend nine hours a day on your book then you watch Westerns on TV. Everything is left up to me. You do nothing to help me. This life we're living is not a life at all. Don't you understand that? It's not living. It's just waiting and hoping that one day it will all be over, and we can go back to what we were doing before. I need that, Robert. I need what we had before."

Today I made an inexcusable mistake. "Eleanor," I said, "with the City having reopened I'll be able to return during the week."

My wife stared at me. "You can't return to the City till all of this is over," she stammered. "Until there's a vaccine.

We can't take the chance. Robert, 40 percent of people hospitalized at your age … what happens if you get sick! What happens if you need to be hospitalized! What happens if you have to be put on a ventilator! I won't be with you. I won't be able to hold your hand. I won't be able to say goodbye. Reid won't …"

Eleanor started to sob. Tears flooded her face.

"Please stop crying, Eleanor. I've had twenty-one years I could never have imagined. Anything left is gravy. Besides, I'm not going anywhere. If I do, Reid will be with you. Your friends. Your sister."

"I can't lose you, Rob. I wouldn't want to live without you. You can't go to the City. Promise me you'll stay here until it's safe. Promise me, Rob. Promise me …"

I come downstairs to get to my novel. I sit in front of the typewriter. The first thought I have is that I'm weary. Before I begin the day I'm fatigued. I'm not going to whine and remind you that I'm the old man in the book, but it has been a struggle to get up early every morning. To work to three, four or five. I'm not close to what I once was. There was a time I could write for fourteen straight hours, then party all night. Now it's so different. It's as if my body has betrayed me. There's hardly anything left. I feel it from the time I wake till the time I hit the pillow. I just don't have much strength left any longer. At the dinner table I don't eat more than half the food Eleanor pushes in front of me. Don't have the energy to watch much TV, take long walks. Managing the steps to our bedroom has become a huge chore. I don't have the stamina needed to keep writing, yet I do keep writing. I have the end of this first draft in sight.

"I'm not quitting now, Eleanor. I'm too close to the finish line."

"I'm proud of you, Robert. In your own way you're teaching Reid a lesson that he'll keep for a lifetime."

Every night before I collapse into my warm bed, a soft pillow, my quilt, I ask myself why I keep going. I have no good answer – but I do.

People are still suffering. All over the globe there is still an urgent need for body bags. At a New York City living facility fifteen people came with their pillows and toothbrushes. They were healthcare workers to stay *not* overnight, but till this plague is over, to take care of people who were in need 24/7. Those helpers don't have college diplomas, Ivy League education. They are first generation people for the most part: people of color. Immigrants. People without creature comforts. They left their own overcrowded homes, stepped up and right now, today and tomorrow, are helping the autistic, the blind, the sick. People who can't help themselves. "I'm so glad I'm a nurse. We're all supporting each other. We're really like family," Rodney Parker's granddaughter said.

Eleanor just called me into the kitchen. "Look," she groused as she pointed to a white marble tabletop that I'd scratched while slicing an apple. I'm not being a jerk in pointing this out. Just showing that we're still alive and as large and small and somewhere in between as we've always been. Reid is concerned that he can't find the focus he had at Georgia Tech. His last summer school exam he did poorly on. He's in a terrible mood. Eleanor and I both know what that means. Leave him alone. Just let him be.

Now Reid is wolfing down lamb chops. My son always has a good appetite. "Leave me a few," I shout.

As much as I reek with self-pity, I have to confess a fair share of me still feels like that 21-year-old who was handing out change to demoralized souls in East Harlem. I still feel as if I want to rush home to my mother's home-cooking, listen to my dad as he practices his scales, see Cal Ramsey boarding, talk basketball with Rodney Parker, and I still believe that people count for something and that just because I took a left turn instead of the conventional right, made much of my money by crook, doesn't necessarily mean that somewhere deep inside, as with many others I know, there isn't something that can be of assistance. Brother can you spare a dime.

I didn't get much in other than to tell Lisa Mendelowitz what I missed most was not baseball but the blue jays on my rooftop in the spring. Neither one of us mentioned what Reid keeps reminding me, "Secretary Mattis said that Duck is the first president in history who does not unite the people. He does not even try."

We continued chatting. "…People can now order drinks, along with food, as restaurants are setting up tables on the street. You can choose what you want. You can't sit down. I run in the Park every day amongst as nearly as many people as before. I don't always wear a mask when I'm exercising outside. But I do inside my building out of respect for the doormen and other tenants. My kids are having fun. We have a ten-foot plastic pool that just about squeezed into our balcony space. It's nothing like the one you have on your rooftop, but it will do. I'm cleaning and cooking and seeing my mother every day. She's doing great. She's off the ventilator. No, I'm not writing. My book will be coming out next spring. It took four years for me to find a publisher but that's okay. I found one. That's about it."

Omkar Bel Iarry drove up to deliver provisions. "Things have changed for the worse, Mr. Singer. This month twelve more tenants have moved out of 1818. One-third of the building is empty. Management is doing things you wouldn't believe. It begins at seven in the morning as soon as I begin my shift. It's my regular time, but Mike Nieves retired after thirty-two years. He went with his family to Florida, but first he had to hire a union lawyer to get his ten weeks of severance pay. They didn't want to pay him. Now they got me taking temperatures and making sure that delivery people wear masks, and nowadays every one of them guys has a chip on his shoulder. They all resent having to make deliveries to the rich white tenants. I tell them, don't blame me, get a different job if you don't like it. As for me, I tell them I might be light skinned, but my mother was blacker than you are. Another thing that's changed is that Marea's down the block, they got the City's permission for outdoor dining. Their customers are eating on the street. Marea did a pretty good job of setting it up. You should see how they're doing it. It's pretty cool."

"Any other changes?" BeHarry thought for a second. "All the veteran tenants are still here. It's the old tenants that have the good rents. Besides, they got nowhere else to go."

"...Hi, Robert. It's Walter. Got some bad news. The deal with those London people fell through. Their top offer was sixteen four. I told them I wouldn't take less than the twenty-three. We'll have to start all over again. I got some outfits in mind that might be interested. What about you? Can you think of anybody I can add to my list? Did I tell you Kana and I are building a lake on the ranch? We're going to be stocking it with fish, outboard boats, everything you can imagine outside of our youth. Oh, here's something else. Kana and the kids came up with this brilliant idea for my birthday. They're having a life-size statue made of me... not sure where we are going to place it. Maybe in front of the main house. Maybe near the hackberry trees at the side of the barn... I told you, Robert, I can't get involved in your homeless project. It's a rough time for me. I'm not liquid."

I'm not Picasso but over the years I've painted my fair share of characters. I grew to know them, stand beside them, look them in the eye, think of them as friends, but with Duck, it's as if he's remained a stranger. I never have been able to get inside his head. At that moment, Reid entered the room. "Hey, Ba, can I interrupt you for a minute? I need to talk." I had been writing for five straight hours. I was ready to take a break. "Ba, I decided to drop patent law as a summer class. It would be six hours in front of my laptop. I just don't think it's manageable. I need that time to study multivariable calculus and physics II electrostatics."

"You know what I always tell you, Reid. Make your own decisions. Mom feels the same way."

"I know, Ba. I just wanted to tell you what's going on."

"How are you doing in that history course you're taking?"

"I've learned more about political executions than I ever wanted to know. What I've found to be fascinating is the assassination of Heinrich Mueller. He was an industrialist during the Third Reich. Mueller was assassinated by a real clever guy. Want to know how the assassin did it? Every day Mueller would go to the same coffee house in downtown Berlin to have a pastry, read his newspaper. The assassin took a job at the coffee house. He planted a miniature chocolate on Mueller's dessert plate. Mueller loved chocolate. It was laced, of course. Pretty cool, huh, Ba?"

Our conversation sounds harmless. It worried me. Reid has been talking more and more to me. Good? No! He's been speaking constantly about regicide and assassinations. When he watches TV, he takes notes on Duck. When Duck appears, he stares at him with this weird look on his face. Last night Eleanor was talking about how we met. She started elaborating on all our years together. Mostly good, but that's not the point. Reid's reaction was, "There's no such thing as perfect love. Love isn't limitless. Not in these times."

"Hey, Ba, I've started to write my own blog. I'll be concentrating on Covid-19 and police reform. Want to see my notes?"

Africans were brought here in the belly of slave ships.

1968, Governor George Wallace's man, Bull Connor, released dogs in Birmingham.

Richard Nixon was elected in 1968 as a 'Law and Order' candidate. Trump is doing the same.

April 8, 1974, Henry Aaron hits his 715th home run against Al Downing in Atlanta, Georgia. Thousands in the stands boo rather than cheer.

Racism coast to coast.

Protests coast to coast.

Police target disproportionately people of color. This system of justice remains thirty years after Rodney King.

Get inside the problem. Don't cover it up.

Ba says I should not be consumed by rage. That's impossible!

Police officer George Chauvin squashed the life out of George Floyd.

"I CAN'T BREATHE!!!"

Minneapolis fired the three police officers.

In Minnesota, 70 percent of whites own their own houses. 27 percent of Blacks.

Trump berates governors as weak in handling of George Floyd protests. Urges them to use force.

Large-scale public protests nationwide continue. Ba says we must move forward. 21st-century policing means: Stop blaming! What we need are more constructive methods! ... Ba says decency, compassion, empathy. I say: War! Discord! Assassination!

People are on top of one another. Protests continue.

Former police commissioner Bill Bratton said that he was unaware that chokeholds have not been eliminated by law in NYC.

Ba says he runs into Commissioner Bratton at Porterhouse. He's a good guy.

Ba says fear elects the right. Riots helped George Wallace and Richard Nixon gain power in 1968. Looting, stealing, destroying, only makes for a stronger base of reactionary people.

Tear gas...Automatic weapons...Rubber bullets...The way Trump flaunted the Bible at a photo shoot. A show of force...The use of force...'Law and Order' President.

Phillip Pannell...Breonna Taylor...Rodney King...Trayvon Martin...Michael Brown...Eric Garner...Systematic Racism...

Who are the victims of the looting – hard-working people who are struggling to survive. Predominantly Black and Brown and Latino small-business owners.

Keisha Bottoms, the mayor of Atlanta, "We are better than this as a city. We are better than this as a country. Go home! This is not the spirit of Martin!"

We must face it. What did King actually accomplish? Look in the streets right now. We have to start all over again.

Police officer Derek Chauvin is the first police officer to be charged with killing a Black man in Minneapolis. Why isn't it Murder Two? His actions should push forward the legal case to Murder Two...And what about the three other police officers? Silence and complicity...

Protesters against police brutality.

There is also the protesters' brutality against the police...

When will we stamp out poor policing in this country? When will we begin to realize that the central issues are policing and oversight? When will we insist on reforms?

On June 1, 2020, Donald J. Trump pushed people one hundred and fifty yards away from the White House.

Pentagon Chief says he does not support the use of active-duty military force to quell unrest, breaking with Trump.

December 5, 1955. Trial – Blacks with Montgomery boycott the buses. Rosa Parks: "What happened to all men are created equal?"

June 4, 2020. The nation mourns George Floyd. 8:46 seconds of silence. The time police officer Chauvin held George Floyd down at the neck.

On the day of celebration for George Floyd, an elected Black official who identified himself before arriving was compliant with the order to move back. "Even then I couldn't stop from becoming a victim. I was pepper-sprayed and handcuffed."

On June 8, 2020, Congressional Democrats unveiled sweeping police reforms legislation in response to protests after the killing of George Floyd. Ba says, "It's just words."

Structural racism in both parties. Police misconduct historic all over the country.

44 percent of Americans are not seeing America through a race equality lens.

Protest! Violence! The war continues!

"Eleanor where is Reid? I haven't seen him all day."

"He went to the City to join the protests."

When Obama took office, we thought things were changing. That it was a giant step forward. I called up Myra Parker, Rodney's wife. I could hear in her voice a ring of joy. "Rodney and I have been waiting for this day. We thought it would never come."

Today I didn't call Myra. I couldn't think of anything worth saying. I participated in the civil-rights movement almost sixty years ago. America has gone through white supremacy protests for four hundred and one years. Nothing much has changed. I remember the movement I took part in. What we learned was that it's only the federal government that can do something, and it took years after the Montgomery boycott and the March on Washington to even get miniscule federal legislation passed.

In a finite amount of time, we'll have a vaccine to combat the virus; what vaccine will we ever have to inoculate people to stop hating, polarizing, feeling insecure? As someone a whole lot wiser than me once said, "If you have an empty milk bottle and I don't, you will feel superior." Who is going to give up their empty milk bottle? Who is going to discover a serum, a pill, a drug, a way of changing our souls? Our ingrained sickness is not on the surface. It's not something you can amputate or pray-to-Jesus away. It's rooted deep inside our primordial instincts, our nervous systems, our DNA. It's there that you won't discover compassion, empathy, decency, love thy neighbor. It's not love one another, it's to devour one another, feed off one another, to survive, not as a tribe or country or globe, as an individual; survival of the fittest is closer to our Darwinian savage truth; so, let's not talk in overblown platitudes about loving one another, and that's what I should have told Myra Parker. Nothing was pretty about George Wallace in 1968, though he came close to becoming POTUS. Nothing to praise Duck for in 2020, and he still is POTUS! Washington does not take protests that seriously. Within three or four months, or at the most a year, this movement, triggered by the murder of George Floyd, will be nothing but a footnote in history. A few crumbs will be given. Maybe a bill or two will be enacted. A law or two decreed. But people are indifferent in the long run; take care of my own ass, my own family, that's about it, everything else is just tweets, words and marches. We're not in this together. History proves we're as far apart today as we were in 1921 when a Black man grazed a white woman's shoulder and caused a race riot, killing three hundred and forty-seven African Americans. When I left the Welfare Department, I thought one of the good things that came out of those real, real years was the book of heart-felt essays I pounded on the racial divide in America. My well-intentioned words I discovered did not improve one thing. Impassioned words don't protect or make us see one another. They certainly don't change housing or employment or income or schooling or … a vaccine will. Where is that vaccine? Rodney Parker would tell me all the time, "There ain't no hope." Rodney died believing that until his last breath. So, did most of my other long-time African American friends. And the sad thing, for me at least, is that Obama came and Obama went and we are still protesting and killing and holding down and for these things and more there will never be a vaccine.

"…Robert, the person on the other end wouldn't give me his name. He sounds terribly upset. I think you should talk to him."

I didn't have the patience to listen to Duck's rationales and deflections. I didn't have the strength to argue over right and wrong.

"People are saying that you do not speak for them or to them. Are you indifferent?…Speak up, Mr. President. I can't hear you…You can help by not sending out your incendiary messaging to protesters. You've been calling them criminals. You've been threatening to attack Americans with tear gas, vicious dogs, the might of the military."

"I didn't say attack, I said combat. And I didn't say Americans. I said Black and Brown thugs."

"What about calming America down. Quieting fears. What about learning how to live together."

"I don't know why you're taking this attitude, Singer. I thought we made up. What have you become, some kind of activist?"

"A week or two ago you were asked some pretty candid questions. You just turned your back and walked off the stage."

"I don't care about those people. Singer, if you don't stop this crap, I won't give a damn about you, either."

"Is that how you feel? You're disgusted and don't care?"

"I didn't say that. Those anarchists. They're the criminals. Not me!"

Duck was in a good mood. "Listen, Singer. I'd like to chat with you, but I have to review my notes. I'm going to be addressing the country tonight."

"What time are you scheduled to speak?"

"Between six and seven."

"Do you have your speech prepared?"

"You know me. I'll be speaking off the cuff. But I do have a good idea of what I want to say."

"My advice is, don't go too far one way. Try and show some concern for what's happening out there."

"Don't worry about me, Singer. I can take care of myself. Why don't you meet me after my address? I'll be going to St. John's church. I promised the rector I'd drop in. He had a little trouble there. Some damage to the basement. It was those thugs. They had a field day last night. They were out of control."

"Is it okay if I bring my son? Reid asked me if it were possible to meet you."

"Bring him along. I'll leave word with John Mertson. He's my security chief. He'll escort you through the barriers directly into the church. And stop worrying about me. I'm putting my hammer down. Incidents like what happened last night will not be happening again. I'm invoking the insurrection act. Bringing in the federal National Guard. If I have to, the military."

"You can't do that. It's against the law. What we need is a more just America, not a reactionary one."

"I can't believe you said that, Singer. I'm telling you like I tell everyone. You put them in jail, and you won't hear from them again."

I walked the city streets. Tried to get a pulse on what was real. I'm not saying I didn't know what was going on, but

I didn't have a clue on how to change things. I observed people in midtown Manhattan, some carrying placards, some screaming and cursing. I went further downtown, as far as Chelsea, witnessed some looting, some skirmishes. I noticed a young woman in tears. She had bloodshot hazel eyes, pouches underneath them, a tormented face. She looked out of place here. The youngster was curled up on 17th street. "I'm afraid to sleep in my own apartment. I'm from Alamo, California. This is my first year in New York City. I graduated Cornell. I took a job here. It's a good job. I like it. I even liked New York until these protests started. I called my parents. They want me to come home. I'm afraid to go back to my apartment. I'm trying to get to my girlfriend's house. It's hard navigating through the crowd. People have been protesting day and night. I saw four fierce-looking, dark-skinned wild-eyed men carrying jerrycans filled to the brim with gasoline. I'm not that kind of person. My boyfriend is. He's marching."

I unlocked the door to my place. Duck was already there.

"I had to be sheltered in a White House bunker with my family the other night."

Before I could say a word, "What about offering a pal some pineapple juice?"

Ten minutes later:

"I know what you're going to say. That the right to demonstrate is a First Amendment right. That I'm here to serve and protect. To bring down tensions. Not add to them. That Black lives matter. Crap like that. What about mine, Singer? What about mine!"

"It's your job to make sure that law enforcement keeps their heads. This is not an insurrection."

Duck gnarled his teeth. Stepped to a window. Peered out at Central Park. When he turned back to me, he looked unhinged.

"Some police chief in Santa Clara said a lot of crap this week. This guy was out there telling the public that the police bring their prejudices to the job. The guy has forty-two years in law enforcement and he's saying garbage like that." Duck paused to swallow his juice. "You're big on police reform. What kind would you suggest?"

"Police recruitment should be improved. Screening methods should make sure that racists are kept off the force."

I went on and on making recommendations that my son cried out every day. Each one of them I had heard all the way back to the 1960s. Animus for Black Americans is as familiar in our country as Jew-hating was in Nazi Germany, as Christians fighting Muslims, as not seeing "the other," condemning one side or the other in all unholy wars. Polarizing never stops. It starts over and over and over again. It is our human virus.

"Singer, I'm having breakfast with Edna tomorrow morning. She'll be telling me what she's told me since I was 2. To be good to as many people as possible."

I must remember this is not all about Duck. It's about combustible national issues, voter protection rights, police reform, civil unrest. It's about four hundred and one years of screwing up. It's knowing that with this protest becoming a movement there are still four out of every ten Americans saying that they disagree. It's about all the positive rhetoric going on, all the vows and prayers to embrace Black and Brown. It's about demanding better schooling, health plans, housing, employment, pay, benefits. Better people to take over the key jobs. It's about putting a stop to chokeholds and knees to the neck. It's about eliminating lynching and the sickness of the Klan. It's about sickening George Floyd moments in an America reeling from a trillion of them. It's knowing that in our past four hundred and one years we haven't moved forward a sea change, only have had a ripple of progress, that it's no longer enough. It's about better utilizing all of our digital media resources. It's about all of us linking hands. It's marching and protesting and plotting and engaging with the established order to pass bills, make stronger laws, make sure that the defensive player beats Duck to the spot, prevents his next move, doesn't allow Duck to get by him, or through him or over him as he's heading for the rim. It's about making sure that Duck and all the other ducks will be stuffed as they attempt to dunk their shots. That's the question. Can we the people do it? That's what I'm waiting around to find out. This is what I've been thinking all day.

My wife dreads my leaving our private acres. Today I remained indoors. At five-thirty in the morning I began writing, for two hours on Duck and all the other ducks, then returned to bed and slept till noon. Went back to the starting gate and wrote for another four. Exhaustion set in. I called it a day. Trudged the eighteen steps that lead to our bedroom. Collapsed onto the bed. Napped till six, then showered, shaved, combed my hair, went down to the kitchen where Eleanor was preparing dinner. "I feel like myself. Maybe for the first time this week. I feel okay," I told her.

After dinner Eleanor wanted to watch TV. The selection she made was a documentary on Michelle Obama. She came off like a deeper Doris Day: good heart, common sense, straight shooter. Definitely a woman Barack Obama was lucky to find. Eleanor started lamenting that this super couple was out and what's in. I started pontificating. My wife said she had heard it all before. Then Eleanor was off to bed. I stayed up and watched television. Found an interview between Chris Webber and The Big O. Webber asked O how Shaq would have done against Wilt. "He'd hold his own for about one half. Shaq was strong." Then Webber asked O about Elgin Baylor. "He never gets his due. It's unfair. The man is one of the five greatest players in NBA history. He scored thirty-seven points a game one year and if he played today, he'd average thirty-eight." The first time I saw Elgin play was when he was in college. Within ten minutes I knew I was seeing Mozart on the court. With Oscar Robertson it took one. "That's not Beethoven or Mozart," I said to Cal Ramsey and Rodney Parker. "We're seeing God on a basketball court."

When the Webber-Robertson interview was over, I switched on a news channel and listened to reports on the virus and the violence on the streets between white police officers and protesters. I turned to another channel and listened for a while to more unwelcome news on Covid-19. Then I turned to the YES Channel, first time in ages I watched a Yankee game. It wasn't the same. I couldn't believe the players could adjust to the cadaverous echoes. The grandstands are without people or noise, without the blood and vitality that make the game come alive, it was as if the ballplayers were androids going through the motions. And the foul balls that go into the stands that, as a boy, I would chase for, dive for, scrape my chin, my elbow, my knees and shins, kill to clutch, they now go unattended as if they were dead vermin in a junkyard. I didn't have the energy to turn off the TV, just left the room, snuggled real close to Eleanor. I asked her if she had spoken to Reid. She said he called, that he was okay. A minute later Eleanor was fast asleep. I was still worried about Reid. I got out of bed. Called him.

"… Ba, it's not young people that need to be taught right from wrong. Most of us are committed to trying to change the way things are. The message has got to reach the grownups who run this freakin' country of ours. Remember what Rodney Parker always said, 'As long as Whitey has the power, it's the way it's going to be.'"

"It's human nature, Reid. People get excited then change hits a wall."

"You're wrong, Ba. A new America starts today. Maybe it will succeed. Maybe it will fail. But, damn, Ba, we must try … Ba, the thing I'm putting in my blog today is that we must eliminate the attitude that white people matter more. Everyone has a momma. Everyone!"

I was wrong. I've watched tons of newscasts. I've talked to people. Lots of people. From Georgia to Vermont. From Baltimore to Los Angeles. In Washington, D.C., people are changing. For the first time since the '60s, I feel there is real hope. There is something happening that has never happened before. My mother would invite my friends to our house for dinner. She never said invite your white friends or your Black friends or your Asian friends or your Latino friends or your Jewish friends or your Christian friends or your Muslim friends. She said friends. Half of my buddies were Black and Brown, the other half were pink. What the fuck's the difference? There isn't any. All of us went out together, double-dated together, played ball together, went to school together, hung out at each other's homes together, became friends with each other's little sisters and brothers, mothers, and fathers. My mom would exchange family recipes with Calvin Ramsey's mother. My dad would talk about Joe Louis and Kid Gavilan and Jackie Robinson to anyone who would listen. Spend hours giving Hector Elizondo voice lessons. That was our family. That was the world Dick and I grew up in. Now I'm thinking I had parents who were ahead of their time. Perhaps they were. I'm not! All these years I bought into, "There ain't no hope! There ain't no hope!" Since the '60s ended. At 83 I'm waking up. It's different now. I can feel it. I just know it. It's like I knew Elgin Baylor was Mozart and Oscar Robertson, God. All over America people are changing. Not all of us. Nothing is ever all of us. When I write a novel, it's one word at a time, one sentence at a time, one paragraph at a time, one page at a time. It takes stamina, it takes focus, it takes commitment. It takes patience, it takes everything that is inside of you to get from page one to realizing your vision. Today's vision is what America could be, should be, ought to be. Attitudes are changing. Some of us are beginning to see we're all in this together. This time I'm almost sure that it's going to stick. I think we're on our way. We're believing in what can be done. I'm listening to my son Reid, "I have no interest in yesterday's newspaper. I want to read tomorrow's. Duck is irrelevant. He's done! Tomorrow is about to begin. Tomorrow has begun."

EPILOGUE

SEVERAL YEARS LATER

One of my old lady friends sent me Mark Nepo's new book. She asked me "AM I PRESENT IN THE LIFE I HAVE?"

Well, there might not be much left of the life I have. My concierge doctor, Ed Goldberg, tells me that I have prostate cancer and a lame heart that has anywhere from one day to nine years. He said that I better start taking life seriously, lose forty pounds, exercise, take long walks, lift some weights, and take the radiation treatments my urologist is recommending. My twin is still around as well, though he has a small tumor in his bladder. Both of us are still scribbling, our new books are coming out next Fall. My wife is getting up there. She's approaching a mature age but is as sincere as ever. She insists that I can live to one hundred if I mend my ways.

I get a hug every morning. We still hold hands, there is nothing better. We watch terrible movies on TV and classic plays as well. I go to New York City at least twice a week. Love that penthouse of mine. Love my ten thousand book library that I haven't figured out whom I will leave it to. No one reads any more. At least not the kind of literature that

I have in my apartment. Ten thousand books and still adding to the sum. Just reading *Augustus* and *Stoner* by John
Williams. I know you never read John Williams. That's
because you're a Twitter guy or a Facebook lady or addicted
to dots and dashes. But there is something to be said for a
life of the mind, for being human, staying in touch with
blood and guts and glory and tenderness. What does your
iPhone and laptop give you: data, status, a digital universe;
but what about flesh and blood and lyrical feelings? Well,
there's not much left.

I walk around, actually hobble around the blocks near
my 1818 Manhattan building. This morning I went to get
some breakfast at one of the diners on Seventh Avenue.
They still have their outdoor dining shed set up with heat-
ers. I ordered breakfast to go and returned with it to the
apartment I have lived in for over fifty years. I started to call
my wife and right then I shivered as I thought of the terrible shock we had a few seasons past. You know when we
lost all those Hall of Famers: Tom Seaver and Joe Morgan,
Don Sutton and Bob Gibson, Whitey Ford and Tommy
Lasorda, Lou Brock and Phil Niekro and several others,
including 'Hammerin' Hank Aaron. Henry Aaron had
humility and dignity. He was from Mobile, Alabama. Why
is it, I thought to myself, that Alabama produced Cleon
Jones and Tommy Agee and Willie McCovey, and Willie
Mays and so many other African American ballplayers who
had a quiet strength like my old friend Cal Ramsey, may
he rest in peace. They had something the Duck never had,
and speaking of the quacking Duck, I just arranged for
Omkar BeHarry to drive me up to visit him. I have visited
him where he's incarcerated several times now, and I love
it when I see him there. It's a joy. He doesn't wear zebra

stripes, but his hair has thinned out to where every strand is accountable to his scalp, and he has dark pouches and creases now that make him look so much more like who he really is. Duck is still ranting how great he is and that he's going to make America great again when he gets out, but the seventy million he once had as devoted followers have found other schmucks to follow. Duck had his day though I don't tell him that. I rather just sit there at the penitentiary and offer him a Snicker's bar or something else from one of the vending machines in the big room where you can sit and visit. There aren't many security people at the prison who pay much attention to him; believe me, the guards pay more attention to me when I enter the correctional facility. They place my wallet, keys, pen, and other personal objects in a steel box before they allow me to go in for my visit. Duck walks into the room, sees me, and actually smiles. When he sits down, he immediately starts one of his rants. "I'm getting out of here, I'm going to be doing great things again. You can be with me if you want. I don't have many friends left. That Rudy. Fuck-him! He turned on me like Michael Cohen did, and all those guys I pardoned on my last day in office. Fuck them too, not one of them visits or writes or is there for me. My wife, what wife? My children, well …" I don't have the heart to contradict Duck. His daughter Ivanka, the one who went to Choate, Rosemary Hall, before Reid did – she's the one who married that thin blooded real-estate silver spoon, well she's now got a wide ass, lost her looks, and is aiming to be President of the United States one day. Her husband, that Jewish boy who now looks more like Haskell Gold, is as cunning, as shrewd, as evil as ever. Duck has dismissed him from his go-to list of comrades.

Duck asked me about the Russian guy Putin, and about Biden. Oh, did I mention that Kamala Harris is preparing to take over for Biden? I mean he's still around but his memory isn't. Kamala is doing the job, according to my blessed wife. I stopped following Rachel and Ari and Hannity and Carlson and the other experts on TV. What for? They are all regurgitating the same things that have been said over and over throughout my entire lifetime.

I'm thinking of Hank Aaron right now. He joined the Major Leagues at nineteen years of age, when I was seventeen. I can recall his first base hit. He flipped his wrists and sent a hardline drive over the shortstop's head. I remember Willie's twentieth at bat in the polo grounds too. First hit Willie got was off Warren Spahn, an elegant lefthander who might be one of the five greatest southpaws in Major League history. Willie hit it over the polo grounds left field roof. Henry hit his single over the shortstop. That was the difference. Willie was spectacular, Henry was quiet and consistent, dignified, and humble. I loved them both of course, but Mickie Mantle remains my all-time hero. He could run like Man O' War and he could hit the ball father than anyone. What he couldn't do was stay healthy.

Back to Duck. He's always been self-absorbed, indifferent to the world he lived in. If he were a novelist, he'd only be writing about himself. Not that different than me, but he wouldn't care about anyone else, and he certainly doesn't flinch about all the deaths he caused in the pandemic. He is and was probably the worst POTUS in American history. But he is still here, and actually he's getting out of the correctional facility in the Fall. I think he has more trials coming up, likely more time to serve, but it is not a fact. The guy had his day, made his noisy cruel mark, left us with more things to stitch up than all the wars we've been in. I recommended to Duck that he read some of the 18th-century novelists, not to change the subject, but to show you how much I progressed. I stopped reading postmodern works like David Markson, and even Beckett. I've gone back to Diderot and *Jacques the Fatalist,* and Cervantes' *Don Quixote* for humor, truth and a better grip on the fact that life is ridiculously short, that I'm leaving soon, and I want to do that with a smile. The only thing that worries me is Eleanor. She will suffer my loss and my son will too.

I have done my thing. I wrote checks out for all the guys at 1818 that I love: Rodriguez, Gonzalez, Torres, Lester, Welch, Camacho, oh too many more to list. The guys and gals that are porters and doormen, building managers and handymen, and I even left a few checks for several friends who are on their ass. My library, my ten thousand books, well, I am going to consult Dick and some of his literary elitist friends to figure that out. I have had the privilege, the honor, the joy, the nourishment of having access to profound writers and artists who had something significant to say, a whole lot more than Duck. But he was POTUS, that's a fact. The truth is I'll visit with him in the graveyard for hours listening while he tells me one quacking duck lie after another about why he is the only man in the entire world who sees things with perfect vision. Some things never change. Though I still believe they will.

The end

PEOPLE I WILL ALWAYS REMEMBER

Rodney Parker: A great friend. Helped more boys realize their dreams than all the billionaires I know.

Abe Margolies: Everyone's best friend.

Stanley Weldon Hill: Decent to a fault. Always striving to do the right thing.

Sidney Bernstein: The promoter's promoter. Stickers was always ready to go to get some ice cream.

Linda Kay Eisenberg: Great girl. Beautiful inside and outside. It was my fault that we weren't married for sixty years.

Donnie Burks: Great talent. Always needed a favor …

Harvey Ross: The Colonel. When you weren't laughing with him, you were laughing at him.

Myra Ross: I stayed with Harvey because he needed me.

Nancy Schreiber: My happiness pill until I fucked it up.

Victoria Kore Grodman:	Maybe, yes, she was, the most inimical person I knew. Seventeen wasted years of trying ... for what?
Calvin Ramsey:	Sober, stable a man of integrity and great depth. MSG; The Knicks; helping others; always there ...
Roger Gibbs:	He loved Carl Braun. He would wolf down my mother's lunch sandwiches in high school. He continued doing that for a long, long time. Great defensive player at Virginia Union.
Harvey Litt:	My closest friend. He was always trying to do better. Never could.
Henry Hasenberg:	A Holocaust survivor. One of the most intelligent and creative men in my lifetime.
Hector Elizondo:	A friend since the age of 5. A man for all seasons.
Michael Jay Feldman:	I thought of him as a younger brother – He was. A decent man with a fine, fine mind.
Jack Defaris:	Commerce High School. Winston-Salem ... One of the very best jump shooters of his generation. A good guy too.
Alan Seiden:	He played his heart out only to be defeated by ego. Lived his life without realizing his dream.

Red Holzman:	Knick coach. CCNY player. Will always remember that I sat on his knee when I was 5.
Fuzzy Levane:	Believed that today's players are bigger, stronger, quicker, better than those of his generation. Open-minded and as likeable a man as there ever was.
Dick McGuire:	Great playmaker. Great friend. Silent to a fault but he was loud on the court.
Carl Green:	Solid as a rock. Loyal, strong opinions, a man with integrity.
Connie Hawkins:	Way before his time. He could play with anyone today, tomorrow, and yesterday too.
Tom Konchalski:	Basketball junkie. Lovely man. Trustworthy.
Howard Garfinkel:	Knew more basketball than anyone this side of Bobby Knight. Knew how to be kind to himself less than the sum of all the people I knew.
Big John Stiloski:	Great friend. Wonderful human being. Strong and intelligent. I wished he hadn't smoked as much as he did. His wife is great, as well.
Joanie Pryor:	Actress, social worker, mother, friend. One of the best people I knew.
Norma Meyers:	From the south and to the north. She could get by anywhere.

Mattie Mixon: Worked with Mattie in Harlem. It was a treat.

Caroline Shipp: Strongly opinionated and austere with her employees. Had a heart too.

Dolph Schayes: Would be a superstar today. Played for a top salary of sixteen thousand dollars. Today would be earning...

Freddy Schayes: Dolph's older brother. A man who would back you up when necessary.

Herman Schayes: Dolph's younger brother. He would play the game as hard as anyone. Great competitor.

Whitey Bucek: Vanilla ice cream and apple pie... Great shooter. Got screwed because he played with the wrong team. He sulked for a lifetime because he was never passed the ball. If it had been, he would have been Whitey Skoog or Paul West-phal or at least have maximized his own very considerable talent.

Sheila Tronn: Did the right thing when she said: "You read too many books. You'll never be happy."

Brenda Lehrer: Five years with her. I was happier than a gambler on a winning streak. She wasn't.

Beverly Weitzman: I liked her so much. She was as grounded as Brooklyn. As kosher as my mom and dad. (As ready to get married as I wasn't.)

Rhona Chezer:	Those were the days …
Bob Korman:	Richie Pryor fucked him. Bob never came back.
Jack Leiser:	Had great potential. Taught school somewhere in Jersey. Pre-school …
Jackie Robinson:	Had the biggest shoulders in America. Great guy. A real champion amongst men.
Howie Puris:	More talent than anyone in my life.
Jason Ressler:	For him to get by means lying, cheating, calculating, thinking, doing whatever it is that needs to be done. He didn't do enough …
Evan Strome:	Some people don't come into their own until they reach 50.
Beau Bernstein:	Getting married for the second time at 50. Best thing he's ever done. This time he's not involved with a bitch. Diane's a great woman with a heart.
Joe Feshbach:	Complicated and enraged. Good mind, not one to be denied. Will compete and win and ruin it and do it all over again. Stop when you're ahead, Joe …
Melissa Joy Tobin:	Hard to figure.
Mickey Mantle:	Boozer, self-destroyer, the man who could fuck up at any moment. More talent than any player of his era. More potential and possibility and more heart and courage and demons too.

Sugar Ray Robinson:	Pound for pound the best fighter I've ever seen. And that pink Cadillac he would drive through the neighborhood. Sugar had his day.
Joe Louis:	He made his bones by destroying Schmeling. Decent man. More than a few of my friends loved him.
Jake LaMotta:	See the movie.
Billy Martin:	When I was a boy, he'd stand outside the old Yankee stadium and talk to me. Talk to the other schoolboys. He always advised us to stay in school.
Joe Torre:	Sober. Logical. Great hitter. Greater manager. Solid man.
Lenore Engel:	My first crush. I was 12 years old.
Judy Isserlis:	My twin's first crush. He was 12 years old.
Gunilla Knutsson:	Miss Sweden … Beautiful. We had one night at Jilly's … I did not take her home.
Sissie Tindell:	The most talented, vivacious, beautiful, and difficult woman I knew. Artist-cook-horseback-riding champion-singer-model – Sissie had everything and chemistry interfered.
Gabriela Blanco:	We had our moments. She loved the opera, the theatre, fine food, a safe life. I disappointed her.
Joe Newhouse:	College friend who disappeared.

Warren Blum:	Congenial and good-looking. "Who needs her," he would say when disappointed by a woman.
Arlene Simpson:	Solid and a good friend. I miss her.
Bob Knox:	Intelligent and mature. He was always accountable.
Sonny Jamison:	Proved to me that you could throw fastballs in a softball game. Great athlete.
Lenny Chappell:	All-American at Wake Forest. A friend of my youth.
Ben Swain:	Played basketball for Texas Southern. Bunked with Ben up at Kutsher's. We scrimmaged together. He played some pro-ball too. Likeable and soft-spoken. Always will remember him.
Freddy Carrion:	Had intelligence, talent, and a great spirit.
Alex Rodriguez:	As complicated as anyone I've known. A better ballplayer than anyone I've known. A man with more insecurities and death wishes than most.
Abbe Wexner Koppel:	The little girl I knew is gone. The woman now rules a very large roost.
Danny Koppel:	One step at a time. Reads books. Tries to overcome. Struggles and succeeds.
Terry Wrong:	One guy I lost contact with. I regret that.
Charlie Price:	Dick wrote a book on him.

Patty Coleman:	A hard worker. A great mother. A greater friend.
Ettore Stratta:	Got lucky when he met Patty. She got lucky too.
Ricki Whatshername:	Inimical. Psychologically challenged. Beautiful when young. Always instrumentalizing. Never winning.
Albert Rolon:	A friend who does everything. Is succeeding.
Justin Schweitzer:	Thank you for all your help.
Dr. Alan Egelman:	Some guys never take the leap.
Champ Harry Segal:	Broadway tough guy and man about town. Loved his wife, Molly.
Tom Hoover:	Known Tom for a lifetime. He once played for Villanova. And then the Knicks. Good guy.
Bertha Paula:	Another young lady I had a crush on when I was 15.
Andy Gargiulo:	If I were in a foxhole, he's the one guy I'd want to be there with me.
Milton Kutsher:	A man with integrity, compassion and decency and did more share of good on this earth during his time than most.
Bobby Knight:	Made me rich. Best college coach in the history of the game. We never had to meet. I followed his games. No conspiracy here.
Karina Hilton:	The best housekeeper in New York City.

Maurice Stokes:	Terrible, terrible disease. Could have been one of the NBA all-time superstars.
Cus D'Amato:	Wise and shrewd. He knew life and he knew fighters.
Floyd Patterson:	A special guy.
Hana Beckerman:	The most beautiful woman in the world. The problem is it doesn't matter. Other things are much more important.
Daniel Litt:	My Godson. He's grown up. He's doing well. He's trying to go somewhere. I would like to think that he'll get there.
Manny Kimmel:	This CEO was a son of a bitch but he knew more about proposition betting than anyone, he knew more about cards than anyone, he knew more about making money. He was money. It was his blood.
Spike Lee:	He came out of Brooklyn. He came out of wherever there is a seed that can realize its possibility.
Dickie Barnett:	Good guy with a real brain. Also, could play a little basketball.
Susan Braudy:	Talented and intelligent and what was missing?
Michelle Obama:	Would like to have called her my friend.
Barack Obama:	Would like to have called him my friend.

Walter Winchell:	… No comment.
Joe Weintraub:	So much more than what life provided him with.
Harry Marcus:	A distant relative of Heinrich Heine. Incredible!
Dennis Stein:	A prankster and a shallow, shallow man.
Elizabeth Taylor:	Never could understand what the fuss was all about.
Zane Weiner:	He realized more than his potential.
Danny Aiello:	Bouncer; Actor; Great friend.
Kevin Conway:	An actor's actor.
Joe Papp:	What he did for theatre. What he did for Shakespeare … What he did for NYC.
Tom O'Horgan:	Hair … great friend and director. One of a kind.
Susan Strasberg:	Dated her when we were teenagers.
Lee Strasberg:	He did some real important things for the theatre world.
Curt Block:	A boy from my past who evolved into a fine man.
Charlie Gonzalez:	Mario's son. Club Coronet … Taft Hotel … Pete Terrace … How many of you remember?
Stanley Amigo:	Going back before I was 10.
Sandy de Sedle: Madison Avenue?	Do you remember de Sedle's on
Rene Wallach:	Still remember her.
Gene Barry:	Bat Masterson. La Cage. He left New York to make it. He did.

Reva Klass:	Gene's sister. Heard she made a life in Australia. Always liked her.
Bonnie Shimkin:	Oh, Bonny, what happened this time…
Keith Hernandez:	Complicated and special. Greatest defensive first baseman in history. Should be in the Hall of Fame.
Mel Allen:	The voice of the Yankees. The voice of my youth.
Dobrinka Salzman:	Ambitious… Hungry… focused… a great mother and loyal friend to my twin.
Steve Salzman:	Devoted father.
Ralph Banks:	Top of the class. Then life took over.
Carl Witas:	Knew him when we were 5 and 6 and 7.
Steve Cohen:	Knew him from 5 to whatever…
Morty Gunty:	Stage Deli. Carnegie. A laff or two.
Myron Cohen:	Copa never did better.
Henny Youngman:	Loved Solomon Lepidus' Rolls. Wanted to be driven around the block.
Dick Shawn:	Master Richard. Kutsher's Country Club performer.
Lenny Bruce:	If I were a comic, I would have liked to have been Lenny.
Jan Peerce:	My father's best friend.
Richard Tucker:	Also a great friend of dad.
Robert Merrill:	Bet you didn't know that this baritone could play a little baseball too.
Lou Carnesseca:	We hit it off in our later years. Not the handicapping ones.

Jim Thorpe:	I will always remember how gracious he was to sign my auto-graph book.
Bill "Pickles" Murphy:	He could play the game.
Bobby Cassotto Darin:	Turned into a prick.
Michael Allen Gluck:	Talented and smooth.
Norman Mailer:	One of my inspirations to be a writer.
James Joyce:	Another one of those special writers who gave me something to live for.
Gabriel García Marquez:	Awesome!
Fyodor:	Who could do more?
Tolstoi:	His wife would say she did more.
Franz Kafka:	Pity his life wasn't as healthy as his fiction.
Samuel Beckett:	The Big O of writers: He sees the whole court.
Margot Fonteyn:	Thank you.
Rudy Nureyev:	Thank you.
Philip Roth:	He was my kind of guy.
Saul Bellow:	Superior and much too keen for low brows like me.
Evelyn Plesser:	My third-grade schoolteacher.
Mickey Fisher:	Boys High. Great coach.
Bill Spiegel:	Benjamin Franklin basketball coach. Mr. Zone.
Frank Neely:	Great friend, brilliant man, fine ballplayer.
Michael Edison:	Whatever happened to him?

Arnie Singer:	Always wanted an easier life.
Ivan Prashker:	Remember that he is a fine, decent man.
Lester Meyers:	Brilliant and good.
David Manfredy:	My friend.
Brendan McKenney:	Great father, husband, fireman, special associate. Makes my life and my wife's more secure.
Michael Roloff:	He could think with Hesse, live with Handke and dream... He always followed his dreams...
Geraldo Camacho:	As loyal as a boulder.
David Levi:	High-school friend.
George Mikan:	I babysat for his wife and him. The child's name was Larry.
John Patrick Ryan:	Loved being an actor. A character.
Red Auerbach:	Tough, competitive, strong, and wise, and loved to play cards.
Jimmy Breslin:	As sharp as anyone.
Mary Breslin:	Worked with her in Welfare. Quite a trip.
Ruth Ramsey:	Cal Ramsey's mother. One of my best friends.
Madonna:	She came and she went and she stayed the course.
Maria Elena Scotto:	Andy's daughter. A princess and a woman of worth.
Elaine Gargiulo:	She chooses her friends carefully.
Phil Rizzuto:	As cheery a time as one could have would be one with the Scooter.
John Farrar:	FSG – the first publisher to tell me to keep writing.

Corky Smith:	Viking…took me and walked me through the ins and outs of being published.
John Romine:	Mr. Slick can carpenter with the best of them but there is something missing…
Meryl Zegarek:	Says the right thing all the time.

ACKNOWLEDGMENTS

My family: Brunde, Knute and Dick...
     All of the people I knew, all the people who are continuing their journey, fighting, struggling, going to war, discovering something better, hopefully not worse, and all those who are realizing that, whatever it means, it's worth taking one more breath for.

A billion, billion more, to say the least...

www.ingramcontent.com/pod-product-compliance
Lightning Source LLC
Chambersburg PA
CBHW021218260626
47172CB00002B/494